ACCLAIM FOR A

"A story of grief as well as new beginnings, this is a lovely Amish tale and the start of a great new series."

—*Parkersburg News and Sentinel*
on *A Place at Our Table*

"This debut title in a new series offers an emotionally charged and engaging read headed by sympathetically drawn and believable protagonists. The meaty issues of trust and faith make this a solid book group choice."

—*Library Journal* on *A Place at Our Table*

"These sweet, tender novellas from one of the genre's best make the perfect sampler for new readers curious about Amish romances."

HEARTS

"Cli   mily
reu   nd a
hap   3.3.22   she
giv

                                                                      rop

                                                                      AYER

"Au   on's
sec

                                                                      HOPE

"Th   ries
is su

                                                                      LOVE

"[Tł   ract
read   lent
writ

                                                                      MAS

THE

Cherished Quilt

OTHER BOOKS BY AMY CLIPSTON

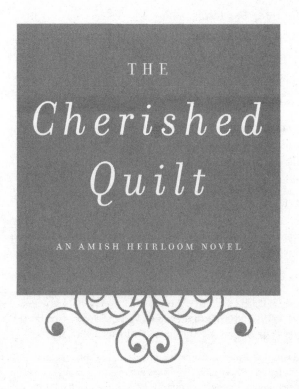

THE

Cherished Quilt

AN AMISH HEIRLOOM NOVEL

AMY CLIPSTON

ZONDERVAN®

ZONDERVAN

The Cherished Quilt

Copyright © 2016 by Amy Clipston

This title is also available as a Zondervan e-book. Visit www.zondervan.com.

Requests for information should be addressed to:
Zondervan, *3900 Sparks Dr. SE, Grand Rapids, Michigan 49546*

ISBN: 978-0-3103-5297-6 (repack)

Library of Congress Cataloging-in-Publication Data

Names: Clipston, Amy, author.
Title: The cherished quilt / Amy Clipston.
Description: Grand Rapids, Michigan: Zondervan, [2016] | Series: An Amish heirloom novel; 3
Identifiers: LCCN 2016031028 | ISBN 9780310341963 (paperback)
Subjects: LCSH: Amish--Fiction. | GSAFD: Love stories. | Christian fiction.
Classification: LCC PS3603.L58 C48 2016 | DDC 813/.6--dc23 LC record available at https://lccn.loc.gov/2016031028

Scripture quotations are taken from the Holy Bible, New International Version®, NIV®. Copyright © 1973, 1978, 1984, 2011 by Biblica, Inc.® Used by permission of Zondervan. All rights reserved worldwide. www.zondervan. com. The "NIV" and "New International Version" are trademarks registered in the United States Patent and Trademark Office by Biblica, Inc.®

Any Internet addresses (websites, blogs, etc.) and telephone numbers in this book are offered as a resource. They are not intended in any way to be or imply an endorsement by Zondervan, nor does Zondervan vouch for the content of these sites and numbers for the life of this book.

All rights reserved. No part of this publication may be reproduced, stored in a retrieval system, or transmitted in any form or by any means—electronic, mechanical, photocopy, recording, or any other—except for brief quotations in printed reviews, without the prior permission of the publisher.

Publisher's Note: This novel is a work of fiction. Names, characters, places, and incidents are either products of the author's imagination or used fictitiously. All characters are fictional, and any similarity to people living or dead is purely coincidental.

Interior Design: James Phinney

Printed in the United States of America

19 20 PC/LSCH 10 9 8 7 6 5 4 3

For my mother, Lola Goebelbecker, with love and appreciation

GLOSSARY

ach: oh
aenti: aunt
appeditlich: delicious
Ausbund: Amish hymnal
bedauerlich: sad
boppli: baby
brot: bread
bruder: brother
bruderskind: niece/nephew
bruderskinner: nieces/nephews
bu: boy
buwe: boys
daadi: granddad
danki: thank you
dat: dad
Dietsch: Pennsylvania Dutch, the Amish language (a German
   dialect)
dochder: daughter
dochdern: daughters
Dummle!: Hurry!
Englisher: a non-Amish person
faul: lazy

faulenzer: lazy person

fraa: wife

freind: friend

freinden: friends

froh: happy

gegisch: silly

Gern gschehne: You're welcome

grossdaadi: grandfather

grossdochder: granddaughter

grossdochdern: granddaughters

grossmammi: grandmother

Gude mariye: Good morning

gut: good

Gut nacht: Good night

haus: house

Ich liebe dich: I love you

kaffi: coffee

kapp: prayer covering or cap

kichli: cookie

kichlin: cookies

kind: child

kinner: children

kumm: come

liewe: love, a term of endearment

maed: young women, girls

maedel: young woman

mamm: mom

mammi: grandma

mei: my

mutter: mother

naerfich: nervous

narrisch: crazy

onkel: uncle

Ordnung: the oral tradition of practices required and forbidden in the Amish faith

schee: pretty

schmaert: smart

schtupp: family room

schweschder: sister

schweschdere: sisters

Was iss letz?: What's wrong?

Willkumm: Welcome

Wie geht's: How do you do? or Good day!

wunderbaar: wonderful

ya: yes

AMISH HEIRLOOM SERIES FAMILY TREES

Martha "Mattie" m. Leroy Fisher
Veronica (m. Jason)　　　Rachel　　　Emily

Agnes m. Wilmer Hochstetler
Paul (m. Rosanna)　　　Christopher　　　Gabriel (deceased)

Rosanna m. Paul Hochstetler
Mamie　　　Betsy

Vera (deceased) m. Raymond (deceased) Lantz
Michael "Mike" (mother, Esther, deceased)　　　John

Sylvia m. Timothy Lantz
Samuel (m. Mandy)　　　Marie　　　Janie

Annie m. Elam Huyard
Jason (m. Veronica)　　　Stephen

Tillie m. Henry "Hank" Ebersol

Margaret m. Abner (deceased) Lapp
Seth (deceased)　　　Ellie

Fannie Mae m. Titus Dienner (Bishop)
Lindann

Susannah m. Timothy Beiler
David　　　Irma Rose (m. Melvin)

Irma Rose m. Melvin Smucker
Sarah

NOTE TO THE READER

WHILE THIS NOVEL IS SET AGAINST THE REAL BACKDROP of Lancaster County, Pennsylvania, the characters are fictional. There is no intended resemblance between the characters in this book and any real members of the Amish and Mennonite communities. As with any work of fiction, I've taken license in some areas of research as a means of creating the necessary circumstances for my characters. My research was thorough; however, it would be impossible to be completely accurate in details and description, since each and every community differs. Therefore, any inaccuracies in the Amish and Mennonite lifestyles portrayed in this book are completely due to fictional license.

PROLOGUE

CHRISTOPHER HOCHSTETLER SHIVERED DESPITE THE HOT June sun beating down on his black church hat. The scent of moist earth assaulted his senses, and calluses stung his palms as he stared at the fresh pile of dirt he had helped shovel over the coffin with his seventeen-year-old brother's body inside. The minister recited a prayer, but it played as background noise to Chris's anguish.

Only a few days ago, Chris and Gabriel had been working side by side in the pasture, helping their father train horses. Now Chris stood next to his older brother, Paul, surrounded by hundreds of community members who'd come to pay their last respects. He was stuck in a dream. No, he was stuck in a nightmare. It was as if he were floating above the crowd, watching the chilling scene play out in front of him.

His mother's keening broke through his thoughts and hurled him back to reality. He turned his head to his right. *Mamm* was holding on to *Dat* for support, and grief grabbed him by his shoulders and shook him.

Gabriel was gone forever.

When the minister's prayer ended, a murmur of conversations spread throughout the crowd. Paul spoke quietly to a friend as some of the community members slowly made their way back to their buggies that lined the long street. To Chris's right, *Dat* spoke

1

softly into *Mamm's* ear. The sight of his parents consoling each other tore at his heart. Chris raised a trembling hand and wiped away the sweat on his forehead.

"Chris."

He turned to where Sallie Zook suddenly stood beside him, wringing her hands. Her dark eyes were red-rimmed and her pink cheeks were tearstained.

A pang of sorrow ripped through him as he recalled the days Gabriel talked about Sallie nonstop. Gabriel had liked her since they were in school together, but he had never shared his feelings with her. Now he never would.

"I'm so sorry, Chris. I can't believe he's—" A sob escaped from her throat. She took a deep breath and swiped at the tears trickling from her eyes. "I just spoke to Gabriel at church last Sunday. I'll never have the chance to talk to him again."

Unable to speak past the lump swelling in his throat, Chris looked at the knot of mourners behind Sallie to avoid her grief-stricken eyes. Salina Chupp was weaving through the crowd. As she hurried toward him, his shoulders tensed. Salina met his gaze, and Chris's stomach twisted with apprehension. He turned to his right, intent on walking away, but he was trapped by people surrounding his parents. If only he could get away and avoid talking to Salina. She was the last person he wanted to see today.

Salina sidled up to Sallie and placed her hand on her slight shoulder while keeping her eyes focused on Chris. She shook her head as her dark eyes misted over. "Oh, Chris. I can't believe it. I don't even know what to say." A tear slid down her cheek. "It's a terrible tragedy."

Chris swallowed and pressed his lips together, fighting against the memory of—

"How could you let this happen, Christopher?"

He flinched at the harsh words and then turned to face his glaring father. "What do you mean?"

"This is your fault." *Dat* pointed toward the freshly covered grave. "If you hadn't been so irresponsible, your *bruder* would still be alive."

Chris heard both Salina and Sallie gasp.

Chris's eyes widened as he took in the fury in his father's hazel eyes. *Dat* blamed him. Even more than he'd been blaming himself?

"You think this is all *my* fault?" Chris jammed his finger into his own chest. When *Dat* merely stared, he added, "I didn't kill Gabriel."

"*Ya*, you did." *Dat* nearly spat the words at him. "You're the older *bruder*, and you knew better. Once again, you ignored my instructions, and you failed Gabriel. In fact, you failed this family. I should've known better than to leave you in charge. You can't handle it." He glared at Salina and back at Chris again. "You're too easily distracted, and you don't think about anyone but yourself."

Chris's breath came out in a whoosh, and he winced as if his father had struck him. "How can you blame me like this? I never meant to—"

"You didn't mean to, but there's nothing you can do to fix this." *Dat* was seething. "Gabriel is gone now. He's dead, Christopher, and we can never bring him back."

Tears stung Chris's eyes. Turning back toward the grave, he could almost feel his father's furious stare boring into him. His younger brother was gone, and as *Dat* said, there was nothing he could do to fix this.

Chris closed his eyes and crossed his arms over his chest in an effort to stop his body from trembling. A tear trickled down one cheek. How could he go on without Gabriel? And with the guilt? *Dat* was cruel to place all the blame on him for Gabriel's death, but he was also right.

Gabriel would be alive if it weren't for him.

CHAPTER 1

EMILY FISHER HUMMED TO HERSELF AS SHE WALKED DOWN the rock path leading from her parents' large farmhouse to the harness shop her father co-owned with their next-door neighbor. The warm September breeze whipped the skirt of her blue dress against her legs and hinted that cool weather was not in a hurry to visit Lancaster County.

The sign for the Bird-in-Hand Harness Shop came into view as she approached the one-story, white clapboard building. The three parking spaces in front of the store were empty, as was the hitching post that welcomed horses and buggies. Her father and his best friend, Hank, were no doubt busy back in the shop's work area while waiting for the day's first customers.

As she stepped into the shop, a bell over the door announced her entrance. As always, she took in the familiar aroma of leather. The showroom in the one-room building was filled with displays of leather harnesses, leashes and collars for pets, saddles, door-knob hangers with bells, rope, pouches, bags, and various other horse accessories such as saddle blankets. The sales counter sat in the center of the packed showroom with small, round displays peppered with leather key chains in shapes varying from cats to horses.

Beyond the showroom was where her father and Hank were

busy creating items to sell. Emily worked her way between displays to their work area.

"*Gude mariye*," Emily sang.

"Hi, Emily." *Dat* gave her a wide smile. Although he was in his early fifties, his light brown hair and matching beard were threaded with gray. His deep brown eyes were bright with question. "Are you done helping your *mamm* in the *haus* already?"

"*Mamm* said I should help you with the books this morning and then help her cook for the *Englishers* tonight." Emily fingered the hem of her black apron. "It's going to be a big group, so we have a lot to do."

"You're hosting a supper on a Wednesday?" Hank raised his eyebrows. Although he and *Dat* were about the same age, Hank's brown beard had a hint of gray. "Don't you normally have *Englishers* come on Fridays?"

"*Ya*, that's true." Emily nodded and the ties to her prayer *kapp* bounced in agreement. "They asked if they could come tonight. They have activities booked through the rest of the week, so *Mamm* agreed to it. We don't want to turn them down and then lose their business."

"You can work on the books another day," *Dat* said. "I know how hard you and *Mamm* work to prepare for the meals."

"It's fine. I can take a look at them and then go back to help *Mamm*. It's too early to start cooking, and I cleaned the *haus* nearly all day yesterday. I have plenty of time to get ready for the meal." She paused. "Is Christopher still starting at the shop today?"

"*Ya*," Hank said. "He should be here shortly. I told him to take his time coming in this morning."

"Oh, *gut*." She smiled. "I can't wait to meet him. I'll send him back to you when he arrives."

"*Danki,*" Hank said.

Emily moved behind the counter by the cash register and pulled out the accounting book from the bottom drawer. She was engrossed in calculating the month's sales when the bell above the door chimed to greet a customer.

"*Gude mariye.*" Emily looked up from the ledger to see a tall young man watching her from just inside the front door. She smiled. "You must be Christopher."

He gave her a slight nod but no return smile. In fact, his expression was so passive he was nearly frowning.

"Welcome. I'm Emily Fisher." When he didn't respond, her smile faded. She took in his appearance. His hair was light brown with flecks of gold reflecting in the sunlight pouring in through the windows behind him and skylights above him. He was handsome, really handsome. His eyes were a brilliant hue of blue-green, and he had a long, thin nose, chiseled cheekbones, a strong jaw, and a clean-shaven face. But his good looks seemed a stark contrast to his bleak, dull expression as he stared at her.

"Well, I'll get your *onkel* for you," Emily offered, turning toward the work area. "Hank!"

"Christopher!" Hank came into the showroom and crossed to where Christopher still stood by the front door. "Come in! This is Leroy's youngest *dochder*, Emily." He gestured toward her. "Emily, this is my nephew, Christopher Hochstetler. His *mamm* is *mei schweschder* Agnes."

"We met." She smiled again in an attempt to lighten the mood.

Christopher nodded again as he came nearer, but his cold expression didn't change.

Dat appeared behind Hank. "So this is Christopher. I've heard a lot about you. I'm so glad you came to work with us."

"*Danki,*" Christopher said softly.

Before more could be said, the bell above the door rang again and two *English* men entered the store. Hank excused himself and started answering their questions about the saddles on display. The phone in the work area rang, and *Dat* hustled to answer it.

Christopher was staring at the toes of his work boots. Emily longed to pull him into a conversation and make him feel comfortable.

"So, Christopher." She leaned forward on the counter. "How was your trip?"

"Fine."

"Oh, well, I guess you're pretty tired, huh?" Maybe a little empathy would get a friendly response. "It's a long trip from Ohio, right?"

Christopher shrugged, still looking at the floor.

"When did you get here?"

"Last night." He suddenly looked up at her, his blue-green eyes locking with hers.

She tried to think of something else to say, but she was dumbfounded by his frosty demeanor.

"Christopher," *Dat* called from the work area. "Come on back and I'll start you off with some simple leatherwork. Today you're going to learn how to make a leash."

Christopher left without giving Emily a second glance. She stared after him. Did this man treat everyone so coldly?

LATER THAT MORNING EMILY ENTERED THE KITCHEN, WHERE her mother sat at the large table, staring down at her favorite cookbook. She glanced up and smiled. Emily had inherited her blonde hair and blue eyes from her mother, but she didn't think anyone could be as beautiful as *Mamm* was.

"What are you looking at?" Emily sank into the chair across from her.

"I was just looking up a few recipes I want to try for our next *Englisher* dinner. I think we should change up the menu." *Mamm* peered up at her. "Is something wrong?"

Emily shrugged before resting her arms on the table and frowning. After her awkward conversation with Christopher, he spent the remainder of the morning in the work area with her father and Hank. As far as she could tell, he never glanced back at her, and he didn't acknowledge her before she left the shop. Christopher had completely snubbed her attempts to be friendly.

"Emily?" *Mamm's* expression filled with concern. "Are you all right?"

"*Ya*, I'm fine. Hank's nephew started today at the harness shop."

"Oh. How is he?" *Mamm* tipped her head.

Emily's shoulders slumped as she scowled. "He's nothing like Hank."

"What do you mean?"

"He's not friendly at all." Emily relayed the brief conversation she had with Christopher, and *Mamm's* eyes widened with surprise.

"I can't figure out why I couldn't seem to make him feel welcome."

"I'm certain it wasn't anything you did," *Mamm* insisted. "You always go out of your way to be nice to people. In fact, you always consider everyone else's feelings before your own."

"I've never had anyone be so rude to me." Emily absently drew circles on the blue tablecloth with her finger. "I tried to pull him into a conversation, but he only gave me terse responses. I just thought we should get to know each other since I work at the shop too."

"Just be yourself and let him warm up to you. Maybe he was nervous about working with Hank and your *dat*. Maybe he's never worked in a shop before."

"*Ya*, maybe that was it. *Dat* said he was going to teach him something easy on his first day."

But her mother's encouragement did little to settle her concern. She couldn't accept the idea of someone not liking her. But she also couldn't imagine feeling uncomfortable at her father's shop. If that was Christopher's problem, she would do everything in her power to help him feel like he belonged.

EMILY WAS SETTING THE TABLE FOR THEIR *ENGLISH* GUESTS when her older sister Rachel rushed into the kitchen. At twenty-three, Rachel was tall like their older sister, Veronica, but she was the only one of the three who had inherited their father's light brown hair and deep brown eyes. Other than being the youngest, Emily's only distinction in the family was that, at five four, she was also the shortest.

"How was your day?" Emily asked.

"*Gut, gut.* How was yours?" Rachel glanced around the kitchen, her eyebrows knitting together. "We have a dinner tonight?"

"*Ya*, did you forget?"

Rachel blushed. "I'm so sorry. I wouldn't have stayed after school to grade papers if I had remembered."

"It's fine." *Mamm* pulled baked chicken from the oven. "Just go get cleaned up and you can help us put the meal together. The group will be here in about thirty minutes."

Rachel disappeared up the spiral staircase.

"Sometimes I think Rachel is so wrapped up in Mike that she forgets things," Emily said as she finished setting the table. She was referring to Rachel's boyfriend, Mike Lantz. Rachel had fallen in love with Mike last spring. "I really can't blame her, though."

Mamm snickered. "From what I remember, that's how young love is. It permeates your mind like a cheerful fog."

Emily sighed. When would she meet the right man and fall in love? She dreamed of having a home and family, but Rachel taught at the special school for children who needed extra help, and their parents needed Emily at home all day. She split her time between working in the harness shop and helping her mother with the household chores. She also made quilts to sell at the market and helped host dinners for *Englishers*.

Rachel reappeared in a fresh green dress. "What can I do to help?"

"Would you get out the glasses and fill a pitcher with water?" *Mamm* set freshly baked bread on a platter. The delicious aroma blended with the chicken and wafted over the kitchen.

"*Ya.*" Rachel headed toward the cabinets. "So how were your days?"

"Emily has a new coworker." *Mamm* set the bread on the table. "Hank's nephew arrived from Ohio. I think *Dat* told you Christopher is going to work with Hank and your *dat* for a while."

"Oh *ya?*" Rachel raised her eyebrows. "How old is he? Is he handsome?"

Emily took the first two glasses from her and set them on the table. "I don't know how old he is, and I don't think he likes me."

"But is he handsome?" Rachel prodded with a grin.

"Rach, don't start, okay?"

Emily wasn't in the mood for her sister's teasing. Lately Rachel had taken to trying to set Emily up with Mike's friends from his church district, but it never seemed to work out. It wasn't that Emily was picky or even that she had unrealistic expectations of what a relationship should be. Yes, she wanted to find someone she could talk to and who would listen to her and relate to her, but that wasn't all.

She wanted to feel a spark. She wanted true love, like Veronica had with her husband. Veronica had once told her Jason was her best friend, but she was also attracted to him. Emily wanted the same thing—a man who was her best friend but also warmed her heart.

"Did I miss something?" Rachel turned toward *Mamm*.

"Let's just say Christopher wasn't very friendly to Emily," *Mamm* said.

"What do you mean?" Rachel asked.

As they finished preparing the meal, Emily told her about her brief conversation with Christopher.

"I can't believe he wasn't friendly to you," Rachel said, frowning. "*Dat* grew up with Hank, so we're practically family."

Emily nodded, feeling more confused than ever.

Rachel's frown softened. "Well, I was awfully rude to Mike the first time I met him, and Mike forgave me."

"What are you saying?" Emily opened a nearby cabinet and pulled out a stack of cookbooks her mother sold for a friend at dinners.

"I'm just saying maybe Christopher will realize you were just being nice and he'll apologize." Rachel shrugged. "Maybe he was having a bad day."

"Maybe." Emily worried her lower lip as her recollection of the coldness in Christopher's face sent a shiver through her. Had she misinterpreted what was going on with him? Had there been sadness or even anger in those cold eyes?

"They're here," *Mamm* said.

The hum of the van's engine and crunch of the tires on the rock driveway drew Emily's attention to the window above the sink. She pushed thoughts of Christopher away and prepared herself for the evening. She needed to concentrate on serving food and answering questions about their Amish culture.

"CHRIS! CHRIS, HELP ME!" GABRIEL CRIED FROM SOMEWHERE IN the distance.

"Where are you, Gabriel? Where are you?" Chris's pulse pounded in his ears as he ran toward the back of the pasture at his father's farm and searched for his younger brother. His body was shaking and his head was spinning with fear combined with adrenaline.

Chris rounded a corner, and a strangled sob escaped from deep in his throat as he found Gabriel lying on the ground, covered in blood. Chris fell to his knees beside him and touched his arm.

"Gabriel?" he croaked as tears snaked down his hot cheeks. "Please open your eyes. I'm so sorry." His voice broke as sobs racked his body.

Chris's eyes flew open. He was drenched in sweat. He rolled onto his side and stared at the plain white bedroom wall.

It was just a dream. Another nightmare.

Gabriel was still dead.

And it was still Chris's fault.

He rubbed his wet eyes. He'd been crying again. As usual, the dream was so real that he was transported back to his father's pasture, reliving the horrible day that changed his life forever. But this time Gabriel begged him for help, and Chris was too late to save him.

He shoved himself to a sitting position. He glanced around the unfamiliar, sparsely decorated bedroom, and for a moment he was disoriented. Then reality whacked him in the gut. He was at *Onkel* Hank's house in Bird-in-Hand. Moving in with *Onkel* Hank was Chris's last-ditch effort to somehow pull his life back together after Gabriel's death nearly three months ago. He scrubbed his hands down his face and inhaled a jagged breath.

Chris swung his legs over the side of the double bed and stood. He turned toward the battery-operated digital clock on the nightstand. The bright green numbers read 1:05. He'd managed to get two hours of sleep, which was a new record. Most nights the nightmares woke him every thirty minutes, like clockwork. He flipped on the lantern and padded down the stairs to the kitchen, careful not to wake his aunt and uncle, who were asleep in their bedroom on the first floor.

After filling a glass with water, he stepped out onto the back porch and sat down on the swing. More tears threatened Chris's eyes, and he took a deep, trembling breath. He didn't want to cry. He'd cried too much already, and he had to find a way to move past his grief. With his hand shaking, he lifted the glass and took another sip of water. His gaze moved to the house next door, the Fisher family's home.

Chris had noticed the large, white clapboard house when the taxi steered into *Onkel* Hank's driveway Tuesday evening after the endless bus ride from his parents' farm in Sugarcreek, Ohio. The Fisher house had a large wraparound porch at the front and a smaller porch at the back. *Onkel* Hank spoke highly of Leroy

Fisher and his family, explaining that Hank and Leroy had gone into business when they were in their twenties.

Just like Chris's brother, Paul, *Onkel* Hank was a man who'd known what he'd wanted at a young age. His path had been settled long ago. Chris admired his uncle, who was warm and forgiving, a stark opposite to Chris's father.

Chris longed to get his life in line too. But he didn't know what he wanted to do with his life.

Chris stared at Leroy's house as an image of Emily Fisher's face filled his mind's eye. She was so pretty—beautiful, actually—with her soft facial features reminding him of a doll, golden hair peeking out from under her prayer covering, and sky-blue eyes. She seemed so sweet and kind.

Chris cringed as he recalled their conversation earlier in the day—as if he could call it a conversation at all. Why had he been so rude to Emily when she tried to talk to him? It was obvious she was straining to pull him into a conversation, but Chris had quashed her kindness as if she were an annoying bug.

Chris lifted his eyes to the sky, taking in the bright, twinkling stars as the cool night air seeped through his T-shirt and into his skin. He knew exactly why he'd been rude to Emily. There was no use trying to be friends with anyone. He wasn't good at relationships, and he certainly did not want to be too friendly with a woman.

Emily's confused stare had weighed heavily on him as he worked beside her father, though. He should apologize to her, but what could he say? She most likely had already written him off as a horrible person. Regret settled on his shoulders and a headache brewed behind his temples.

Chris stood and wandered back into the house, set the glass

in the sink, and quietly made his way up to the spare room. He placed the lantern on the nightstand, climbed back into the bed, and stared at the ceiling.

Mamm had once told him he should lay his burdens at God's feet. If only he remembered how to pray. His ability to talk to God had died the day Gabriel was killed.

Chris hoped coming to Bird-in-Hand would somehow lead him back to God and heal his soul.

But as he lay awake for the next few hours, he wondered if that was even possible.

CHAPTER 2

EMILY SAT AT THE COUNTER IN THE HARNESS SHOP Thursday morning and chatted with a customer as she rang up two key chains, a saddlebag, a horse blanket, and two reins. The bell above the door chimed, and she had the sense that whoever had come in was looking at her.

She glanced to her left and saw Christopher standing by the door with his intense gaze locked on her. His demeanor was different than the day before. This time she was sure his eyes seemed sad.

"Here you go." The customer handed her a stack of dollar bills.

"Thank you." Emily was suddenly self-conscious. She counted out the man's change and handed it to him. Then she put his items into two large paper bags for him. "Have a nice day," she said as he walked out the door.

Emily sat back on the stool and smiled up at Christopher. *"Gude mariye."*

"Gude mariye," he said softly.

Shock nearly knocked Emily off the stool when Christopher answered her nicely. She was silent for a moment. He had dark circles under his eyes, which looked more green than blue today in the light of the skylights. The clock behind his head read nearly nine thirty. Had he just gotten out of bed?

"*Wie geht's?*" she asked, hoping to engage him in conversation.

Christopher's gaze moved to the work area, and he shrugged.

Emily remembered all the reasons Christopher could have been so distant before, and an idea struck her.

"Do you have plans for lunch?"

Christopher met her gaze and looked hesitant. "What?"

"Would you like to have lunch with me?" Her words came out in a rush. "I have some leftover baked chicken from last night, and it's always *appeditlich* reheated. I also have homemade rolls, so we could make chicken sandwiches."

Christopher was silent for a moment as if puzzling out something. "*Danki*, but I don't think so."

"Oh, okay." Her shoulders deflated as her happy mood dissolved. "You'll have to stop by and meet the rest of my family sometime."

"I'll try." Christopher looked at her for a moment longer and then walked into the work area.

Emily stared after him, feeling like a buffoon. Why had she invited him to lunch? And when he'd turned her down, why had she told him he had to meet her family? He obviously didn't want to meet her family if he couldn't accept an invitation to lunch.

Did Christopher think she was trying to ask him out on a date, as though she were one of those pushy girls? She gritted her teeth and resisted the urge to cover her face with her hands. She had to stop trying too hard to be his friend. Even if he was going through a tough time, it wasn't her place to try to fix his problems. As much as she hated giving up, she had to take a step back and let Christopher come to her. If he wanted to be her friend, then he'd be nicer to her and actually take the time to talk to her.

Emily let the idea settle in her mind. Christopher's rejection had stung, but she couldn't dwell on it. She pulled out the ledger and flipped through it, but her thoughts were still stuck on the surprise in Christopher's eyes when she'd asked him to join her for lunch.

He looked as if he wanted to say yes. So why had he told her no?

Chris tried to concentrate on Leroy's instructions as he sat next to him on a stool. He was explaining how to cut out a key chain in the shape of a cat.

But Chris's curious eyes kept moving toward the front of the store where Emily was staring down at a ledger on the counter as Hank spoke to a customer about a saddle. Had she even turned the page since she'd pulled it out of the bottom drawer fifteen minutes ago? Was she rereading the same page over and over again?

She was so beautiful with her bright blue eyes and golden hair that she could gain the attention of any young man in her youth group or possibly any man in the entire Pennsylvania Amish community. He had been thinking more and more about finding someone special before Gabriel died, though he hadn't had much success getting to know women. But a girl like Emily wouldn't waste her time on Chris. She probably had a boyfriend anyway.

"Christopher?" Leroy asked. "Did you hear me?"

"Huh?" Chris turned to him, his face burning with humiliation. "I'm sorry."

Leroy grinned. "Do you have something on your mind, Christopher?"

Oh no. He caught me staring at his dochder. "It's Chris."

"What?" Leroy asked.

"Mei freinden call me Chris."

"Oh." Understanding flashed in Leroy's eyes, and he smiled. "I'll call you Chris, then."

"Danki." Chris pointed to the piece of leather. "You were saying?"

"Oh, *ya."* Leroy launched into his lecture about cutting out the shape.

Chris tried to listen, but his thoughts turned back to the wounded look Emily had given him when they met. After how cold he'd been to her, he certainly didn't deserve any kindness from her. Why would she even acknowledge him when he saw her again?

Instead, to his complete surprise, she invited him to share her leftover chicken. Chris longed to accept her invitation to lunch and also to meet her family. But he couldn't risk letting her get close to him. He just wanted to be left alone. He didn't want to care.

"So do you want to give it a try?" Leroy asked.

"Ya." Chris hoped he could somehow figure out how to cut out the correct shape. He didn't want to disappoint his uncle or Leroy.

Chris had tried over and over again to impress *Dat,* but all *Dat* ever said was, *"Paul was training horses by himself by the time he was nineteen. You need to work harder."*

Chris closed his eyes as more of his father's criticisms filled his mind.

"Chris?" Leroy leaned in close. "Are you all right? Do you have a headache? Do you need some aspirin? I can send Emily to the *haus* to get you some."

"No, no." Chris opened his eyes and forced a smile. "I'm fine."

"Okay." But Leroy continued to frown.

"I can do this." *At least I hope I can.* Chris began cutting out the shape while hoping with all his might he was doing it correctly. He absently stuck his tongue out while concentrating.

"*Gut, gut!*" Leroy clapped a hand on Chris's shoulder.

"Really?" Chris hated how desperate for approval he sounded.

"*Ya,* really." Leroy's smile was genuine. "You did well both yesterday and today. Are you sure you've never done leatherwork before?"

"No, never."

"Then you're a natural." Leroy lifted the key chain he was creating. "Let me show you the next step."

"How do you like the baked chicken?" *Aenti* Tillie asked as Chris sat across from her later that evening.

"It's *appeditlich. Danki.*" Chris forced a smile and then turned his attention back to his plate. Why had his *aenti* chosen to make baked chicken tonight? Was it to make him feel even guiltier about declining Emily's invitation? Chris stifled a sigh. Of course not. She didn't even know about that.

Chris forked another piece of chicken into his mouth. He had spent all morning thinking about Emily, even after she'd left to go home at lunchtime. Even though he'd declined the invitation to have lunch with her, she still took the time to say good-bye to him.

"Christopher?" *Aenti* Tillie asked.

He glanced up to find his aunt and uncle studying him. Had she said his name more than once? "*Ya?*"

"*Was iss letz?*" *Aenti* Tillie set her fork down beside her plate.

"I'm not sure what you mean," he admitted as he fiddled with the condensation on his glass of water. "I'm fine."

"No, you're not fine." *Aenti* Tillie was not convinced. "You have dark circles under your eyes, and you're preoccupied. You know you can talk to us." She turned to her husband. "Right, Hank?"

"Absolutely." Hank wiped his beard with a paper napkin.

Chris swallowed. He couldn't possibly tell his aunt and uncle about his nightmares. He'd never shared them with anyone, and he wasn't ready to open up about them now.

"I don't sleep well," Chris finally said. *Actually, the whole truth is that I don't sleep much at all.*

"Oh, dear," *Aenti* Tillie said. "Is it that bed? I know it's old, but it's hardly ever used." She turned to Hank again. "I told you we should've bought a new mattress."

"You're right." Hank gave Chris an apologetic look. "We can still get one."

"No, no," Chris insisted. "It's not the bed at all. It's . . . well, it's me." He shrugged. "I just don't sleep well."

"Oh." *Aenti* Tillie's eyes filled with understanding. "It's because of Gabriel's accident." Her words were soft and full of sympathy, but they still sliced through Chris's gut.

"*Ya,*" Chris said, his voice shaky. When would he stop being so emotional when he heard his younger brother's name? "It's not a big deal. I'll be fine." His voice scraped out of his throat. When she continued to stare, he added, "Really, I will."

"Have you called your parents yet?" she asked.

Chris shook his head before sipping from the glass of water. He was certain a lecture was coming, and he steeled himself for her response.

"You should call them," she said gently. "Just let your *mamm* know you got here safely and you're doing okay."

"All right," Chris said, surprised her lecture wasn't harsher.

His aunt and uncle were so different from his father, who would've chastised him instead of nicely asking him to make the phone call.

"So Leroy told me you're a natural at leatherwork," *Onkel* Hank said, and Chris was thankful for the change of subject. "He said you just picked up how to make key chains like it was something you did every day."

Surprised at the compliment, Chris sat a little straighter in his chair. He wasn't used to such encouragement.

"Are you enjoying the job?" *Onkel* Hank asked.

"*Ya*, I am." Chris forked some peas.

"I'm *froh* to hear that." *Onkel* Hank spooned some mashed potatoes. "I was worried you wouldn't like the work."

"You were?" Chris nearly dropped his fork. When his uncle nodded, he asked, "Why?"

"It's so different from horse breeding and training, which is what you've known your whole life." *Onkel* Hank shrugged. "I thought you'd find leatherwork boring."

Chris opened his mouth to tell his uncle he didn't like horse training because he wasn't good at it. And that because it was a horse that killed Gabriel, he'd never look at horse training the same way again. In fact, Chris would be happy if he never stepped foot on another horse farm.

But he was a coward and kept those feelings inside. "I really like working in the harness shop. *Danki* for letting me invite myself down here."

Aenti Tillie reached across the table and touched Chris's hand. "You're always welcome in our home, Christopher. We're *froh* you're here, and you can stay as long as you want."

"*Danki*." Chris took a deep breath, hoping to assuage the emotions warring inside of him.

CHAPTER 3

"Mike and John came to visit our church district today," Rachel whispered to Emily during the service at the Glick family farm on Sunday morning. They sat together near the back row of the single women's section. "I saw Veronica and Jason here too. I like it when they come to visit our district."

"*Ya.*" Emily kept her eyes focused on the section where the young, unmarried men sat.

"What are you staring at?"

Emily turned toward her sister, who was grinning. "Shh," Emily hushed her as the minister continued to talk in German.

"Nope," Rachel whispered.

Emily swung her gaze back to her sister. Rachel had been acting strangely all day. She seemed happier and more upbeat than usual. "What's going on with you?"

"What do you mean?"

"You've been really *froh* today. In fact, you nearly skipped to the buggy this morning. Were you that excited to come to church?"

Rachel waved off the question. "You're changing the subject. You've been staring over there." She pointed toward the bachelor section. "Who has captured your attention?"

"No one." Emily was a terrible liar. She'd been looking at Christopher, wondering if he was uncomfortable visiting a new church district for the first time. He sat next to Mike, Rachel's boyfriend, and Emily imagined her father or Hank had introduced them so Christopher had someone to sit beside. He stared down at the hymnal throughout the service, never looking up and never smiling. Did he ever smile? She tried to imagine what he would look like if he smiled.

"What's his name?" Rachel asked, leaning in closer.

"What? Who?" Emily stammered, caught off guard by the question.

Two sisters whom Emily knew from her youth group turned around in their seats and shushed Emily. Her face flamed with embarrassment.

Rachel leaned in close again and snickered. "You need to learn how to whisper."

Emily closed her eyes and prayed for patience with Rachel. She glanced across the barn to where Veronica sat beside *Mamm*. Veronica looked serene today with her hands resting on her lap. She also seemed somehow different, but Emily couldn't put her finger on what had changed. What was going on with her sisters?

"Tell me his name," Rachel whispered. "Have you met someone new? Is he a *bu* from youth group?"

Emily wanted Rachel to drop this subject. "No, it's not someone from youth group."

"So who is it?" Rachel insisted. "You're definitely distracted by someone."

"It's Hank's nephew," Emily finally admitted with a resigned sigh.

"Christopher?" Rachel's brown eyes glimmered with curiosity. "So you like him?"

"I hardly even know him. I'm just worried about him."

Rachel continued to look intrigued. "Why?"

"Because he's a loner, and he looks so *bedauerlich*."

"If anyone can help him, it would be you." Rachel gave her a knowing smile.

"What's that supposed to mean?"

Rachel looked across the barn, and her smile faded. "We'd better be quiet. *Mamm* is watching, and she's not *froh*."

Emily followed her sister's gaze to *Mamm* glaring at them.

Emily redirected her attention to the sermon, taking in the message and concentrating on God. She could think about Christopher later.

"So what did you think of the service?" Mike asked Chris as they helped convert benches into tables for the noon meal.

"It was *gut*," Chris said, glancing around the barn for *Onkel* Hank. He spotted him talking to Leroy and another man over in the corner. His *onkel* was a social butterfly, yet another stark contrast to Chris's taciturn father.

"Was it different from services back in Ohio?" Mike asked.

Chris turned to see Mike looking at him with interest. "No, not really. I think most services are the same, right?" *Except that mei dat wasn't preaching today.*

"*Ya*, I suppose so." Slightly taller than Chris's six-foot-one stature, Mike had been pleasant and welcoming ever since Leroy introduced Chris to him and his little brother, John, that morning. Mike was dating Leroy's middle daughter, Rachel.

Chris wondered if one of the other young men in the congregation was Emily's boyfriend. Not that it was any of his business whether or not she was dating someone.

"Mike!" John rushed over from the other side of the barn. "Where are we going to sit? Can we sit with Leroy and Hank? Jason is here too!" John had sat quietly next to Mike during the service, and he was the mirror image of his older brother with blond hair and bright blue eyes. He guessed John was about seven or eight years old.

"*Ya*, that sounds *gut*." Mike mussed his brother's hair, then looked up at Chris. "Have you met Jason?"

"No." Chris slid his hands into the pockets of his trousers.

"Jason is Veronica's husband," John explained.

"Oh, okay." Who was Veronica?

"Veronica is Rachel's older *schweschder*," John said as if reading Chris's thoughts.

"Oh." Chris glanced across the barn at Leroy. *How many daughters does the man have?*

"I'll introduce you to him." John took Chris's hand, steering him across the barn toward Leroy and Hank. "Jason is nice. You'll like him."

"John is really shy," Mike joked as he walked beside them.

"I can see that." Chris tried to suppress a grin as John guided him toward the group of men. John reminded him of Mamie, his gregarious four-year-old niece. An unexpected pang of homesickness kicked him in the gut.

"Jason." John interrupted the men. "This is Christopher. He's Hank's *bruderskind*."

A man with light brown hair, a short brown beard, and brown eyes smiled and shook Chris's hand. He was only slightly shorter than Chris and looked to be in his midtwenties.

"Hi, I'm Jason Huyard."

"Nice to meet you. You can call me Chris."

"Jason is my son-in-law." Leroy clapped a hand on Jason's shoulder. "He's married to Veronica, my eldest *dochder*."

"*Ya*, John was just telling me all about that." Chris looked down at the boy.

"Why don't we have a seat?" Hank offered. "The women will be bringing the food soon."

"Sit by me." John pulled on Chris's sleeve.

"All right." He sat down on a bench between John and Jason, and Hank and Leroy sat down across from them. Mike slipped in beside John and whispered something to him. While observing the brothers' interaction, Chris recalled his late-night chats with Gabriel, and his lungs squeezed with renewed grief.

Chris looked up when he heard his name. "What's that?"

"I asked what you did for a living in Ohio," Jason said.

"I'm sorry. I was lost in thought." Chris was sure his cheeks were bright red. "*Mei dat* owns a horse farm. He breeds, trains, and sells horses."

"Wow." Mike looked impressed. "That's a great business to be in."

"Oh *ya*," *Onkel* Hank agreed. "My brother-in-law, Wilmer, is very successful. His farm has grown over the years. I believe he started it just before Paul was born. Now Paul has his own successful horse farm, right?"

Chris nodded, but his shoulders stiffened and his jaw set at the sound of his father's name. How long would *Onkel* Hank continue to brag about *Dat* and Paul?

"*Mei dat* and *onkel* own a shed business," Jason said. "*Mei bruder* and I work there, along with my cousin and a few *freinden*." He pointed toward Mike. "Mike and his *onkel* own a lawn ornament business, and they stay busy."

John sat up taller and gazed at his brother. "I'm going to work there when I get bigger, right, Mike?"

"That's right, Johnny." Mike smiled at him.

Chris frowned. He didn't want to follow in his family's business, so he couldn't relate to Jason, Mike, and John. The men sitting around him were honored and eager to continue their families' businesses, and as usual Chris just didn't seem to fit in with the rest of the community. He had no idea where he belonged.

"Oh, here comes the food," Leroy announced.

A parade of women fluttered by the long table, dropping off napkins, cups, plates and utensils, bowls of peanut butter spread, and plates filled with lunchmeat, bread, pickles, and pretzels.

When the men bowed their heads in silent prayer, Chris's thoughts wandered. *Dat* and Paul were probably sitting down with his home church district to eat now too.

When the prayer was over, the men began loading their plates, and soon a murmur of conversation overtook the large barn. A hand brushed Chris's shoulder and startled him. He peered up at Emily smiling down at him. At the sight of her, his breath caught.

Where did that reaction come from?

"*Kaffi?*" She held up the pot.

"*Ya. Danki.*" He handed her his cup and she poured coffee into it.

"Have you met Emily?" John asked, chewing bread smothered in peanut butter.

"Johnny, we've told you not to talk with your mouth full," a brunette standing on the other side of the table reminded the boy as she filled Leroy's coffee cup.

"Sorry, Rachel," John said with a toothy grin before turning back to Chris. "Rachel is *mei bruder's* girlfriend, and Emily is her *schweschder.*"

"Christopher and I have met already," Emily told John. "We work together at the harness shop."

"So you're Christopher." Rachel grinned. "It's nice to meet you." She turned to his uncle. "Would you like some coffee, Hank?"

Emily gave Chris another smile. "I'll see you later."

Before Chris could respond, Emily moved down the table, smiling and talking as she poured coffee into cups. He couldn't pull his gaze away from her. Emily was so sweet and genuine, even though he'd repeatedly given her the cold shoulder. Chris could never gain the attention of a *maedel* as special as she was.

So why couldn't he stop staring at her?

"You and Johnny are coming over to visit, right, Mike?" Rachel grinned at her boyfriend while standing next to his buggy.

"*Ya*, we are." Mike smiled back at her.

"We're coming over too," Veronica added.

Rachel clapped. "I was hoping you'd say that."

Emily stood beside *Dat's* buggy as Veronica and Jason whispered to each other and held hands. She thought again about how both of her sisters seemed so different today. Rachel couldn't stop grinning at Mike as if they shared a wonderful secret. Veronica and Jason were holding hands, and they rarely displayed affection in public. Emily had never felt so overlooked by her own family before. Her sisters always shared their secrets with her, but now she felt as if she were invisible.

Emily crossed her arms over her apron and was suddenly aware that someone was watching her. She turned to see it was Christopher. When her gaze met his, he quickly looked down at John, who was telling him a story. Christopher leaned down and nodded. He looked as if he was hanging on to every word the little boy said. Emily was grateful John had latched onto Christopher. Perhaps that sweet little boy could melt Christopher's cold exterior.

"Well, let's all go back to *mei haus*," *Dat* announced. "The men can visit on the porch, and the women can have the kitchen to themselves."

"I have a couple of apple pies to share," *Mamm* chimed in.

John took Christopher's hand. "Can I ride with you?"

"Sure. I'm riding with my *aenti* and *onkel*, and we have plenty of room." Christopher looked over at Emily, and she smiled. He gave her a curt nod before climbing into Hank's buggy.

Emily hoped someday soon Christopher would converse with her as easily as he spoke to John.

CHAPTER 4

EMILY CARRIED THE COFFEEPOT TO THE KITCHEN TABLE as Rachel sliced an apple pie. The low hum of the conversation from the porch filtered in through the windows, and she hoped Christopher was enjoying visiting with the men.

Emily filled the cups on the table and then sat down next to Tillie. She gave her sisters, seated across the table from her, an accusing look. "What's going on with you two today?"

Veronica raised an eyebrow. "What do you mean?"

"You're both acting peculiar." Emily pointed at Rachel. "You've been giddy all day." Then she pointed at Veronica. "And you just seem different. I can't explain how, but you are."

"Emily." *Mamm* gave her a warning glance. "What's gotten into you?"

"They're keeping secrets from me." Emily cradled her coffee cup in her hands. "I can feel it."

Veronica and Rachel exchanged glances, and then both started talking at once.

"Wait." Veronica held up her hand toward Rachel. "You go first."

"Okay." Rachel took a deep breath and then blurted, "Mike asked me to marry him last night."

"What?" Emily screeched.

"Oh my goodness!" Veronica flung her arms around Rachel and pulled her in for a hug.

"This is *wunderbaar* news," Mamm said, already wiping her eyes. "I had a feeling it was coming soon. You and Mike both seem so *froh*."

"Why didn't you tell me last night?" Emily demanded.

"Have you picked a date?" Tillie asked.

"Whoa." Rachel held up her hand. "I'll answer one question at a time." She met Emily's gaze. "I wanted to tell you and *Mamm* right away." She looked at *Mamm*. "I did, really, but I wanted to tell Veronica and Tillie too. I was hoping we could all get together today after church." She looked back at Emily. "I'm not keeping secrets from you, okay? I just didn't want to leave Veronica out."

"*Danki*." Veronica took Rachel's hand in hers. "I'm so thrilled for you. Mike is wonderful, and you will be so *froh* together."

"*Danki*," Rachel said, her eyes wet.

Emily frowned as guilt climbed up her shoulders. She should've known Rachel wanted to include Veronica.

"So what about a date?" Tillie asked.

"The first Thursday in November." Rachel's face contorted as if awaiting an explosion.

"What?" *Mamm* said. "Next week is October! How are we supposed to get everything ready in time?"

Rachel leveled her gaze on Emily. "We can do it, right, Em?"

Emily gaped. Was her sister crazy? "Well, I don't know. We'll have only about a month to get it all together."

"Of course we can do it," Veronica said. "I'll come over and help you sew the dresses. Emily and *Mamm* are fantastic with menus. It will all come together."

"I'll help too," Tillie offered.

"Why are you in such a hurry?" *Mamm* asked. "Why not wait until December or even in the spring, like Veronica did?"

"I just can't wait." Rachel beamed. "I know Mike and I have been officially dating for only about five months, but everything feels right. And he already has a *haus*, and we're just so *froh*. I don't see any reason to wait. Mike and I want to start our new life together as soon as possible. I just adore him and John. We're already a family, you know?"

Mamm's eyes gleamed with tears. "I understand." She reached across the table and squeezed Rachel's hand. "I'm overjoyed for you, *mei liewe.*"

"*Danki, Mamm.*" Rachel looked back and forth between Emily and Veronica. "What do you think about purple dresses? Since Veronica wore blue, I was thinking I should have something different."

Veronica nodded. "*Ya*, purple is perfect. We can go look at material sometime this week."

"Wait." Rachel held up her hand and looked at Veronica. "What's your secret?"

Veronica's cheeks flushed and she touched her abdomen.

It was *Mamm's* turn to screech. "You're expecting?"

Veronica started to laugh, her blue eyes misting over. "*Ya*, I saw my doctor last week. I can't believe it."

"Oh, Veronica!" Rachel hugged her older sister.

Mamm hopped up and joined them in a group hug.

"This is so wonderful!" Emily clapped and then turned to Tillie, who was wiping tears off her cheeks.

"I can't tell you how excited Jason and I are," Veronica said. "It seems like we've been trying for a while, and I was starting to worry we couldn't have—" She stopped speaking, embarrassment overtaking her face, and looked at Tillie. "I'm sorry, Tillie. I didn't mean to be insensitive to you and Hank."

"It's okay," Tillie said. "I understand. I'm so thrilled for you. You will be a *wunderbaar mamm.*"

At the mention of the word *mamm*, Rachel started squealing, and Emily laughed.

"What's going on in there?" Leroy asked as the women yelled in the kitchen.

Chris looked up from where he sat on the bench next to John at the far end of the porch. He'd been quietly sipping a cup of water while listening to the men discuss work and politics.

The women continued to yell, and Leroy popped up from the porch swing. "Let's go see what's going on." He headed into the house with Hank, Jason, and Mike trailing closely behind.

John stood and gestured for Chris to follow him. "Come on, Chris."

Chris stilled, holding on to the edge of the bench. He felt awkward about joining them, and he wanted to stay on the porch. After all, this wasn't his family. He was only a visitor. A stranger, really.

But he reluctantly followed John into the house through the mudroom, stopping in the doorway to the kitchen. He leaned one shoulder against the doorframe as Mattie, Leroy's wife, hugged Veronica and Rachel. Emily stood and came around the table to join them. Emily was much shorter than her mother and sisters, but she was easily the most beautiful of the four. Her face glowed with her dazzling smile. When her gaze met his, Chris yearned to look away, but he couldn't bring himself to break the connection.

"What's all the commotion?" Leroy asked with a grin.

"Oh, Leroy," Mattie gushed. "We have *wunderbaar* news! Veronica and Jason are expecting, and Mike and Rachel are getting married!"

Leroy clapped his hands together before hugging his wife. Then he embraced Veronica and whispered something in her ear before moving on to hug Rachel. Jason approached Veronica and held her hand, and Mike moved over to stand by Rachel.

"That means you need to quit teaching," Leroy told Rachel.

"*Ya.*" Rachel sniffed and wiped her eyes. "I'm going to request a meeting with the school board next week. We want to get married the first Thursday in November."

Mike looked at John. "You're going to stand up for me in the wedding, right, Johnny?"

John scrunched his nose, his brow wrinkling. "What does that mean?"

As Mike explained the wedding service to John, another memory assaulted Chris. He and Gabriel were Paul's attendants when Paul married Rosanna five years ago. It had been a great honor. Now he and Paul barely talked; he was so busy with his family and farm. And Gabriel was gone. Grief clutched his chest.

Chris rubbed the stubble on his chin as the conversation moved to Veronica and Jason's baby. Someone asked when she was due, and Veronica announced May. The crowd broke out in more cheers and gasps. Chris felt like an outsider, an intruder invading this private family discussion. He was relieved when John sidled up next to him, and an idea struck him.

"Hey, John." Chris tapped his shoulder. "Do you like to play catch?"

"*Ya!*" John jammed a thumb toward the door. "We have a ball in the buggy. Let me go ask Mike if I can play." He trotted off toward his brother.

"Great." Chris looked across the kitchen at Emily. She was watching him. Her pink lips turned up in a pretty smile, and he nodded a greeting at her.

"Mike said yes!" John announced, rushing over to Chris. "Let's go play."

Chris followed John outside, and after John retrieved a softball from Mike's buggy, they walked over to an empty patch of grass beyond the Fishers' garden. John tossed Chris the ball, and Chris tossed it back. Chris was grateful for his new little friend and their comfortable game of catch.

"Mike is going to marry Rachel," John said before throwing the ball again.

"I heard that." Chris tossed it back to him. "Are you *froh* about that?"

"Oh *ya*. Rachel makes Mike *froh*, and that makes me *froh* too. Mike is *mei bruder*, but he's sort of like *mei dat*." John tossed the ball back and forth in his hands as he spoke. "Mike is actually my half *bruder* because we had different *mamms*. His *mamm* died a long time ago, and then *mei mamm* died when she was having me. Our *dat* died last spring. He was on dialysis and needed a kidney transplant, but he was really sick."

Chris's response was trapped in his throat as he contemplated what the little boy had just shared. Suddenly Mike and John's close relationship came into clear focus. They had only each other.

"I'm so sorry," Chris finally said, his words thin.

"It's okay." John tossed the ball to Chris. "I can't wait until Mike and Rachel are married. Rachel is going to move in with us. And if they have any *kinner*, I'll be the *onkel*."

"That's right." Chris smiled as he tossed the ball back to John. He really liked this little boy.

"Are you an *onkel*?"

"*Ya*." Chris's happiness faded as he thought of his two little nieces. He missed them. "My older *bruder* has two *dochdern*."

"What are their names?" John threw the ball back to Chris.

"Mamie and Betsy."

"Do you play ball with them?" John wiped his brow with the back of his hand.

"No, they're a bit too young for that, but maybe someday I will." He threw the ball back to John. He hoped he'd see his nieces again someday, instead of being cut off from his family for the rest of his life after leaving them. What if he never saw them again?

A wave of distress hurtled through him, leaving him feeling hollow inside.

As CHRISTOPHER TRAILED JOHN OUT THROUGH THE MUD-room, Emily squelched the desire to follow them. The friendship blossoming between them tugged at her heartstrings, and she longed to know more about Christopher. What had that look he'd given her earlier meant? The intensity in his eyes had sent her senses spinning like a tornado.

Emily glanced across the kitchen to where Tillie stood beside *Mamm* as Rachel talked on and on about her wedding plans. Perhaps Tillie would answer some of her questions about Christopher.

Emily walked over and touched Tillie's shoulder. "Could I speak to you for a moment?" she whispered.

"*Ya*, of course."

Emily followed Tillie over to the far window, where they peered out and spotted Christopher and John playing catch just beyond her mother's garden. Christopher grinned at something John said before tossing the ball back to him. The scene warmed her heart, and just as she had suspected, Christopher had a beautiful smile that complemented his handsome face.

"What's on your mind?" Tillie stepped closer to Emily. "You look like you're trying to figure out a complicated puzzle."

"Actually, that's really accurate. I've been wondering about Christopher," Emily began, careful to keep her voice soft. "He seems very . . ." She searched for the correct word. "Well, he seems complicated. I've tried to talk to him, but he doesn't really respond. I also asked him to join me for lunch, and he turned me down. I've wondered if I've somehow offended him or if he just doesn't like me or . . ." She hated the tremble in her voice, but she couldn't hide the fact that Christopher's reactions had hurt.

Tillie shook her head and touched her arm. "Emily, it's nothing you've done, and I'm sure Christopher doesn't dislike you." She frowned and turned back to the window. "He's dealing with a lot of emotions right now, and I think he's a little lost."

Emily held her breath, sure there was more.

Tillie turned toward Emily again, and her eyes glinted with tears. "His younger brother died in an accident in June. Christopher found him, but it was too late to save him."

Emily gasped and tears stung her eyes. Now it all made sense. Christopher was grieving. And then she remembered that Hank and Tillie had traveled to Ohio in June to attend a funeral for one of Hank's nephews. Since Hank had two sisters who lived in Ohio with their families, Emily hadn't made the connection.

"Christopher asked to stay with us to get a new start." Tillie sniffed and looked out the window. "I don't think he means to turn you away. He's a *gut bu* and has a *gut* heart. He just, well . . ."

"He just needs a *freind*," Emily whispered, and Tillie nodded.

Emily silently vowed to be Christopher's friend and to find a way to help him.

CHAPTER 5

CHRIS LEANED BACK AGAINST ONE OF THE SUPPORT POSTS on Leroy's back porch later that evening. He was stuffed after Mattie had served pork chops, applesauce, and green beans before offering another apple pie. Chris had sat across from Emily at the table during supper, and out of the corner of his eye had caught her looking at him again. Part of him wanted to run from her steady gaze, but another part of him wanted to bask in the attention.

His emotions were seriously confused when it came to that *maedel*.

After supper, the men had returned to the porch for another round of talking shop and guessing when the first snow would fall on Lancaster County. Chris just observed, taking in the camaraderie. What would it be like to be part of this family?

The screen door opened and then clicked shut as Veronica and Jason stepped onto the porch with Mattie and Rachel in tow.

"We'd better get going," Jason said. "Work comes early in the morning, and Veronica is getting tired. She's too stubborn to admit it, but I caught her yawning earlier."

She gave him a feigned look of annoyance before hugging her mother. "Tell Emily I said good-bye. I know she's busy doing the dishes, but I don't want her to think I forgot her."

"I will," Mattie promised. "Be safe going home, and I want to go with you to your next appointment, okay? I want to be a part of this."

The women started discussing the baby again, and Chris stared down at the porch floor. Should he walk away to give them their privacy?

"Chris." Jason reached out and shook Chris's hand. "It was nice meeting you."

"You too. Congratulations," he added awkwardly, wondering if that was the appropriate thing to say.

"*Danki*." Jason radiated with pride, reminding Chris of when Paul announced that Rosanna was expecting their first child.

Chris looked toward the pasture as the family continued to say their good-byes and congratulations to Veronica and Jason. Soon Jason and Veronica were on their way, and Chris longed to head back to the sanctuary of his little bedroom next door.

"Have a root beer." Leroy pushed a cold bottle into Chris's hand. "I brew it every summer. This is just about the last of it."

"*Danki*." Chris took a sip and relished the feel of the cool carbonation on his dry throat. "It's fantastic."

"*Danki*." Leroy lowered himself onto the swing and patted the bench next to him. "Have a seat, son. The night is young."

Son? Chris stared at Leroy, stunned by the affection in his tone.

Chris sat down, then glanced out toward the barn and spotted Mike and Rachel talking as Mike hitched the buggy to the horse. John stood nearby, watching his brother and trying to help.

When the horse and buggy were ready, John bounced up on the porch and stuck his hand in front of Chris. Chris raised an eyebrow with confusion.

John scrunched his nose. "Don't you know how to give a high five?"

Chris chuckled. "Of course I do." He gave John a high five.

"*Danki* for playing ball with me. Can we do it again sometime?" John's eyes were bright with hope.

"Absolutely." Chris grinned as John gave him another high five.

"See you soon!" John waved and then said good-bye to the rest of the family before hurrying down the porch steps to climb into the buggy.

"Chris," Mike called. "Thanks for playing with John today."

"Anytime," Chris said.

Mike said good-bye to the rest of the family and then climbed into the buggy. He and John both waved as the horse and buggy moved down the driveway. Chris looked over at Hank. He was talking to Leroy. Could he just climb down off the porch and head unnoticed toward Hank's house? He craved some quiet time alone with his thoughts.

Rachel, Mattie, and Tillie climbed up on the porch and sat down together on a bench beside Chris's.

"So," Mattie began, "you're thinking of purple dresses for the wedding?"

"*Ya,*" Rachel replied with enthusiasm.

"We'll need to get started on them right away," Mattie said. "We don't have much time. November will be here before we know it."

"I told you I would be *froh* to help," *Aenti* Tillie said. "I just love weddings. Since Hank and I never had any *kinner* of our own, we'd love to be involved in your wedding, Rachel, just as we were with Veronica's."

Chris's eyes moved to the door in search of Emily. Was she still washing dishes? Somehow he had a feeling this wouldn't bother her. She seemed like the type of thoughtful and generous *maedel* who loved to take care of everyone else.

He stared off toward the harness shop. He couldn't allow himself to get emotionally attached to Emily or the rest of the Fisher family. He didn't belong here, and he didn't plan to stay long. Hopefully he could make enough money to afford a place of his own in Sugarcreek. But what would he do to make a living?

The front door opened and clicked shut, but Chris kept his focus on the harness shop and his future. Something brushed against his arm, and then cold glass moved lightly against his hand.

"Would you like another?"

Chris looked over at Emily. She was sitting beside him and smiling, holding out another bottle of root beer. Her leg touched his, and the contact sent an intensity radiating through his body. He stared at her, wondering how he could make a quick escape. Yet he was frozen in place, trapped on the bench beside her and held captive by her beauty.

"Don't you like root beer?" Raising her eyebrows, she held the bottle suspended between them.

"*Ya*," he managed to say as he took the bottle from her. "*Danki*."

"*Gern gschehne*." She opened a bottle and sipped. "It looked like you had fun with John earlier."

"*Ya*." Chris nodded, and she looked at him as if waiting for him to say more. "He's a nice *bu*."

"*Ya*, he is." Emily rested her bottle on the arm of the bench. "Rachel teaches at his school. That's how she met Mike a year ago." She stared off toward the pasture. "And now they're getting married. Life moves so fast sometimes."

"It does." Chris took another sip of root beer. What should he say to her? He had nothing to offer her, but he suddenly longed to know her better.

Emily turned back toward him, and her eyes seemed a deeper

shade of blue in the flicker of the lanterns her father had set on the end of the porch. Instead of a sky blue, they were sapphire blue.

"Do you like the fall?" she asked.

The question caught him off guard. "Uh, sure. *Ya,* I do."

"I do too." Emily rubbed her hands over the sleeves of her green dress. "It feels like it's getting colder. Do you like the cold?" Her eyes searched his. What was she trying to find?

"Not really."

"I've never been to Ohio. I'd love to see it someday."

"Oh." Chris wasn't sure how to respond to that comment.

"Well, I guess we should head on home," *Onkel* Hank announced. "My boss expects me to be at work early tomorrow."

"Your boss?" Leroy asked with a laugh. "I thought you were the boss."

Emily grinned and rolled her eyes. "I've heard this argument my whole life. They act like such *gegisch buwe.*"

Chris snickered and then grinned, and Emily's face lit up. "What?"

"You have a great smile," she whispered. "I like seeing it."

Chris blinked. She'd rendered him speechless with one little compliment. No one had ever told Chris he had a nice smile. Not even his mother. He knew *Mamm* loved him, but she had never been one to spoil her sons.

Tillie stood. "We can talk about your wedding plans tomorrow. I'm so *froh* for you, Rachel."

"*Danki,* Tillie." Rachel stood and hugged her.

Tillie faced Mattie. "*Danki* for supper. We had a nice time."

"You know you're always welcome here," Mattie said. "You all are family." She turned toward Chris. "We enjoyed having you over too."

"*Danki*. The food was fantastic." Chris stood.

"Come over again soon," Rachel said.

"I will." Chris faced Emily. "I guess I'll see you at work."

"*Ya*, you will." Her expression seemed to hold something special just for him. Had she become his friend? Did he need her as his friend?

"I'M GOING TO TRY TO TALK TO THE SCHOOL BOARD THIS week," Rachel said as Emily followed her into the kitchen after Tillie, Hank, and Christopher left. "I'll agree to stay on and train my replacement, but I have to quit as soon as possible. I have so much to do."

Emily walked over to the sink and began to dry the remaining dishes sitting in the drainboard.

Beaming, Rachel leaned against the counter. "I'm going to be Rachel Lantz. I can't believe it. I've finally found the one. I wasted so much time hoping David would ask me to marry him, but I guess I had to wait to meet Mike at the right time."

"*Ya*, that's true," *Mamm* said. "God has the perfect plan for all of us."

"And Veronica is going to have a baby in the spring," Rachel gushed. "I can't believe it." She touched Emily's arm. "We're going to be *aentis*."

Emily nodded. "*Ya*, I can't wait."

Rachel started for the stairs. "I need to go make a list of everything I have to do. The wedding is going to come so fast."

Emily leaned against the sink as she listened to Rachel's footfalls on the steps. While she was thrilled for both Veronica's pregnancy and Rachel's engagement, she couldn't stop wondering when it would be her time to celebrate. When would she fall in love, get married, and start a family?

Emily closed her eyes as jealousy clawed at her. She tried to smother the feeling. Jealousy was sin! What kind of horrible person was jealous of her sisters' happiness, as if they were somehow stealing happiness from her? It wasn't as if either of them was standing in the way of her own hopes and dreams.

"Emily?" *Mamm* stepped over to the sink. "*Was iss letz?*"

Emily opened her eyes and forced a smile. "Nothing. I'm fine."

Mamm crossed her arms over her apron. "You don't look fine. You know you can talk to me."

"*Ya*, I know." Emily couldn't bring herself to tell her mother the truth. "I'm just concerned about Christopher." It wasn't a lie.

"Why are you worried about him?"

"Tillie told me he came here because of his younger *bruder's* death a few months ago. He needed a new start." Emily dried another glass as she spoke. "Tillie said he really needs a *freind*, so I'm going to try to be his *freind*."

Mamm touched Emily's cheek. "You have such a kind heart. You will be a *wunderbaar freind* to him."

"I hope so," Emily said softly. "You can go to bed, *Mamm*. I'll finish this up."

"Are you sure?" *Mamm* asked, and Emily nodded. "*Danki. Gut nacht.*"

While she dried the rest of the glasses, Emily reflected on the day. Christopher was such a complicated puzzle. But he seemed to be slowly warming up to her, and that was encouraging.

Emily set the last glass in the cabinet and then dried her hands as her thoughts spun like a tornado. It had been such an emotional day, and life was zipping by too fast. Soon Rachel would move out, and Emily would be the last one left at home.

Heaving a deep sigh, Emily padded toward the spiral staircase to the second floor. As she climbed the stairs, she hoped she would see Christopher's dazzling smile again soon, but more than that, she hoped he would allow her to become his *freind*. Maybe she needed his friendship as much as he needed hers.

CHRIS'S EYES FLEW OPEN AFTER ANOTHER NIGHTMARE. ONLY this time he made it to the middle of the pasture in time for Gabriel to say good-bye to him before he died. As the image of Gabriel dead in a pool of blood violated his mind, he shuddered.

He draped his arm over his eyes, trying to erase the scene. If only Chris could've pulled Gabriel away before that horse kicked. If only Chris could've stopped *Dat* from buying that wild horse in the first place.

Chris stared up at the ceiling for a moment and took deep breaths through his nose until his breathing steadied. Then he ran his hand down his sweat-drenched face before rolling to his side and focusing on the clock. Midnight.

He rubbed the heels of his hands against his eyes and then sat up, throwing his long legs over the side of the bed. He'd give anything for a full night of sleep, but that would never be possible again. Every time he closed his eyes he would relive that horrible day. This would be his lifelong punishment for not saving his younger brother.

Chris stepped over to the window, raised the green shade, and looked out toward Emily's house. He imagined her asleep in her bed, and he closed his eyes, trying to remove that image from his mind. He had to stop thinking about her before he drove himself crazy. Emily was nothing more than an acquaintance, and that was all she'd ever be to him. Yet he couldn't stop his senses from remembering the feel of her leg brushing his and the color of her eyes in the light of the lanterns.

Why was he torturing himself by even thinking about her? Emily was . . . unattainable.

Chris yanked himself away from the window, pulled on a pair of trousers, grabbed the lantern from his nightstand, and quietly walked down to the kitchen. After drinking a glass of water, he stepped out onto the porch, enjoying the cool air as it seeped into his skin through his trousers and T-shirt. He always woke up numb after the nightmares, and the sensation of the cold biting at his skin was better than feeling nothing at all.

He looked over at the harness shop. He could locate the key and then work until exhaustion overtook him, but work wasn't permitted on Sundays. Although it was after midnight, he still didn't feel comfortable breaking the rules that had been pressed upon him since childhood. His eyes moved to the pasture. He decided to take a walk, and went inside to slip on his boots.

Holding the lantern at his side, Chris trudged toward the pasture fence, hoping exhaustion would find him and obliterate all thoughts of both Gabriel and Emily.

CHAPTER 6

CHRIS'S EYES FLEW OPEN AND LIGHT POURED INTO THE
room from the sliver of space between the edge of the green shade
and the window casing. Where was he? What day was it?

Then the sleep haze clogging his brain dissipated. Chris was at
his uncle Hank's house, and it was Tuesday morning. He'd awoken
after a nightmare at one in the morning, and instead of walking
around the pasture as he'd done the night before, he found the key
to the harness shop and made key chains until exhaustion robbed
him of his focus.

He'd gone back to bed around five thirty. Now it was nearly
ten, and he needed to get to work before his uncle fired him and
threw him out of the house. Where would he go if he lost his job
at the harness shop?

Chris quickly rose from the bed and dressed. Once downstairs,
he expected to find *Aenti* Tillie in the kitchen, but the house was
empty and silent. He stood by the counter, trying to decide what
to do. He craved something to eat, but this wasn't his house or his
kitchen. Since he didn't feel at liberty to search through the cabinets without asking permission, Chris stepped out onto the porch
and then walked to the harness shop, his work boots crunching on
the rock path.

When he entered the shop, he saw Emily at the counter, working on the books. She glanced up at him, and when she smiled, his

heart stuttered. She seemed to glow with her blue dress complementing her eyes.

Chris had missed her since they hadn't spoken since Sunday evening. He'd only seen her from afar yesterday when she was outside hanging laundry on the line. He'd hoped she would stop by the harness shop to say hello, but she hadn't come by.

Why was he allowing himself to get attached to her?

"*Gude mariye,*" she said.

Chris attempted to speak, but his response was interrupted by his uncle.

"Christopher!" *Onkel* Hank crossed the showroom floor and stood beside him. "I can see you were busy last night."

Christopher's cheeks were aflame with embarrassment.

"You made nearly a dozen key chains. When did you work?" *Onkel* Hank asked with concern in his brown eyes.

Chris was keenly aware of Emily's gaze locked on him. He lifted his straw hat and raked his hand through his hair. "I think I was here from about one until a little after four."

"Why?" Leroy approached from behind *Onkel* Hank. "Are you ill?"

Could this get any more humiliating? Chris longed to crawl under the counter to hide from the three sets of curious eyes scrutinizing him. "No, I'm not ill. I have insomnia."

He turned toward Emily, and the concern in her face twisted something deep in his gut.

Chris's stomach growled, increasing the shame already suffocating him. Why hadn't he stayed in bed this morning?

Because I can't afford to lose this job.

He folded his arms across his abdomen in a futile attempt to silence his hunger.

"Have you eaten?" *Onkel* Hank asked.

"No. I didn't see *Aenti* Tillie, and I wasn't sure what I could eat."

"Don't be *gegisch*, Christopher," *Onkel* Hank said with a laugh. "You can eat anything you want. *Mei haus* is your *haus*, remember?"

"Tillie went shopping with *mei mamm* this morning," Emily chimed in.

"Oh." Chris's stomach roared again and he longed for this embarrassment to end.

"Go get something to eat," *Onkel* Hank said.

"But I'm already late. I don't want to abuse my position here."

"Abuse your position here?" *Onkel* Hank laughed again. "You're working circles around us old guys. You accomplished more in the wee hours of the morning than we do some days. Go eat something and then come back."

Emily came around the end of the counter and stood beside Chris. "We have plenty of food." She looked at her father. "Is it all right if I make Christopher breakfast at our *haus*? We won't be gone long."

"Sure." Leroy shrugged. "Go ahead."

Chris shook his head while looking down at her. "No, I don't want to impose. I can't let you—"

"Go on," *Onkel* Hank said. "Take your time."

"Let's go." Emily looked up at him.

Chris reluctantly followed her to the door. What would they possibly discuss while they were alone?

"What do you like to eat?" Emily asked as she walked beside Christopher up the path to her parents' house.

"Oh, I don't know." He shrugged. "Anything really. You don't have to do this. I can make some toast and find some peanut butter."

"I don't mind," she insisted. "I like to cook."

"That makes one of us," he muttered, and she laughed.

Christopher looked over at her and raised an eyebrow, causing her to laugh again. He was adorable. No, he was handsome, the most handsome man she'd ever met, but he was also the saddest. She longed to break through his cold exterior and force him to talk to her. She had so many questions she wanted him to answer.

They approached the porch and Christopher slowed, allowing her to climb the steps first and open the back door. He followed her into the mudroom and then stepped into the kitchen behind her.

"Have a seat." She crossed the kitchen and began to open cabinets in search of food. "What do you like besides peanut butter toast?"

Christopher sat at the table. "I'm not picky."

"Okay." Emily faced him while standing by the counter. "Do you like eggs, bacon, and potatoes?"

"Oh no. You don't have to make all of that for me."

"I'll take that as a yes." She pulled two frying pans out of a cabinet and set them on the stove.

"Emily, you really don't have to go to so much trouble for me."

She spun and gasped. He was standing right behind her. He towered over her, and she hadn't until that moment realized just how tall he was. He looked to be as tall as her brother-in-law, Jason, if not taller. For a moment, she couldn't speak.

"Sorry. I didn't mean to startle you." He gave her an embarrassed grin.

"It's okay." Emily pointed toward the table. "Go sit, and I'll get started."

Christopher paused and seemed to be thinking about something. "Fine," he finally said. "But I'll have to make this up to you somehow. I'll do the dishes."

She retrieved a carton of eggs, a potato, and bacon from the refrigerator. "You will not do the dishes, Christopher, and I—"

"Call me Chris."

"What?" She glanced over her shoulder at him as she broke the first of two eggs into a bowl to scramble them.

"I said you can call me Chris." He sat with his elbow resting on the table, chin in his palm. Was he going to fall asleep while she cooked his breakfast? "*Mei freinden* call me Chris."

"Oh, but Hank and Tillie always call you Christopher." She poured the eggs into one of the pans.

"I think it's like a parent thing," Chris said. "Do you have a nickname?"

"*Mei freinden* and *schweschdere* sometimes call me Em." She started chopping the potato as she spoke.

"Do your parents call you that?"

"No." She shook her head. "I see what you mean. So your parents call you Christopher?"

"*Ya.*" His face hardened with anger, or maybe it was frustration. "All the time. I'm never Chris to them."

"That's interesting."

His smile returned, and Emily swallowed a sigh of relief. "Parents are always formal, but our *freinden* use the nicknames. I can't stand it when *mei freinden* call me Christopher. I always feel like I'm in trouble for something."

Emily made a mental note to never call him Christopher again. She slid the slices of potatoes into the second pan and then flipped his eggs.

"I feel *faul* sitting here while you do all the work." His tone held a hint of teasing, and she suppressed a grin. Was she finally breaking through his wall?

"Don't be *gegisch*," she scolded. "You worked during the wee hours of this morning. You're certainly not a *faulenzer*. Do you like cheese with your eggs?"

"Sure. *Danki*."

She reached into the refrigerator for a piece of cheese and tossed it onto the eggs before folding them over in the pan. After removing the eggs from the pan, she dropped in a few slices of bacon and then put two pieces of bread in the toaster.

"I didn't plan this right," Emily lamented as she brought him the plate with the eggs. "I should've started the potatoes before the eggs so you can eat your breakfast all at once."

Chris beamed. "Do I look disappointed? You heard my stomach growl so rudely earlier." He rolled his eyes.

Emily set the plate in front of him. "You don't need to worry about that around me." She handed him utensils. "*Kaffi?*"

Chris paused as if debating if it was too much to ask.

"I'll have a cup with you," she offered.

"Okay." He bowed his head in silent prayer and then dug into the eggs.

A comfortable silence fell over the room as Emily finished making his breakfast. She brought the toast, potatoes, bacon, and peanut butter to the table before bringing two cups of coffee, creamer, and sugar and sitting down across from him.

"This is a feast," Chris said in awe. "You shouldn't have troubled yourself."

"I've already told you I don't mind." Emily sipped her coffee. How could she convince him to open up to her?

"Would you like some bacon or a piece of toast?" He moved his plate toward her.

"No, thanks. I already ate."

"Come on," he coaxed her, holding out his plate. "I can't eat all of this by myself. If I do then you'll think I'm a pig."

"Fine." Emily couldn't refuse his cute expression. She took a piece of bacon and bit into it as he scooped up potatoes. She recalled the key chains he'd created earlier this morning. Had she finally earned the right to ask him questions? "How long have you had insomnia?"

He stopped eating and held the spoonful of potatoes in mid-air as his gaze snapped to hers. She immediately regretted the question, which seemed to float in the air between them. If only she could start the conversation over again with a less personal question.

"I've had it for a few months now."

"Do you always work when you can't sleep?" Maybe he would answer her questions after all.

"No." He set the spoon on the table. "Sometimes I walk outside and other times I just stare at the ceiling and hope sleep will come and find me."

"Did you sleep at all last night?"

Chris shrugged and lifted his cup of coffee. "I got a few hours in. Maybe four." He sipped the coffee and then scooped more potatoes into his mouth.

A silence gripped the kitchen again, interrupted only when Chris's utensils scraped across the plate. After he finished the potatoes, he spread peanut butter on his toast. She wanted to pull more information out of him, including why he came to stay with his aunt and uncle, but she didn't know how to get him to really talk.

"What kind of work did you do in Ohio?" she asked.

Chris's gaze locked with hers, and his face hardened. The invisible wall he'd built around himself suddenly reappeared, and Emily longed to take the question back.

"*Mei dat* owns a horse farm."

"Oh," Emily said. "So he breeds and sells horses?"

"Right."

"Did you like working on the horse farm?"

He kept his focus trained on the toast as he responded. "I'd rather work in the harness shop, if that answers your question."

"I see." She yearned to know the whole story.

Chris looked up at her. "Did you want to ask me something else?" The question wasn't brusque.

"Why did you leave Ohio?" she asked softly. Tillie told her she thought he needed a new start after his brother died, but Emily hoped Chris would share his burdens with her.

He leaned back in the chair and was silent for a moment. "I was tired of disappointing my father and constantly arguing with him. Leaving seemed to be the only option."

Surprised by what he'd said, Emily looked at him, taking in the anguish and frustration in his eyes. She started to ask him another question, but he quickly interrupted her.

"Everything is *appeditlich*." Chris wiped his mouth with a napkin. "Do you work only at the harness shop or do you also work as a baker or something?"

Emily blinked. He was deliberately taking the focus off of himself and pushing it onto her. She took the hint. It was time to back off and allow him to recover from her probing questions.

"No, I don't work as a baker. Veronica has a bake stand, and she sells pies, relishes, and pickles. I used to help her when she lived at home. Now I work in the shop and help *mei mamm* with the chores around here. I also make quilts, and we host dinners for *Englishers* periodically. I'm never bored."

"You make quilts?"

"*Ya. Mei mamm* and I sell them at stores and charity auctions."

"*Mei mammi* made me a quilt a long time ago. I think I was about eight or ten when she gave it to me for my birthday. I wish I'd brought it with me. I left it on my bed."

The regret in his words settled over her. She'd never imagined he would miss a quilt his grandmother had made for him. Only a couple of days ago she'd considered him rude, but now she realized he was a deeply emotional man. She looked into his eyes. What else did he miss about his home in Ohio?

"You're staring at me." Chris smirked. "Do I have egg on my face or potatoes up my nose?"

She laughed, and the tips of her ears blazed. "No, you don't have food on your face."

"What is it then?" He lifted a piece of bacon. "Do I look ridiculous or something?"

"No, it's not that at all. It's your eyes."

His amusement faded. "What about my eyes?"

"They change color. When I first met you in the harness shop, your eyes were blue-green. Then the second day I saw you in the harness shop, they were bluer. Sunday night, they were green in the light of the lanterns when we sat on the porch together. But today they're like a turquoise color. They seem to change color depending on the lighting in the room."

"Really?" He smiled.

Emily took a deep breath and pushed on. "You have the most beautiful eyes I've ever seen," she whispered, her voice trembling.

Chris's grin vanished, and he set the bacon back on the plate.

"I said too much." Emily longed to bury her face in her hands. She once again spoke without thinking. Her cheeks might explode from the heat of her humiliation.

"No, no." Chris leaned forward and reached for her hand, but then pulled back before making contact. "I didn't mean it that way. I'm just not used to getting compliments. You've complimented me twice in the past few days, and I don't know how to handle it."

"I've complimented you twice?" she asked, and he nodded. "When was the first time?"

"It was when we were sitting on the porch Sunday night. You said I had a great smile and you liked seeing it. No one has ever said that to me. And no one has ever complimented the color of my eyes."

"I find that difficult to believe."

"It's the truth," he said simply. "*Danki.*"

"*Gern gschehne.*"

Chris studied her, and something shifted between them. His eyes grew intense, and a thrill shivered through her body. She had to escape his gaze. She reached across the table, gathered up the empty dishes, and carried them to the sink.

"I'd better start cleaning this up." She tossed her words over her shoulder as she began to fill one side of the sink with hot, soapy water.

"I told you I can do the dishes."

"Oh no. Don't be *gegisch*. I'm sure *mei dat* has plenty for you to do at the shop today." She started filling the other side with clean water for rinsing.

"I appreciate the breakfast." Chris pushed his chair back from the table. "I do need to make it up to you sometime."

"That's not necessary," Emily insisted as she washed her coffee cup.

Chris appeared at her side and handed her the last plate and his cup. *"Danki* for everything."

"Gern gschehne." She looked up at him. "Maybe I'll see you later?"

"I hope so." Chris turned and headed for the back door.

As the door clicked shut, Emily replayed their conversation in her mind. She'd learned a little bit about Chris, but how had his brother's death played into his issues with his *dat*? No one had ever told Chris his eyes and smile were attractive? If he'd ever had a girlfriend, then she certainly would have told him he was handsome.

Emily looked at the clock above the sink. She couldn't wait for *Mamm* to get home. She had so much to tell her!

CHAPTER 7

"So you made Christopher breakfast?" Mamm asked while sitting across from Emily later that morning.

"Chris," Emily corrected as she lifted her mug of hot tea. "He likes to be called Chris. He says Christopher is too formal."

Mamm gave her a knowing smile. "I see. And he told you he has problems with his father, which is the reason he left home?"

"Right." Emily recalled the quilt his grandmother had made for him. "I want to make him a quilt. Maybe it could be his Christmas gift. He'll probably still be here at Christmas, and I think we're *freinden* now." She was justifying making such an extravagant gift, but Chris needed a gift that would make him feel special.

Mamm raised her eyebrows. "You want to make him a quilt for Christmas? That's a lot of work for one gift."

"*Ya*, I know." Emily cupped her warm mug in her hands. "What if I made him a lap quilt to keep him warm in his buggy? That won't take as long."

"That's a great idea." Mamm snapped her fingers. "I made one for your *dat* when we were first married. I think it's in my hope chest."

"May I see it?" Emily asked.

"*Ya*, I'll try to find it." She pushed back her chair and stood.

Emily followed Mamm into her bedroom on the first floor.

Emily turned toward the far end of the room and spotted the cedar chest. *Mamm* fished around in the top drawer of her dresser and then pulled out the brass key. She bent over the hope chest and turned the key, and the lock clicked.

Emily wondered why the chest was locked, but she didn't ask. It was *Mamm's* chest, and she had the right to lock it if she chose.

Emily stood by *Mamm* as she opened the chest, and she breathed in the sweet aroma of cedar. *Mamm* sifted through the linens and a few small boxes until she pulled out a small quilt.

"I believe this is it," *Mamm* said, holding it up. "*Ya*, it is. It was the first gift I ever gave your *dat*, and he used it for years. It was really special to him. In fact, I had to mend it several times because he wore it out."

"*Mamm*, it's so *schee*." Emily gasped as she touched the quilt, which was stitched with a traditional log cabin pattern featuring blocks of different shades of tans and browns. "I'd love to make something similar to this." An idea struck her and she looked at her mother. "Do you have any more of *Mammi's* material?"

"*Ya*, I do." *Mamm* glanced down at the cedar chest. "I'm sure there's some in here somewhere."

"Could I please use some to make Chris's quilt?" Emily held her breath, praying *Mamm* would say yes. She loved feeling the connection to her grandmother, especially when she was creating a special gift.

Mamm dug in the cedar chest, pulled out some material, and handed it to Emily.

"*Danki*." Emily sank onto the edge of her parents' bed and sifted through the small pile. It wasn't enough material, but at least it was a start.

Mamm frowned. "I know I had more than that." She snapped

her fingers. "The closet! How could I forget?" She disappeared into the walk-in closet and started moving things around.

"Do you need some help?" Emily offered as bumps, thumps, and mutters sounded from the large closet.

"No, no." *Mamm* called back. "Aha! I found it!" She emerged pushing a large cardboard box. Emily read "Ruth" on the side in *Mammi's* elegant, slanted handwriting.

Mamm pushed the box over to Emily. "It's all yours."

Emily opened flaps at the top of the box and gasped with delight at the rainbow of colors staring back at her.

LATER THAT EVENING, EMILY SAT ON THE FLOOR OF THE sewing room as she sifted through *Mammi's* material box. She'd divided the material by color and had decided to create a log cabin quilt for Chris using different shades of blues and greens, which reminded her of his gorgeous eyes. She had a pencil in her hand and was sketching out the design on a notepad when she heard footsteps rushing up the stairs.

"Em! Em!" Rachel burst into the sewing room and flopped down onto the chair by the door. She took deep breaths to calm herself. "I have to tell you about my day. I met with the school board this evening, which is why I'm home late, and they let me resign. They already have a new teacher picked out, and Malinda is going to train her. That means I can quit now and just concentrate on my wedding."

"That's great." Emily got up from the floor and sat down in the chair by her sewing table, across from Rachel. "I'm so *froh* for you."

"*Danki!*" Rachel beamed. "I'm starting to doubt what color material we should get for the dresses. Do you think purple is the best color?" She frowned. "Do you think cranberry would be better? What if we went with an emerald green?"

Emily took a deep breath as frustration bubbled inside of her. Rachel had already decided on the color for the dresses. Why was she changing her mind now? They had more important things to discuss than the color of her dresses.

"Purple is fine, Rach," Emily said, her words measured.

"You think so?" Rachel ran a finger over her chin. "Cranberry might look better with my dark hair."

"You're *schee* no matter what color you wear. You should stay with the purple. It's what you picked first, so it's your favorite."

Rachel's smile was back. "We could go shopping for material tomorrow. I'll call Veronica and see if she can meet us in town. What do you think?"

"That sounds great. Do you want me to leave a message for Veronica?"

"No, I'll do it. I'm starving too. I'll make something to eat and then call her." Rachel stood and started for the hallway. She turned and grinned again. "I'm so excited, Em. *Danki* for sharing this with me."

"That's what *schweschdere* are for, right? *Mamm*, Veronica, and I will do our best to make your day perfect." She meant every word, but she longed for her sister to take an interest in her life too. Rachel could at least ask how Emily's day had gone. Did she only care about her wedding?

"*Danki*." Rachel's gaze moved to the center of the room and then back to Emily. "What are you doing?"

Emily was grateful Rachel noticed her project. "I'm putting material together for a quilt."

"Really?" Rachel stepped into the room, glancing first at the material and then at the sketch. "What kind of quilt will it be?"

"It's going to be a buggy lap quilt like one *Mamm* made for *Dat* when they were first married." Emily held up *Dat's* quilt. "This is the one *Mamm* made."

"Wow." Rachel touched it. "That's *schee.* Are you going to sell it?"

"No, it's going to be a gift."

"A gift?" Rachel grinned. "And who is the special person who will receive this gift? Is it for Christopher?"

Emily frowned and tugged *Dat's* quilt from her sister's hand. "He prefers to be called Chris."

"Is that so?" Rachel smirked. "I knew you liked him."

"Stop," Emily said, her tone strained with the touch of a moan. "It's not like that. Don't make more out of it than it really is." She sat back onto the floor and examined the material to avoid her sister's knowing look.

"You like each other." Rachel squatted next to her.

"He doesn't like me, Rach, so just stop teasing me." Emily longed for her sister to leave. She'd rather listen to Rachel drone on and on about her wedding plans than discuss her nonexistent relationship with Chris.

"Em, look at me."

She frowned up at her sister. "What?"

"He likes you." All teasing disappeared from Rachel's eyes. "I could tell by the way he reacted when you sat next to him on the bench Sunday night. He looked *naerfich.*"

"Just stop, Rach, okay?" Emily cringed. "I'm not in any mood for your teasing."

"Will you just listen to me?" Rachel snapped. "I'm not teasing you at all. Chris hung on to your every word. He stares at you as if you're the most *schee maedel* he's ever seen. I'm not kidding at all."

Emily swallowed as she looked at her sister's serious eyes. "You really mean it?"

"*Ya*, I really mean it, Em. And this quilt will mean the world to him. I can't wait to see it when it's done. You're an amazing quilt maker."

"*Danki*." Emily pointed to the piles of material. "I'm using *Mammi's* material. *Mamm* gave me a whole box."

Rachel's eyes suddenly glimmered with tears. "That makes it even more special."

Emily smiled. Despite all the teasing, she was thankful for Rachel.

CHRIS GASPED AND SAT UP STRAIGHT IN BED. HE TOUCHED the tears streaming down his face. He'd been crying. No, he'd been sobbing.

The dream came back to him, and he swallowed against another sob. In this dream, Chris heard Gabriel's screams and ran to the pasture, his steps bogged down by an invisible force. By the time he reached Gabriel, he was motionless, lying on the ground in a pool of his own blood. Chris rushed to him, and with his pulse pounding in his ears, he gave his younger brother mouth-to-mouth resuscitation between screams for Gabriel to wake up. Despite his efforts, Gabriel remained motionless. He was dead.

Once again, Chris was too late.

The nightmare had been so real that Chris could feel Gabriel's clammy skin, and when he looked down, his hands and clothes were covered in Gabriel's blood.

Chris took deep, trembling breaths until his pulse slowed to a normal pace. He had to find a way to stop these nightmares. But how?

He glanced at his clock; it was midnight. He could fall back to sleep, but the nightmare was too much to bear again. One nightmare per night was already too difficult for him to handle. He pulled on his trousers, pushed his hands through his thick hair, grabbed his lantern, and started down the stairs.

After locating the key hanging on the nail by the back door, he pushed his feet into his boots and walked out to the shop. He took a quick inventory of the items for sale on the round displays and saw that only a few doorknob hangers were left. Hank had shown Chris how to create them yesterday, and he was confident he could do it. Chris located the tools and supplies and then set to work.

While creating the first one, Chris's thoughts turned to his breakfast with Emily. He'd spent all day analyzing their conversation. None of the girls he'd known at school or in his youth group had commented on his eyes or his smile.

Of course, he had never felt comfortable letting any of them get close enough to him for that. He didn't even have close male friends—except for Gabriel.

But maybe now Emily could be his friend.

Suddenly the memory of the pity in Emily's eyes when Chris told her about his father clobbered him square in the chest. He didn't want her pity.

He'd give anything to have someone to talk to and listen to him—yes, someone who would really and truly *listen* to him. His

AMY CLIPSTON

soul yearned for a true friend, and he hoped he'd be blessed with one someday.

EMILY ROLLED OVER AND RUBBED HER EYES. HER ROOM WAS cloaked in darkness, and the house was deathly silent. She looked over at the digital clock on her nightstand to see 12:15 a.m. What had woken her up?

Was Chris awake too? Was he working in the harness shop as a way to deal with his insomnia?

Emily jumped out of bed and opened the shade. She peered over toward the harness shop and spotted a light burning. Chris *was* there! She should go help him. She'd mentally kicked herself earlier for not telling him to try warm milk. She could take him some milk now and offer it as a possible solution to his insomnia.

Emily pushed a brush through her waist-length hair, quickly braided it, and tied her pink robe over her white nightgown. Retrieving a lantern and padding down the stairs to the kitchen, she quickly heated a pan of milk and poured it into a mug. She pulled on the first coat she found in the mudroom and pushed her feet into a pair of boots before walking out the back door.

The air smelled of rain, and a cool mist kissed her cheeks as she followed the rock path to the harness shop. She pulled open the door, and the chiming bell somehow sounded louder than usual. Two lanterns on the counter illuminated the front of the shop, the lights she'd seen from her bedroom window.

At the sound of the chimes, Chris looked up from the workbench at the back. "Emily? What are you doing here?"

"I woke up, and when I looked out the window I saw the

lanterns burning out here." Emily held out the mug of warm milk. "I thought this might help you."

Chris looked at her with his eyebrows drawn together.

"It's warm milk." She took a step closer to him, and when he wouldn't take the mug, she set it on the workbench beside him. "I should've suggested it to you earlier. When I was little, *mei mamm* always made me warm milk when I couldn't sleep. Milk might help you too." She sat on a stool across from him.

Chris looked at the mug for a long moment and then met her gaze again. "I don't think warm milk can help me." His words were thin and his voice shaky. His eyes were red-rimmed. Had he been crying?

Her chest tightened. Why hadn't she woken up earlier? Maybe she could've offered him solace.

"Do you want to talk about it?" she whispered.

His eyes flashed with frustration and then hardened, stealing her breath.

"No." The word was terse and laced with contempt. Suddenly, the man who had teased her and smiled during breakfast was gone, and the angry man who had rebuffed her his first day in the harness shop was back.

Panic seized her. She had to get out of there.

"Okay." Emily scrambled to stand, nearly knocking over her stool in the process. "I'm sorry I bothered you. I only wanted to help." His tone had sliced right through her, but she couldn't allow Chris to know how deeply his rejection hurt her. *Keep it together, Emily! Don't let him see you cry.*

She headed for the door, and as she grabbed the doorknob, tears trickled down her cheek. A light tapping sound caught her attention. She glanced up at the large shop windows and saw raindrops hitting the panes.

"Emily!" Chris called, his tone urgent and pleading. "Emily, wait. Please, Em. Don't go."

CHAPTER 8

EMILY FROZE AT THE SOUND OF HER NICKNAME. SHE turned and faced Chris, who was now standing next to the counter. The fury was gone from his features, and instead, he looked humble and forlorn.

He studied her, and his eyes widened. "Oh no. I made you cry." His face contorted with what seemed to be regret. "I'm so sorry, Em. Please, please don't go."

"Are you sure?" She brushed away the tears. "I don't want to intrude."

"I'm absolutely positive." He held out his hand, but she didn't take it. "I'm tired of carrying this burden around all by myself. I need someone to talk to. What I really need is a *freind* who will listen to me."

"I'll listen to you anytime, Chris. I thought I was your *freind*."

"You are, but you shouldn't be because I haven't been a *freind* to you." He pinched the bridge of his nose as if battling a headache. "Em, I'm sorry I was awful to you again tonight, and I'm so sorry I was cold to you the first day I met you. I keep pushing you away, but you still come back to me." He tipped his head to the side and looked at her, his brow creased. "Why is that?"

"Because you need a *freind*."

Chris shook his head. "But I don't deserve your friendship."

"Everyone needs a *freind*, Chris." She pointed toward the work area. "Do you want to sit back there and talk?"

"*Ya*, I'd like that." He looked relieved—as if he were dying of thirst and she'd offered him water.

She followed him to the work area and perched on the stool beside him. He rested his elbow on the table and dropped his chin into the palm of his hand just as he'd done this morning during breakfast. She drank in the sight of his handsome face, observing his red-rimmed eyes. Something was tearing him apart emotionally, more perhaps than his relationship with his father or losing his brother, and she yearned to find a way to encourage him to open up to her.

"You've been crying," she whispered, hoping he wouldn't explode again.

"*Ya*." Chris blew out a deep sigh. "I woke up sobbing in my sleep."

Emily gaped with confusion. "I don't understand. You said you had insomnia."

"I do, but sometimes I sleep a little and then wake up." Chris looked up at her and his eyes were green in the soft glow of the lantern sitting on the worktable in front of him. "You asked me earlier why I left Ohio."

"That's right." She held her breath, awaiting his explanation.

"My younger *bruder* died in an accident in June, and it was my fault. That's why I have . . . insomnia. But tonight, when I did get to sleep for a while, I also had a dream." He looked down at the unfinished doorknob hanger. Was he avoiding her gaze?

"I'm so sorry, Chris. What happened to your *bruder*?"

He kept his gaze focused on the worktable as he spoke. "I told you *mei dat* owns a horse farm. He's bred, trained, and sold horses since my older *bruder*, Paul, was born. I was never *gut* at horse training, but Paul always has been. *Mei dat* has told me more than once that he doesn't understand why I struggle with horse training when it came so naturally to Paul. He said I should be more like Paul."

He took a long breath and his body trembled. Emily longed to reach out and comfort him, but she didn't want to appear forward.

"*Mei dat* wanted to buy this horse with a bad reputation to prove he was the best horse trainer in town. Paul has his own successful horse farm now, and he told *Dat* not to buy the horse because he was dangerous. Of course, *Dat* wouldn't listen, so he got this horse named Mischief."

Chris shifted his body so he was leaning back against the wall and facing her. His eyes misted over. "*Dat* went to town for supplies, and he left Gabriel and me alone on the farm. He told us to do our chores but not to train any horses until he got back. I was too immature and headstrong to follow his instructions."

His voice faltered and he paused, licking his lips. "I told Gabriel we should get Mischief out and try to train him to show *Dat* how *gut* we were, though I really meant I wanted to prove both to myself and *Dat* that I could be good enough. Gabriel was only seventeen. He looked up to me, so he always went along with my idiotic schemes."

He turned his attention back to the worktable again, running his thumbnail over the edge of it. "I got Mischief from the stable and told Gabriel to take him to the pasture, promising I'd be right there. I got distracted and then—" His voice hitched and he made a noise deep in his throat that sounded like a sob.

Emily scooted her stool over to him and placed her hand on top of his. "If it's too painful, then you don't need to tell me."

He looked up and the tears rushing down his face shattered

her heart. "I need to tell you," he whispered. "I need to get this off my chest."

"Take your time." She reached up with her free hand and wiped away his tears, enjoying the feel of the stubble on his cheeks. It was bold of her to touch him, but she couldn't bear the agony in his eyes. She longed to find a way to comfort him.

Chris kept his eyes focused on her as if she were his lifeline. "By the time I got to the pasture, Gabriel was dead." His lower lip trembled with every word, but he pushed on. "Mischief had kicked him in the head, and it was too late. He was lying in a pool of blood, and there was nothing I could do. I think Gabriel walked up behind the horse and startled him. It's a horse's natural instinct to kick if they are spooked or scared."

Emily tried to hold back her tears, but she couldn't. She sniffed as they streamed down her hot cheeks. She attempted to share her condolences, but she couldn't speak.

"I called nine-one-one, but there was nothing the paramedics could do." Chris looked down at his lap where Emily's hand remained on top of his. "My parents were devastated. After Gabriel was buried, *mei dat's* grief turned into fury, and he directed it all at me. One way or another, he reminded me almost daily that I killed Gabriel by blatantly disobeying his instructions that day."

Emily gasped. "He couldn't possibly blame you. It wasn't your fault. It was the horse that killed Gabriel, not you."

Something flashed in Chris's eyes, and Emily was almost certain it was appreciation.

"He does blame me. And the tension got so bad that all we did was argue—about anything and everything. He hasn't always said it directly, but in so many ways *Dat* has let me know for a long time that I'm a failure, an embarrassment, and a disappointment to him—especially when it comes to working with the horses. After Gabriel's death it only got worse. And this time, he said, there was nothing I could do to make up for my mistake. I couldn't take it anymore, so I called *Onkel* Hank and asked if I could stay with him until I earn enough money to live on my own."

"Chris." Emily squeezed his hand. "This is so unfair. You made one mistake, but you don't deserve to be treated like that. I don't understand your *dat*. He's already lost one son, so how could he let you leave?"

He shoved his free hand through his light brown hair. "*Mei dat* didn't look at me when I told him I was leaving. He didn't even say good-bye to me. *Mei mamm* begged me not to go, but I couldn't stay there and continue to see the disappointment in *mei dat's* eyes. It's better that I'm gone. I've embarrassed my parents enough. I just wanted to come here and find some peace. I need to find a way to move past this grief and move on with my life."

He paused and looked at Emily as if pondering something intently. She held her breath again, waiting for whatever he wanted to tell her.

"I'm such a coward, Em." He squeezed the back of his neck with his free hand. "I don't even have the courage to call *mei mamm* and tell her I'm okay. Can you believe that? Do you still want to be *mei freind* now that you know the truth about me?" His eyes begged her to say something encouraging. He broke the trance and stared down toward his boots.

Emily leaned forward. She placed a finger under his chin and tilted his face, forcing him to look directly into her eyes. He sucked in a deep breath and the air around them seemed to crackle with electricity.

"Look at me, Christopher Hochstetler, and listen to what I'm telling you," she said, her voice quavering with each word. "I don't think you're a coward. I think your *dat* is wrong to berate you for Gabriel's death when it was clearly an accident. And if you want me to, I'll call your *mamm* and give her a message for you. And to answer your question, I've wanted to be your *freind* since the first time I met you. I just had to figure out a way to make you realize I was here for you."

Chris stared at her with what looked like a combination of awe and bewilderment.

Their faces were so close that if Chris leaned forward merely a few inches, his lips would brush hers. An unfamiliar shiver of wanting danced up her spine. She had never experienced such a strong attraction to a man, but she had already gone too far when she touched his shoulder, held his hand, and brushed tears off his cheeks. She had never been comfortable enough to touch a man, and here she was talking to one alone when she should be asleep in her bed. She had to put some space between them before she broke even more rules tonight.

Emily lowered herself back down onto the stool and released her hand from his. Rain drummed a steady cadence on the roof and skylights, and the sound filled the thick silence hanging between them as they stared at each other.

She was suddenly aware of her attire, sitting in front of a man with her hair uncovered. She touched her braid and then hugged her arms over her father's large coat.

What would Mamm *say if she saw me now?*

A TREMENDOUS WEIGHT HAD BEEN LIFTED OFF CHRIS'S chest, and he could breathe, truly breathe, for the first time since

Gabriel died. Opening up to Emily had released something deep in his soul and allowed some of the grief he'd been carrying to melt away. He'd never felt such a close connection to anyone in his life, and he suddenly wasn't lonely anymore. Emily had changed his life just by listening to him. For the first time since he'd lost Gabriel, he had a friend. No one had ever listened or responded to him the way Emily had.

He'd never given anyone the chance.

He yearned to pull Emily into his arms and hug her until she was breathless. If he were that forward with her, he risked scaring her away, which was the exact opposite of what he needed. Fantasizing about touching her was wrong, but he couldn't deny an invisible magnet was pulling him toward her. Emily was like no other *maedel* he'd ever met, and he longed to hold on to her and never let her go.

Chris had taken a terrifying risk by pouring out his soul to Emily and sharing nearly all his secrets. He had worried she would reject him, but to his astonishment, instead of running she'd defended him fiercely, insisting he wasn't a coward.

He didn't deserve Emily's friendship. He'd hurt her feelings more than once and even made her cry with his stinging words, but she remained by his side. And now he didn't know what to say to her. The most logical thing would be to thank her.

"*Danki*," he finally said. "*Danki* for listening and not running away."

"*Gern gschehne*," she said, hugging her arms over the giant coat she wore. "I've already told you I don't plan to run away from you."

Emily looked adorable sitting there on the stool. She was obviously dressed in her father's coat and boots, which were much too big for her. Her golden hair, styled in a braid, hung to her small waist. Her skin was almost ivory in the soft light of the lantern. She reminded him of a painting of an angel he'd once seen in an *Englisher* church when he attended a funeral for one of his father's frequent customers. What would it be like to have a *maedel* like her at his side, supporting him emotionally and telling him everything would be all right during the bad times?

A hurricane of emotion swept over Chris—admiration, grief, worry, regret, and longing. He wasn't good enough for her, but he couldn't bring himself to push her away again. He couldn't risk losing her. He needed her too badly.

She yawned and covered her mouth with both hands.

"You need your sleep," he said. "It's late."

Another yawn overtook her pretty face.

"You can barely hold up your head," he said. "You should go home."

She shook her head like a petulant child and then grinned. "I'm not going home until you do."

Chris leaned forward and breathed in her aroma. Was it the smell of strawberries? "I'm not the only one with a great smile."

Emily's eyes widened, and her cheeks flushed bright pink. She was even more attractive with her rosy cheeks. "I don't have a great smile."

"*Ya*, you do. In fact, you have *schee* eyes too," Chris said as she continued to look flabbergasted. "Your eyes remind me of the summer sky." He reached forward to touch her braid and then stopped, quickly setting his hand in his lap. *Hands off, Chris!* "Your hair is like spun gold. It reminds me of the summer sun."

Emily blinked. "*Danki*." She yawned again, her eyes glistening in the warm yellow light.

"Come on, Em. You need to sleep." He stood and held out

his hand. To his surprise she took it, allowing him to lift her to her feet. He enjoyed the feeling of her warm skin against his. He turned off the lantern on the workbench and then started toward the door.

"Wait." She grabbed his hand and pulled him back.

"*Was iss letz?*"

"I'm not leaving until you drink your warm milk." Emily pointed toward the mug on the worktable.

Chris raised his eyebrows, and she scowled. "You're serious."

She crossed her arms over her enormous coat. "I made that milk for you because I was worried about you and wanted to help you. The least you could do is drink it."

Chris sighed. "You're right, and I'm sorry. I've been thoughtless again."

"That's not what I meant." Emily's face softened. "I don't want you to be sorry. I only want you to sleep. You need your rest just as much as I do."

The empathy in her eyes calmed something deep inside of him. "*Danki* for caring about me," he said as he lifted the mug.

"That's what *freinden* do, Chris. They care about each other." She pushed her thick braid behind her shoulder, and he again yearned to touch it.

He sipped the milk instead.

"Is it still warm?" she asked with a little laugh.

"*Ya*, a little." Chris gulped the milk and then handed the mug to her. "*Danki*."

"I hope it helps you sleep." She yawned once again, and he took her hand.

He relished her soft skin as he gently tugged her toward the door. "You need to get back to bed."

When they reached the door, Chris peered out at the pouring rain. "I didn't even realize it was raining. Do you know if there's an umbrella in the shop?"

"No, I don't think so, but it's okay. I won't melt." She pushed on the door.

"Wait." He rested his hand on her arm.

"What?" She looked up at him, and he was speechless. But he didn't want her to leave just yet.

"I, uh," he stammered, rubbing the stubble on his chin. "Well, I just . . ." He chuckled. "I have no idea what I was going to say."

Emily laughed. "Is the warm milk working already?"

"*Ya*, maybe it is." Chris touched her arm again. "*Danki* for everything, Em."

"I didn't do much."

"You actually did more than you know."

"*Gern gschehne*," she said. "*Gut nacht*. Go get some sleep. I'll see you sometime tomorrow."

"*Gut nacht*," he echoed.

Emily wrenched the door open and hurried up the path.

She hustled through the rain with her father's coat billowing around her legs. Emily Fisher was a very special friend, and he was thankful he'd met her.

CHAPTER 9

"I THINK THE MATERIAL WE PICKED OUT IS PERFECT," Rachel said as she sat across from Emily in the booth at the Bird-in-Hand Family Restaurant the following afternoon. "I love the shade of purple we picked, don't you?"

"*Ya,*" Mamm said, sitting next to Emily. "What do you think, Emily?"

"*Ya,* I do." A yawn suddenly overtook Emily.

"Are you all right?" Rachel leaned forward in the seat. "You look wiped out."

Emily yawned again. "*Ya,* I'm fine."

"Didn't you sleep well last night?" *Mamm* asked.

Alarm surged through Emily. She didn't want to lie to her mother, but how could she admit she'd been up in the middle of the night talking with Chris? She couldn't imagine also admitting she had stayed awake for nearly two hours after their conversation as she replayed what Chris had shared with her.

And then there was the other issue—the way Emily's body had reacted to Chris. She'd actually wanted him to kiss her! She could never admit those feelings to her mother. *Mamm* certainly wouldn't approve, especially since Emily had been alone with Chris in the harness shop and they had plenty of opportunity to kiss.

"May I take your order?" A young waitress with auburn hair appeared at the table, and Emily swallowed a sigh of relief.

Emily quickly perused the menu while Rachel and *Mamm* gave their order. She'd been so consumed with Chris that she hadn't decided what she wanted for lunch.

"And you, ma'am?" the server asked Emily.

"Um, I'll have the Bird-in-Hand club sandwich on wheat."

"Are fries okay?" the girl asked.

"Yes," Emily said. "Thanks."

The girl retrieved the menus and left.

Emily took a sip from her glass of water and once again turned her thoughts to Chris. How could his father treat him so badly and blame him for Gabriel's death? Her father had always been loving, understanding, and patient with Emily and her sisters. Emily couldn't comprehend the kind of emotional turmoil Chris had been dealing with.

"Emily?" Rachel's voice broke through Emily's mental meanderings.

"*Ya?*" Emily looked up at her sister watching her.

"Did you hear a word I said?" Rachel asked with a suspicious expression. When Emily didn't respond, Rachel just shook her head. "I said it's a shame Veronica couldn't meet us today, but I'm glad she can join us Friday for sisters' day. She said she'll help us get started on the dresses."

"Great." Emily yawned again. She needed some caffeine or maybe even a nap to perk up.

Mamm turned in the booth, angling her body toward Emily. "What's going on?"

Emily was caught. She couldn't count on the waitress to save her again. Instead, she had to tell the truth. "I didn't get much sleep last night."

"Why not?" Rachel asked.

"Are you ill?" *Mamm* inquired.

"I'm not ill." Emily swirled the straw in her glass of water and stared at the small ripples the motion created to avoid their worried eyes. "I woke up in the middle of the night, and when I looked out the window, I saw a light on in the harness shop."

"Did someone break in?" Rachel asked with a gasp.

"Why didn't you wake your *dat*?" *Mamm* demanded.

"No one broke in. In fact, I knew who was in there." Emily paused while contemplating how much to share.

"I don't understand," *Mamm* said.

Without looking up, Emily told them she assumed Chris was working because of his insomnia and she'd gone out to take him some warm milk. Then she had stayed for a while because he needed to talk to someone. When she raised her eyes, both her mother and sister were staring at her. She braced herself for their questions, and they began talking at the same time.

"You were out in the harness shop with Chris in the middle of the night alone?" *Mamm* asked.

"Why does he have insomnia?" Rachel asked.

Emily blew out a deep sigh, and her shoulders clenched. She couldn't bear disappointing *Mamm*. "*Mamm*, I knew you wouldn't be *froh* when you found out I was alone with him, but please trust me when I tell you nothing bad happened. He just needed someone to talk to, and I listened. He's been through a really rough time."

"What did he tell you?" Rachel asked.

Emily summarized what Chris had told her about his father and brother, leaving out his most vulnerable details. Rachel and *Mamm* listened, their eyes wide.

"I had no idea," *Mamm* said. "Tillie didn't tell me anything about Chris's *dat*."

"I can't believe his *dat* actually blames him for Gabriel's death." Rachel wiped her eyes. "That's so *bedauerlich*. I'm sure Chris feels guilty enough without having his *dat* constantly criticize him."

"He does. And I just want to help him. He was so desperate for someone to listen. I have a feeling no one has ever given him a chance to explain how he felt after losing Gabriel. Or at least he hasn't felt comfortable talking to anyone."

"You care about him." A grin tugged at the corner of Rachel's mouth.

"No." Emily blew out a puff of air. Who was she kidding? "Well, *ya*, I do, but it's more than that. I'm worried about him. I want to show him he's worthy of someone's friendship."

Mamm patted Emily's shoulder. "Just be careful with your heart."

"I will." Emily needed to take the focus off herself. "So, Rachel, what else do we need to shop for today?"

"I've been thinking about the table decorations." Rachel pulled a notepad out of her purse. "What if we did something with vases and silk flowers?"

CHRIS EXAMINED THE DOORKNOB HANGER ON THE WORK-table in front of him. It had to be the twentieth one he'd created today. After sleeping for nearly five hours, Chris had come in early this morning and started working before *Onkel* Hank and Leroy even arrived. He worked straight through the morning, only taking fifteen minutes to eat a quick sandwich before getting back to work.

Although his hands had been working methodically, he kept remembering how emotional Emily had been, crying along with him when he told her about Gabriel and becoming angry when he shared how *Dat* had treated him.

Last night Chris was certain Emily cared for him, but as the day wore on and she didn't come to work at the harness shop, doubt crept into his mind and displaced his security. Had he scared her away by sharing too much? Perhaps he should've lied when she asked if he needed to talk and told her he was fine. He could've blamed his insomnia on having too much caffeine in his diet.

"Christopher?" *Onkel* Hank called from his seat at the cash register. "Are you going home today?"

Chris glanced up from his current project. "What do you mean?"

"It's almost five thirty." *Onkel* Hank pointed to the clock on the wall. "Leroy left thirty minutes ago."

"He did?" Chris scanned the shop in search of Leroy.

Onkel Hank chuckled. "He said *gut nacht* to you before he left."

"I never heard him."

Onkel Hank grinned and chuckled again. "You've been in your own little world just working away today. I think it's time you quit for the night. I put the Closed sign out, and I'm sure supper is on the table waiting for us."

"May I just finish this one last doorknob hanger?"

"*Ya*, you may, but don't take too long." *Onkel* Hank jammed his straw hat on his head. "Will you lock up for me?"

"Sure." Chris pointed toward the cashier counter. "Just leave the key on the cash register."

"See you in a bit," *Onkel* Hank said before exiting the shop.

Chris finished the last doorknob hanger and then stood and stretched. His shoulders and neck were stiff after hunching over the workbench all day long. He switched off the lanterns and grabbed his hat from the peg on the wall by the front door. After stepping outside, he locked the door.

Wondering where Emily was, Chris looked toward the Fisher house. He had missed her today. Had she thought about him too? He doubted it. Unless it was to plan how she could get out of being his friend after what she'd learned about him. With a glower, he started walking toward his uncle's house.

"Chris!"

He spun to find Emily waving as she hurried toward him. His heart tripped before catching itself. He met her halfway down the path.

"Chris," she said again, smiling up at him. "I'm so glad I caught you. How was your day?"

"It was *gut*." He shrugged. "Busy. How was yours?" He braced himself for a lame excuse as to why she'd avoided him.

"I spent all day shopping with *mei mamm* and Rachel." She gestured toward the house behind her. "Rachel bought the material for the dresses for the wedding, and then we went to about a hundred places looking for decorations and favors." She frowned. "I was hoping to come and see you, but Rachel wanted to make sure we visited all her favorite stores before we came home."

"Oh, I understand." *She isn't avoiding me!* Relief flooded him. "It takes a lot of time to put a wedding together."

"*Ya*, that's the truth." She searched his eyes for a moment. "You look better today. Did you get some sleep last night?"

"*Ya*, I did. How about you?"

"It took me awhile to fall asleep, but I made it through the day." She paused. "I've been worried about you. How are you feeling?"

"I'm okay." He hooked his thumbs in his suspenders. "I'm

sorry for keeping you up last night. You shouldn't worry about me." But it warmed his soul to know she cared.

"Emily!" Rachel called from the porch. "Supper is ready." She waved. "Hi, Chris!"

Chris waved back at Rachel and then turned to Emily. "You should go."

"I know. I'll see you tomorrow."

"I look forward to it." As Emily made her way back up the path, Chris started toward his uncle's house. He was grateful Emily was his friend, but he wondered what it would be like if Emily was his girlfriend. He couldn't deny the attraction he'd felt the night before.

If only the circumstances were different and he could offer her a solid future.

"How's Chris doing?" Rachel asked with a grin as she placed the dinner plates on the table.

"He's fine." Emily ignored the teasing in her sister's tone. She took utensils from the drawer and set them next to the plates. Emily was grateful she had prepared a casserole before she left with *Mamm* and Rachel to go shopping this morning. As soon as they arrived home, *Mamm* had preheated the oven and put the casserole in. Now the aroma of the hamburger pie filled the kitchen, causing her mouth to water with anticipation.

"Did he sleep better last night after talking to you?"

Emily looked at her sister. Was Rachel ever going to stop teasing her?

"Why are you looking at me like that?" Rachel bristled. "I was wondering if your conversation with him helped."

"I thought you were making fun of me again," Emily admitted before placing a fork and knife by her father's plate. "He said he slept, and he actually looked better today. His eyes were brighter."

"That's *gut*. I think you're really helping him. You've always been so helpful to Veronica and me, so I know you can help him too."

Stunned, Emily stared at her sister.

"What?" Rachel released a dramatic sigh. "Can't I compliment you without getting a defensive look?"

Emily closed the distance between them and hugged her sister. "That's the sweetest thing you've ever said to me."

Rachel laughed. "You've been so unpredictable lately, Em. I never know if you're going to take my head off or hug me."

"I'm sorry." Emily leaned her hip against a kitchen chair. "I've just been so worried about Chris. I promise I won't be so moody."

"It's okay. I know I've been wrapped up in my wedding plans."

"You're allowed to be, Rach. This is going to be one of the happiest days of your life." She gnawed her lower lip. "I need your help with something."

"What is it?" Rachel placed the last plate on the table and then faced her.

"I want to do something nice for Chris besides making him the quilt. Do you have any ideas?"

Rachel shrugged. "Make him lunch. You mentioned the other night that he loved the breakfast you made for him. Mike liked the meals I brought him, and that's how I won his heart."

Emily snapped her fingers. "I love the idea. I'll make a nice lunch tomorrow and have *Dat* invite him to join us. Would you help me plan the menu?"

Rachel smirked. "I'd love to."

EMILY STARED DOWN AT HER QUILT DESIGN AS SHE SAT ON her sewing chair later that evening. The material she'd chosen for the quilt was arranged in piles by color on the floor, and she was ready to get started. She ran her fingers over the quilt her mother had made. She wondered how *Dat* had reacted when he'd received it as a gift. *Mamm* said the quilt was special to him, and he must have thought of her every time he used it. Would the quilt she made for Chris be special to him as well?

"Emily?"

She looked up at her mother, standing in the doorway. "*Mamm.* I thought you'd gone to bed."

"I was just getting ready to, but I wanted to talk to you first."

"Come in." Emily pointed to the chair across from her sewing table.

Mamm looked down at the material on the floor. "You're going to use blue and green shades for the quilt?"

"*Ya.* Do you think it will look okay?" She couldn't admit the colors reminded her of Chris's eyes.

"I think it will be beautiful."

"*Danki.*" Emily ran her finger over her mother's quilt again. "I just hope he likes it."

"I'm certain he'll love it." An uneasy frown melted *Mamm's* smile as she rested her hands on the arms of the chair. "I didn't want to say anything to you in front of Rachel earlier. I thought it would be better if we talked in private."

Emily sat up straight as her spine tensed with apprehension. "*Was iss letz?*"

Mamm folded her hands and was silent for a moment. "I'm concerned you went to meet Chris alone in the harness shop in the middle of the night."

"*Mamm.*" Emily held up her hands. "All we did was talk. I'm telling you the truth when I say nothing inappropriate happened between us. Chris just needed someone to listen, and that's what I did. Nothing else is going on between us."

"I believe you, Emily, but you're *mei dochder*, and it's my job to look out for you and keep you safe."

"I'm almost twenty-one," Emily said. "I know what's appropriate and what's not appropriate. You've already had that talk with me, and I've never gone against the rules of the community."

"I know that too." *Mamm* heaved a deep sigh. "Christopher is older than you."

"Only by three years," Emily cut in. "He's younger than Veronica."

"He's still older than you, and he's very handsome."

Emily's face flamed. *Can* Mamm *sense my attraction to Chris?*

"Sometimes older men have a way of talking *maed* into, well . . ."

Emily's eyes widened as *Mamm's* words clicked into place in her mind. "You can trust me. I'm not going to go against my beliefs. You've raised *mei schweschdere* and me with solid values. You don't need to worry about us, okay?"

Mamm's frown softened. "I'll always worry about my *kinner*. It's my job as your *mamm*. Just promise me you won't meet him in the shop in the middle of the night ever again."

"I promise."

"And one more thing," *Mamm* said, lowering her voice. "Don't ever tell your *dat* you were out there alone with Chris at night. He would be very upset with both of you."

"It was my fault," Emily said. "Chris didn't ask me to come out there. I went all on my own."

"I know that, and I believe you, but you know how protective he is of you and your *schweschdere*."

"Okay," Emily said.

"*Danki*." Mamm stood. "The quilt will be *schee*, Emily. I'm certain Chris will love it. Please just remember what I said earlier about protecting your heart. You have a tendency to think of others before you think of yourself. I don't want to see you get hurt." Mamm headed for the door. "*Gut nacht*."

"*Gut nacht*."

A prickle of doubt skittered through Emily's thoughts as Mamm headed for the stairs. Would Chris break her heart? Emily stared down at the quilt and said a silent prayer, asking God to help Chris realize how important he was to Emily, and to make the quilt a balm to his broken spirit.

CHAPTER 10

"Go on to lunch," Chris told *Onkel* Hank and Leroy as he sat on his stool in the work area. "I can handle things here."

"Why don't you come eat with my family and me?" Leroy suggested as he stood up from the stool beside Chris.

"No *danki*. You and *Onkel* Hank hardly ever get a break. I can wait until you get back."

"I'm certain we'll have enough food for you," Leroy pressed. "You really should come with me."

"I don't mind," Chris insisted. "I have some work I want to finish up anyway. We were completely out of the horse key chains, and I want to finish at least six of them today. The work hasn't been going as quickly as I'd hoped." He glanced over toward the display of items for sale and spotted a coin purse. He was tired of making key chains and doorknob hangers and was eager to create something with more detail.

"Leroy, would you show me how to make coin purses when you get back from lunch?"

Leroy grabbed his straw hat from the peg on the wall and shoved it onto his head. "*Ya*. That sounds like a great idea. I think you're ready for something more challenging."

"*Danki*." Chris sat up a little straighter, just as he had when

Onkel Hank told him Leroy was pleased with his work. He was grateful to have someone compliment his abilities.

Leroy hesitated. "I'd really like you to join me for lunch. Are you certain you don't want to?"

Chris raised an eyebrow. What was going on with Leroy and his determination to have Chris share his lunch? "Really, I'm fine. I promise you I won't starve before you get back."

Leroy hesitated for a moment and then gave him a curt nod. "Fine, then."

Onkel Hank stood by the shop door, holding his straw hat. "Do you want me to bring you something to eat?"

"No, it's okay." Chris waved off the offer. "You two just get out of here already."

Onkel Hank chuckled. "You remind me of your *mamm* sometimes. She always shooed me away when we were *kinner*. Sometimes she acted like she was the older sibling instead of one of the younger ones."

Chris grinned. "Really?"

"Absolutely." *Onkel* Hank gestured for Leroy to follow him. "Let's go before Christopher loses his patience with us."

"Take your time," Chris called before the bell over the door chimed.

Chris turned his attention to the horse-shaped key chain he was creating and chuckled to himself. He'd never been told he reminded someone of his mother. He frowned, wondering how *Mamm* was doing and if she worried about him.

Did *Dat* even care Chris was gone?

He pushed the troubling thought away and concentrated on the key chain. When the bell above the door suddenly chimed,

Chris jumped up and moved to the front of the store, where a middle-aged woman with bright red hair stood in front of one of the round displays. She was clad in jeans and a red jacket with a camera slung around her neck.

"May I help you?" Chris approached her.

"Hi there," she said, grinning. "I was just driving by and saw your store. I was looking for some cute souvenirs for my grandkids back home. Do you have anything with a horse and buggy on it?"

"I don't think so, but let me look." Chris perused the displays and then held up one of the horse key chains he'd created earlier in the day. "I don't see anything with a horse and buggy on it, but we have these horse key chains."

"Hmm." The woman held the key chain and turned it over in her hand. "It's not exactly what I'm looking for, but it will work." She pointed toward the displays. "I'm going to look around for a bit."

"Okay. Let me know if you have any questions." Chris moved behind the counter and saw Emily's ledger. He opened it and flipped through the pages, taking in her neat penmanship and precise calculations. He imagined her poring over the numbers, maybe even chewing on the end of her pencil while she worked. He couldn't wait to see her again. Their short conversation yesterday wasn't enough to quench his eagerness to spend time with her.

Chris looked out the window. She'd told him last night she'd see him today, but she still hadn't come by. Perhaps she had some chores to do at the house before she could help out at the shop. Or maybe Rachel had needed Emily to work on wedding plans today.

Maybe she's not as eager to see you as you are to see her.

Chris closed the book and tried to ignore that negative voice that always choked back his hopes and dreams.

"I think I'm done." The woman appeared in front of him and placed three horse key chains, two horse doorknob hangers, and a dog collar and leash on the counter.

"Great," he said with surprise before ringing up her merchandise and taking her money. He handed her the change and stuffed the items into a paper bag. "I hope you'll come see us again."

"I will." She started for the door and then stopped and faced him once again. "You have a really nice store here."

"Thanks." Chris crossed his arms over his chest. "I'm actually just an employee, but I'll let the owners know."

"Definitely tell them. You might also want to consider making some horse and buggy souvenirs. Tourists like me love that stuff." She pushed the door open and waved. "Have a nice day."

"You too." Chris returned to his key chain project. The woman's suggestion echoed in his mind while he worked. He glanced over at the display of coin purses and wallets. Could he somehow incorporate a horse and buggy design on one of the leather items they already sold? If so, would *Onkel* Hank and Leroy think it was a stupid idea?

He filed the idea away and concentrated on the key chain again. He was adding the ring to the finished product when the bell above the door chimed again.

Chris stepped out of the work area and stopped. Emily stood by the front door. She held a large picnic basket, and she was frowning at him. Although she apparently was annoyed at something, he couldn't help but think she looked cute.

"Hi, Em." Chris fought back the grin threatening to appear. "Is something wrong?"

"*Ya*, something is wrong." Emily dropped the basket on the

counter with a loud thunk. "I want to know why you turned down *mei dat's* lunch invitation. I took the time to make you a nice lunch, but you didn't have the decency to show up to eat. That meant I had to pack everything up and carry it down here to you."

"You made me lunch?" He was stunned.

"*Ya*, I made you lunch. I planned it all last night." She jammed her hands on her small waist as she glared up at him. "*Mei dat* said you kept insisting you had work to do. You know, you do have to eat sometime."

"I'm sorry for ruining your plans. I didn't realize the invitation was actually from you."

"It's fine," she said, suddenly calm. She pointed toward the large worktable. "Do you think we can make room to eat back there?"

"Sure." He reached for the basket. "Let me carry this for you, and you can make room."

Emily entered the work area and moved the tools and projects to the far end of the table before unpacking containers, bread, plates, utensils, napkins, and two bottles of water.

"I hope you like chicken salad," she said. "I made it earlier this morning, but then I realized you might not like mayo. Some people don't like mayo."

"It's fine. It's *wunderbaar*, actually." Chris sat on a stool beside her. They had sat on these same stools only two nights ago when he poured out his soul to her. Their friendship had blossomed tremendously since then. It was as if he'd known her for years instead of only a week.

Emily raised her eyebrows as she opened the container of chicken salad and stuck a spoon in it. "Why are you looking at me that way?"

"How am I looking at you?"

"You look stunned, like someone just told you you've inherited a thriving farm." She chuckled a little. "It's just lunch, Chris."

"It's more than just lunch to me." He rested his hands on the table. "No one has ever done anything like this for me."

Her smile faded, and her intelligent eyes looked earnest. "Maybe if you let people in, you'd see how many people want to do things for you and help you."

Chris gaped as her words soaked through him.

"Are you ready to eat?"

"*Ya.*"

She bowed her head, and he joined her. After the silent prayer, they made chicken salad sandwiches. She pulled out a bag of potato chips and shook a pile out onto his plate.

"So how is the day going so far?" Emily asked before biting into her sandwich.

"It's gone well." Chris told her about the projects he was working on and shared what the customer had bought earlier. "I asked your *dat* to show me how to make a coin purse later today. I think I'm ready for something a bit more detailed."

Emily picked up two of the key chains from the pile beside her. "Did you make these?"

"*Ya.*" He wiped his chin with a napkin.

"You definitely need something more challenging, then."

"Why?" he asked before taking another bite of his sandwich.

"Because these are fantastic." She turned a key chain over in her hand. "You can handle the more difficult projects already. You've picked up leatherworking quickly."

Her words sent euphoria expanding inside of him. Why did her simple compliment mean the world to him?

She gave him a small smile. "You're doing it again."

He lifted his water bottle. "Doing what?"

"Looking at me as though I just gave you the world."

Chris gave her a half-shrug. "No, not really."

Emily smiled broadly now. "You can't fool me, Chris."

"Fine, Emily." He sighed, knowing he was caught. "I appreciate your compliments. I can't remember the last time someone told me I was *gut* at anything, so it's nice to hear I've done something right for once."

"Really?" Her eyes widened.

The shock and pity in her eyes were almost too much to bear. Why had he admitted that out loud? Now he looked like even more of a failure. He fought the urge to hide under the workbench. He needed to redirect the conversation—fast.

"*Danki* for lunch. It's wonderful. You make a fantastic chicken salad."

Emily blinked. Chris held his breath, awaiting a snappy comment about how he had obviously dodged the uncomfortable discussion of his low self-esteem.

To his surprise, she beamed. "I'm glad you like it. I made brownies for dessert." She pulled out a flat container. "I hope you like chocolate."

The tension in his shoulders released. "Who doesn't like chocolate?" He took a brownie from the container. "This is fantastic. *Danki.*"

"*Gern gschehne.*" She bit into a brownie and then placed it on her plate. "What's your favorite kind of cake?"

He shrugged. "I haven't met a cake I didn't like." He bit into the brownie and closed his eyes, enjoying the warm, sweet flavor as it melted in his mouth.

"I'm serious. What would you choose for your birthday cake?"

Chris's eyes snapped open. "My birthday cake?"

She nodded, and something unreadable flashed in her eyes. Why was she asking about his birthday?

"I don't know. I guess I like chocolate cake the best. What's your favorite birthday cake?"

"When's your birthday?" she asked, ignoring his question.

He set the brownie on his plate and wiped his hands on a napkin. "You didn't answer my question."

"I like chocolate cake too," she said quickly. "So when is your birthday?"

"It's in a few weeks."

"But what date is it?" Her eyes gleamed with excitement, which sent an unexpected warmth surging through him.

"October fourteenth."

"And you'll be twenty-five?"

Chris shook his head. "Twenty-four. And when is your birthday?"

"January twenty-second. I'll be twenty-one," she said simply before breaking a brownie in half. "Rachel wants to have sisters' day tomorrow since we have to start on the dresses right away. Veronica is going to come over to help us sew. I'll have to show you the material Rachel picked for the dresses. It's a *schee* shade of purple. It's sort of a plum color. It looks great with Rachel's dark hair. Purple has always been her favorite color."

Chris finished eating his brownie as Emily shared the details of the wedding plans. He relaxed, enjoying both the sound of her sweet voice and the ease of the conversation.

"Jason, Mike, and John are going to come over for supper tomorrow night," she said. "You'll have to join us."

"Oh no. You don't need to feel obligated to invite me to come over." Chris recalled how awkward it was on Sunday when Emily's family celebrated Rachel's engagement and Veronica's pregnancy. He was out of place, like a voyeur invading their special occasion.

"Why would you think I felt obligated to invite you?" She looked perplexed.

"I'm not family, so I don't want to intrude."

"Aren't we *freinden*?"

"*Ya*, of course we are."

"Then you need to come. It's time you started socializing more. Supper is at five." Emily's lips formed a thin line, indicating the conversation was over and she'd made up her mind. She snapped the top onto the chicken salad container.

Emily began to detail the menu for tomorrow night's meal, but Chris's thoughts spun. He could join her family for supper tomorrow night, but the invitation was still cloaked in doubt. He took in her astute, bright blue eyes and her excitement as she shifted to discussing her plans with her sisters. Chris longed for the closeness Emily cherished with her family. And deep down, he ached to feel that closeness with her.

"WHY DIDN'T YOU COME HOME FOR LUNCH TODAY?" *AENTI* Tillie met Chris at the back door later that evening, after he finished taking care of the animals.

"Emily brought me lunch at the shop." Chris hung his straw hat on the peg on the wall and smiled to himself as he contemplated his afternoon.

After lunch, Emily had gone home to take care of the dishes. She returned later to work on the books, and Chris spent the afternoon learning how to create coin purses. He not only enjoyed having a more challenging leather project but relished working with Emily nearby.

"Emily brought you lunch?" *Aenti* Tillie's eyebrows rose.

"*Ya.*" Chris pushed his hair off his forehead and breathed in the aroma of his aunt's good cooking, making his stomach rumble. The kitchen table was set with a platter of goulash and bowls of carrots, mashed potatoes, and noodles. He stepped into the kitchen, and his stomach gurgled with the promise of food.

The back door clicked shut and *Onkel* Hank came up behind him.

"Oh. I didn't realize you ate with Emily." After a few moments, *Aenti* Tillie's face clouded. "You haven't called your *mamm.*"

Chris's pleasant mood vanished. Several seconds ticked by as *Aenti* Tillie waited for him to respond, her brow creasing as she looked at him. He could feel the weight of *Onkel* Hank's eyes observing him from behind. Had his aunt and uncle planned this? Would they kick Chris out if he didn't say he'd call his mother right away?

"No," Chris finally said. "I haven't."

Onkel Hank moved past him to the sink, where he began washing his hands.

"She left a message on our voice mail today." *Aenti* Tillie rested a hand on the back of one of the kitchen chairs. "So I called her back."

"How is she?" Chris felt the hitch in his voice. Why was he so emotional when it came to his family members? He doubted they were equally emotional about him. Even his mother was probably glad by now that he had eliminated so much of the tension in her home.

"She's doing all right." *Aenti* Tillie frowned. "She misses you. She said she'd love to hear from you."

Chris's stomach cramped. His mind reeled with the memory of the grief in his *mamm's* eyes when she finally stopped begging him to stay. Tears rolled down her cheeks as she said good-bye and told him she loved him. He took a deep breath in an attempt to release his burning grief and guilt, and then he glowered.

"Did she mention if *mei dat* misses me too?" His tone was hard and laced with acrimony.

Aenti Tillie blanched as if the words had hit her in the face, and Chris immediately regretted taking his rancor out on her. She was only a witness to his family's turmoil, and after all, Chris's mother was Hank's sister. He tried to apologize, but she cut him off.

"You need to call her," *Aenti* Tillie said, keeping her tone even despite his disrespect. "She needs to hear from you."

"I know." Chris still couldn't imagine himself using the phone. Stubbornness and pride kept him from walking out to the phone shanty and picking up the receiver.

"Everything smells *appeditlich, mei liewe.*" *Onkel* Hank kissed *Aenti* Tillie on the cheek. "Let's eat." He gave Chris a sympathetic nod as he sat down at the head of the table. "Wash up. You worked hard today in the harness shop and the barn. Let's enjoy this meal together."

"All right." Chris moved to the sink to wash his hands. Shame and anger meshed inside of him as he scrubbed off the dirt and grime. He looked out the window above the sink, and his gaze settled on the Fisher home, where he imagined Emily enjoying supper with her parents and sister. He was certain the Fisher daughters had never been estranged from their parents.

Would time heal his wounds, as the old adage promised? Somehow the chasm in his heart seemed too large and too deep to heal.

CHAPTER 11

"We got a lot done on the dresses today." Rachel stirred a pot of chicken and noodles on the stove late Friday afternoon. "*Danki* for your help."

"You don't need to thank us." Veronica leaned against the counter and wiped her hand across her sweaty brow. Her cheeks were rosy as she blushed.

"Veronica," Rachel said with alarm in her tone. "You don't look well."

"Are you feeling all right?" Emily rushed to her side and touched her hand. "You look like you're burning up."

"I think it's hormones." Veronica fanned herself with her hand. "I'm hot all the time, and I'm so tired." She placed her other hand over her mouth to stifle a yawn, then touched her abdomen, although no changes to her slender frame were yet visible.

"Have a seat." Emily gently tugged Veronica's hand, steering her to the table. "You look like you need to rest."

"*Ya*, you need to rest," Rachel echoed.

Veronica lowered herself into a chair.

"Are you sick?" *Mamm* entered the kitchen from the family room and rushed to Veronica's side. "Do you need to lie down?"

"Don't fret over me. I'm fine." Veronica waved them both away. "I just need to relax and cool off."

Emily poured a glass of water from the pitcher in the refrigerator and set it in front of Veronica. "Take a drink." She smoothed her hands over her apron as she took in her oldest sister's pink cheeks.

"*Danki.*" Veronica sipped the water and then gave Emily a tired smile. "I will be fine, Em. Stop worrying."

"Okay." Emily continued to observe her sister, hoping she'd feel better soon.

"Is your stomach upset? Do you want something to eat?" Rachel started rifling through the cabinets. "I'm sure we have some crackers here somewhere." She found a sleeve of saltines and brought them to Veronica.

"That's a *gut* idea, Rachel." *Mamm* rubbed Veronica's shoulder.

"*Danki.*" Veronica bit into a cracker and then looked up at *Mamm* standing over her. "You stop worrying too, *Mamm.* I'm okay. I promise you."

A faraway look overtook *Mamm's* eyes. "I remember the first trimester with all my *kinner.* It was an exciting but exhausting time. There was so much I wanted to do, but I knew I had to rest. Listen to your body, Veronica. If you're tired, then your body is telling you to slow down."

Veronica took another bite of cracker. "*Ya, Mamm.* I will."

Emily and Rachel exchanged knowing smiles. *Mamm* always gave the best advice.

Emily glanced at the clock above the sink. It was almost a quarter after five. "I think everything is ready for supper. The men will be here anytime, right?"

"*Ya,*" Rachel said, peering out the window above the sink. "Mike and John should be here soon. Mike left work early so he could be here by suppertime." She looked over her shoulder at Veronica. "Jason did too, right?"

"*Ya*," Veronica agreed before taking another cracker.

"Your *dat* should be closing up the shop at five." *Mamm* set a large bowl of salad on the table. "I'm surprised he's not home yet."

Emily brought out bowls for the chicken and noodles. She hoped Chris would join them for supper tonight, but he hadn't agreed to come. She frowned as doubt settled over her.

"Is something wrong, Em?"

Emily glanced over to where Veronica observed her intently. "No, I'm fine."

Veronica raised an eyebrow. "You wear your emotions on your face, so you're not a *gut* liar. You look like you're upset about something."

"No, I—" Emily began.

"Did something happen with Chris?" Rachel asked. "I thought you said he liked the chicken salad and brownies you took him for lunch yesterday. Isn't he coming tonight?"

"You took Chris lunch yesterday?" Veronica asked as a grin formed on her lips. "Was he surprised?"

Emily loved her sisters, but she wasn't in the mood for their endless barrage of questions about Chris.

The sound of horse hooves and buggy wheels moving up the rock driveway drew Rachel's attention to the window.

"Oh! Mike and John are here." Rachel rushed through the mudroom and out the back door.

A few moments later, the door opened then clicked shut again, and *Dat* stepped into the kitchen. "Oh, I smell chicken and noodles." He rubbed his hands together. "My favorite!"

Emily looked at the doorway, expecting Chris to appear in the kitchen behind *Dat*, but he didn't.

"*Dat*, did Chris say he'd be over soon?" Her fingers sought the ribbons on her prayer covering. She held her breath, hoping he would say yes.

"I don't think he mentioned it before he went to work in Hank's barn." *Dat* frowned and rubbed his cheeks as if trying to remember their conversations throughout the day. "No, I don't think he mentioned coming over tonight. Did you invite him?"

Emily's spirit sank as she tried her best not to permit disappointment to invade her face. "Well, I did say something to him." She could feel the weight of Veronica's stare at her back.

Dat gestured to the door. "You should go ask him. I'm certain he'd love to come."

"*Ya.*" Emily forced a smile. "Maybe I will."

"*Gut.*" He started toward the family room.

"How was your day?" *Mamm* said, following him out of the kitchen.

Emily busied herself with bringing food to the table. As she set down a large bowl of green beans, Veronica gently grabbed her arm.

"What's bothering you?" Concern flashed in her blue eyes.

Emily paused, debating what to tell her sister.

"It's Chris, isn't it?"

"*Ya,* it is." Emily frowned. "I don't think Chris is going to come tonight."

Veronica pointed to the chair beside her. "Sit and talk to me."

The sound of another horse and buggy poured in through the window above the sink.

"I think Jason is here," Emily said.

"*Ya,*" Veronica said with an impatient nod. "And that means we don't have much time to talk alone. Tell me what's wrong. Please."

Emily examined a dish on the table to avoid Veronica's eyes. "I invited Chris yesterday when we had lunch together, but he said he didn't want to intrude. Now that I think about it, I don't think he feels comfortable coming over here. I don't understand it." She met Veronica's sympathetic gaze. "I know *Mamm* told you how Chris poured out his heart to me about his *bruder* and his father, but it's like he's afraid to get too close or something."

Veronica's eyes softened and she gave a knowing grin. "You care about him."

Emily's cheeks flushed. "*Ya,* I do. I want to get to know him better, and I want to help him. He's dealing with a lot of guilt after losing his *bruder.*"

Veronica leaned close to Emily. "Well, if you think Chris needs to be here, then you need to find a way to get him to come over."

Just then, John bounded into the kitchen and took in a big breath. "I love chicken and noodles!"

Emily stood as an idea flashed in her mind. "Hi, John. Would you do me a favor?"

CHRIS STEPPED OUT OF THE BATHROOM AND WALKED TOWARD the kitchen, stopping to drop his dirty clothes in the hamper. After getting ahead on his projects in the harness shop this afternoon, he offered to do all Hank's chores in the barn as a way to thank his uncle for allowing him to stay with him. He'd spent nearly two hours mucking out stalls and feeding the animals. After he finished the chores, he was certain he smelled like the barn, so he'd taken a shower and changed into fresh clothes before supper.

In the kitchen the aroma of pot roast wafted over him. *Aenti* Tillie stood at the stove as she stirred gravy in a saucepan.

"That smells *appeditlich*." He pushed his hand through his damp hair. "Would you like me to set the table?"

Aenti Tillie looked at him over her shoulder. "*Ya*, if you want to. I'm running a little behind this afternoon. I was quilting and lost track of time."

Chris fetched three dinner plates from the cabinet and placed them on the table. He took utensils from the drawer and began to arrange them at the place settings. Emily's sweet face came to mind. He'd been consumed with thoughts of her as he worked in the harness shop and on the farm.

Chris had debated joining her and her family for supper tonight. As much as he craved spending time with her, the awkwardness he'd experienced when her sisters announced their engagement and pregnancy news still reminded him he was a stranger. Chris didn't belong with Emily and her family. In fact, he didn't belong anywhere.

"You like pot roast, right?"

At his aunt's question, he looked up from the table to where she was still standing at the stove.

"*Ya. Mei mamm* makes it from time to time."

"I used her recipe. Hank and I enjoyed it when we visited your family in Ohio once, so I asked your *mamm* to write it down for me. I thought you might like to have something that reminded you of home."

His neck tightened as memories hit him in the face. Family dinners. *Mamm* bringing a pot roast to the table. Sitting across from Gabriel at the table. He wondered what *Mamm* was cooking tonight and whether Paul and his family would join his parents for supper just as Emily's sisters and their extended family planned to do.

A knock at the back door startled Chris.

Aenti Tillie raised her eyebrows as she glanced at him over her shoulder. "Would you please get that?"

"*Ya.*" Chris crossed the kitchen and walked through the mudroom. When he reached the screen door, he didn't see anyone standing outside. Chris wrenched the door open and saw John Lantz standing on the porch. "Hi, John."

"Hi, Chris." John grinned up at him, his blue eyes twinkling with excitement as he held a softball in his hand. "Can you come out and play ball with me?"

Chris rubbed his clean-shaven chin, trying hard not to grin. "You want me to come out and play?"

"*Ya.*" John held up the softball. "I brought a ball and bat. We can play softball in Rachel's field."

"Who's at the door?" *Aenti* Tillie appeared at his shoulder. "Oh, hi, John. How are you today?"

"Hi." John waved up to her. "I was wondering if Chris could come out and play with me. I know it's suppertime, but Emily said I should convince Chris to come for supper, and then he can stay and play ball with me for a while."

Chris looked toward the Fisher house and spotted Emily standing on the back porch. She waved at Chris, and everything clicked into place. Emily knew Chris would never refuse John's invitation. She was so determined to convince Chris to join her and her family for supper that she sent John to fetch him. He was amazed Emily would go to so much effort.

"Chris?" John's voice was full of enthusiasm and his eyes pleaded with Chris to say yes. "So can you play after we eat supper?"

Chris turned and met his aunt's gaze. "I know you made the pot roast for me."

"Go. You can have leftovers for lunch tomorrow." *Aenti* Tillie waved him off. "Emily is waiting for you."

His stomach pitched. *Emily is waiting for you.* "*Danki, Aenti* Tillie."

"Great!" John took Chris's hand and tugged him toward the porch steps. "See you later!" he called to Tillie.

Chris permitted John to propel him across the porch and down the steps to the rock path leading to the Fishers' house. John released Chris's hand and took off running. Chris fixed his eyes on Emily standing on the porch, leaning on the railing and watching them.

John rushed up the porch steps. "I got Chris to come to supper," he told Emily. "So that means I can play ball with him after we eat, right?"

"Right." Emily's cheeks looked pinker than usual. Was she blushing?

John rushed into the house, the screen door clicking shut behind him.

"Hi." Emily gave Chris a tentative smile as he climbed the steps.

"Hi," he echoed as he approached her. "That was a dirty trick." She smelled like cinnamon, strawberries, and . . . sunshine?

"I did what I had to do." She lifted her chin, and her eyes twinkled. "It's obvious how fond John is of you. I couldn't get you to agree to come to supper when I asked you yesterday, but I knew you wouldn't want to hurt John's feelings."

"I worry about your feelings too, Em."

She blushed again. "We'd better get inside. *Mei dat* is hungry."

CHAPTER 12

EMILY COULDN'T KEEP HER EYES OFF CHRIS DURING SUPPER. She stole glances at him as he sat across from her. He was so attractive in his blue shirt, which brought out the blue hues of his gorgeous eyes. His light brown hair was damp as if he'd just stepped out of the shower, and he smelled like soap and a musky aftershave that made her think of a fall breeze. She'd wanted to reach up and run her hand over his clean-shaven chin. His earlier comment to her on the porch knocked her off balance for a moment.

I worry about your feelings too, Em.

Did that mean Chris cared about her? But if he truly cared about her, would she have had to send a seven-year-old to convince Chris to come over for supper?

"Isn't that right, Em?" Rachel's question brought Emily back to the present.

Everyone's eyes focused on Emily, and her ears burned. "What's that, Rach?" She turned toward Rachel beside her and hoped her words sounded casual instead of nervous.

"I said you did the bulk of the sewing today," Rachel explained as she buttered a roll. "You're the best seamstress in the family, other than *Mamm*, of course."

"That's not true." In her peripheral vision, Emily could see Chris looking at her intently, and she longed for her galloping pulse to slow to a normal pace. Why did Chris have such a strong effect on her? "*Mamm* taught us all to sew, and she is the best. I just happened to do the most sewing today, but that doesn't make me better than anyone else."

"*Ya*, she's very humble, but she's the best out of all of us," Rachel insisted, turning her attention to Mike. "But we did get a lot done today, thanks to Em."

"That's *gut*," Mike said, swiping a roll from the basket. "You think you'll have everything done in time?"

"Oh, *ya*," Rachel said. "I know we will. Right, Em?"

Emily shrugged. "*Ya*, I think so. I told you I'll do my best to help you finish the dresses in the next couple of weeks."

Mike raised an eyebrow. "Are you sure you're not trying to accomplish too much in a short period of time? It's okay if we wait until December or even January to get married."

"I don't want to wait," Rachel's tone held a hint of a whine.

"She's stubborn," *Mamm* teased.

"Don't I know it," Mike countered with a grin.

"I'm sure everything will come together just fine," Rachel insisted. "Trust me."

"I do trust you." Love gleamed in Mike's eyes as he gazed at his future bride.

Would Emily ever find that kind of love? That familiar pang of jealousy shook her to her core, and she tried to push it away.

Emily glanced at Chris. He was still looking at her, and warmth built in her chest as she gave him a shy smile. He responded with a nod.

"How do you like working in the harness shop?" Jason asked, sitting on the other side of him.

"I like it." Chris spun his fork in the noodles. "Leroy and *mei onkel* have taught me a lot about leatherworking."

"He's a talented student," *Dat* chimed in. "Chris has quickly learned the basics and is now working on more complicated projects. He makes it look easy, but it took me much longer to get to the level of quality work he's already reached."

"No, I'm really not that *gut*." Chris shook his head, and his cheeks turned pink.

Emily fought the grin threatening her lips. He was actually blushing!

"Don't listen to him, Jason," *Dat* continued between bites of chicken. "He's very *gut*."

Chris met Emily's curious gaze and he shrugged. "Your *dat* likes to exaggerate."

Emily turned toward the head of the table where *Dat* sat, shaking his head. "Are you exaggerating, *Dat*?"

"No, I'm not." He lifted a forkful of noodles. "Chris is talented. We're blessed to have him working at our shop."

Chris's face darkened as he stared at *Dat*. He'd told her he didn't know how to handle compliments, but that was in reference to his smile and eyes, and this was about his work. Chris had shared, however, that his older brother was better skilled at horse training than he was, so maybe he'd never received compliments about his work before either.

Sadness settled over Emily as she tried to imagine Chris's painful home life. Why couldn't his father appreciate what a wonderful man Chris was?

After supper the women started cleaning the kitchen and the men went outside.

"Dinner was *appeditlich*," Veronica commented as she finished washing a glass in the sink.

"*Ya*, and your pies were too," Rachel agreed, taking the glass to dry it. "I ate too much. I have to be careful or my dress won't fit."

Emily stopped sweeping the floor and peeked out the window toward the field behind the house. She spotted Chris playing softball with John, Mike, and Jason as *Dat* leaned on the fence nearby and watched. She held on to the broom and beamed as Chris pitched the ball to John and then clapped when John slugged the ball out toward Mike in the makeshift outfield. Chris seemed to fit in so well with her family.

Did that mean he was the man God meant for her? A shiver raced through her as she imagined spending her life with him.

"You should invite him to go to your youth gathering Sunday night."

Emily glanced over her shoulder to where *Mamm* stood by the table holding a stack of dishes and smiling at her.

"I don't think it's a *gut* idea." Emily held the broom tighter. "I think he would've mentioned going to youth group with me if he wanted to go."

"I think Chris would enjoy meeting your *freinden*." *Mamm* placed the dishes on the counter. "He seemed to enjoy talking to Jason and Mike during supper." She crossed the room and stood next to Emily. She peered out the windows that overlooked the back porch and the field. "Chris is having fun out there, isn't he?"

"*Ya*, he is," Emily said as Mike pitched the ball to Chris and Chris hit it out toward the pasture. John cheered and Chris laughed as he jogged toward a fence post that must have served as first base.

"*Mamm* is right," Rachel cut in as she dried another glass. "I imagine Chris would enjoy going to a youth gathering with you. Maybe he could take you in Hank's buggy."

"Oh, *ya.*" Veronica beamed, gazing over her shoulder at Emily. "It would give you and Chris an opportunity to get to know each other better."

"No." Emily plucked at a loose piece of wood on the broom handle. "I don't think so."

A cool evening breeze drifted into the kitchen through the open windows, carrying the aroma of moist earth.

"Why not?" Rachel's brow wrinkled. "I thought you liked him."

"I do like him." Emily continued to pick at the loose wood. "I just don't think I should push him too much. I already forced him to have supper with us. What will it look like if I invite him to youth group too? That might make me look too eager."

"You *forced* him to have supper with us?" Rachel snorted. "He didn't look like he was suffering to me. What do you think, Veronica?"

Veronica shook her head. "He looked as if he wanted to be wherever you were, Em." She returned to her washing.

"I think it would be nice if you invited him." *Mamm* gathered utensils from the table and brought them to the counter. "Maybe it would help him feel more a part of our community."

Emily looked out the window again as Chris gave John a high five.

"What are you afraid of?" Rachel asked.

"I'm not afraid to ask him." Emily pushed the broom around the floor to force herself to stop fixating on Chris. "I just don't want to give him the wrong impression."

"Em." Rachel set her towel down on the counter and padded over to her. "You once told me you didn't date any *buwe* in our youth group because you couldn't connect with them. You said you wanted someone you could talk to."

Emily stopped sweeping and shrugged. "What are you getting at?"

"I've never seen you so interested in a man before you met Chris." Rachel pointed toward the window. "I think you found that connection with him." She dropped her hand and paused. "You know, I just want to encourage you, Em. You were instrumental in helping Veronica and me find our husbands."

"That's not true." Emily fiddled with the loose piece of wood on the broom handle again.

"*Ya*, it is," Veronica chimed in as she began to wash the utensils. "You found Jason at the mud sale and brought him over to my booth so we could talk, and that was the day I finally agreed to date him. Remember?"

"And you invited Mike over for supper the day we met him at the post office. That was the first time his *dat* met our family. Do you remember that too?" Rachel rested her hand on her hip and gave Emily a knowing look. "You're always taking care of the rest of us. It's time you started taking care of yourself."

Emily frowned. It was no use arguing with the three of them.

"All right. I'll invite him."

Rachel grinned and gently squeezed Emily's shoulder. "I know he'll say yes. And maybe then he'll ask you to be his girlfriend."

Emily wasn't convinced. And what would she do if Chris said no?

"GREAT JOB, JOHN!" CHRIS CHEERED AS THE BOY SLUGGED the ball past Mike, who was pitching, and out toward Jason in the makeshift outfield. Chris marveled at how well John hit the ball. He had hit it at least six times, and he'd only missed once or twice.

John took off toward first base, which was actually the fence post next to where Leroy stood clapping, and Jason trotted over to retrieve the ball.

He threw the ball to Chris and then lifted his chin as if to instruct Chris to allow John to make it to first base. Chris nodded and grinned as John stood panting when he got there.

"You made it." Chris tossed the ball up in the air and caught it. "You're better at this game than you let on." He eyed the little boy with feigned suspicion. "Were you setting me up to think you weren't *gut* at this game so you could beat me and then make fun of me?"

John guffawed. "No!"

Chris held up the softball and shook it at John. "I think you were. You like to take advantage of old guys."

"Old guys." Leroy chuckled. "You have no idea what old is."

Mike and Jason joined in the laughter.

"Are you guys ready for a break yet?" Jason clapped Chris on the shoulder. "I want to see if there's any pie left."

"I'm not tired yet," John quipped without missing a beat. "I think Jason is the old guy."

Leroy roared with laughter, and Chris couldn't help but join in with the infectious chuckling.

"Thanks, Johnny," Jason muttered on his way toward the back porch. He looked back at John and winked at him before climbing the back steps.

"Jason is going to wind up fat if he keeps eating Veronica's pies," Leroy commented as he walked toward the house.

"I guess he'll gain weight along with her, huh?" Mike joked.

Leroy laughed again as he started toward the house. "That is very true, Mike."

Chris grinned, enjoying the comfortable teasing and joking. Warmth settled over him as he recalled the conversation at supper. Not only had he enjoyed sitting across from Emily and admiring her during supper, but he'd been part of the family tonight. When Leroy called Chris a blessing, the sentiment nearly shoved him off his chair. He'd never felt so appreciated.

"Can I have a piece of pie?" John asked Mike.

"*Ya*, sure." Mike waved him off. "Just ask Rachel to cut you a piece."

John took Leroy's hand and tugged him toward the porch steps. "Come with me, Leroy."

Chris retrieved the bat from where John had tossed it. He rested it on his left shoulder while tossing the ball up in the air and catching it with his right hand. "Are these yours?" he asked Mike as they walked toward the house.

"Yeah, they are." Mike pointed toward the porch. "You can just leave them here, and I'll pick them up when we leave tonight."

"All right." Chris set the ball and bat on the porch. "John is really *gut* at softball."

"*Ya*, he is." Mike smiled, pride shining brightly in his eyes. "He's been going to a special school since last year, and it's done wonders for his self-esteem. He was struggling with both reading and math, and he also had problems making *freinden*. Now he's doing really well in school, and he's made quite a few *freinden*. The school has been a blessing to us in quite a few ways. That's actually how I met Rachel. She was his teacher."

"Oh. That's great."

Mike hopped up to sit on the porch, his legs dangling over the side. "You're really *gut* with John. Do you have *bruderskinner?*"

"I have two, both girls. They're young. Four and two." He wondered if they would remember him if he ever went back home to Ohio or if they would look at him as if he were a stranger, maybe even cry when he greeted them.

"You definitely have a gift with *kinner.*" Mike leaned back on his hands. "You have siblings, then."

"I have two *bruders.* I mean, one." Chris's fingers took to the monotony of rolling the bat back and forth on the porch. He looked up at Mike observing him with an indecipherable expression. "My younger *bruder* died in an accident in June."

"*Ach*, I'm so sorry." Mike blew out a deep sigh. "*Mei dat* died in May. It's tough losing someone you love." He looked out toward the pasture as he shared that he'd lost his mother when he was ten and then lost his stepmother when she was giving birth to John. "Some days are easier than others, but grief has a way of sneaking up on you. I'll be doing something mundane and remember something *mei dat* said or something *mei mamm* did, and I just feel like laughing or even crying."

He faced Chris and gave him a hesitant smile. "Grief is an unpredictable emotion."

"*Ya*, it is."

Mike's face brightened. "I appreciate how nice you are to John. He really likes you."

"I like him a lot too." Chris absently moved his hand over the smooth bat. "He's a great kid."

"*Danki.*" Mike grinned, reminding Chris of a proud father.

"Are you two coming in for pie?" Rachel stood at the screen door.

"*Ya*, we'll be there in a minute." Mike gazed up at her over his shoulder. "We were just talking."

"Well, if you keep talking, you may not get any pie. I suggest you bring your conversation inside." Rachel gave Mike a coy smirk and then disappeared into the house, the door clicking shut behind her.

Mike rubbed his chin. "Rachel keeps me on my toes. When I first met her, *mei dat's* health was failing, and I was convinced I didn't have room in my life for a *maedel*. Of course, I was wrong. I met her at the perfect time because it was when I needed her the most." He sat forward and wiped his hands across his trousers. "It's funny how God works. As Rachel once told me, we think we know God's plan for us, but we don't know what his plan is until he reveals it to us."

"I suppose that is true." Now Chris held the ball.

Mike gave a sheepish smile. "I'm sure you didn't come here tonight to listen to me preach." He stood up. "Let's go get some pie."

"Sounds *gut*. I've worked up an appetite for more dessert." Chris climbed the porch steps as Mike's words marinated in his mind. What was God's plan for him? Where did he belong?

As he stepped into the kitchen, Chris shoved the haunting thoughts away and relished the sight of Emily cutting a piece of chocolate pie as she smiled at John. He hoped he'd get a chance to talk to her alone later.

EMILY WAVED GOOD-BYE AS THE TWO BUGGIES STARTED down the driveway toward the main road later that evening. The crisp evening breeze sent the skirt of her purple dress fluttering around her legs. She hugged her sweater to her chest as the sunset stained the sky with vivid streaks of orange, pink, and yellow.

"I'm going to finish cleaning up the kitchen," Rachel said after the buggies had disappeared from view. "Do you want to help me, *Mamm?*"

"*Ya*, of course."

"I'll help too." Emily walked with Rachel and *Mamm* toward the house.

"No, you don't have to." Rachel winked.

"Why not?" Emily asked, annoyed. "Why wouldn't I help?"

Rachel looked at the porch and then widened her eyes as she glanced back at Emily.

Emily followed Rachel's gaze toward the porch, and when she spotted Chris sitting on the glider, her stomach fluttered with the wings of a hundred butterflies. Was he waiting for her? Perhaps after their talk the other night, Chris was just as eager for them to have some time alone as Emily was.

She followed her mother and sister up the porch steps and then lingered behind as they headed toward the back door.

"*Gut nacht*, Chris," Rachel said.

"*Gut nacht*," he said, moving his hand down the arm of the glider. "*Danki* for supper, Mattie. It was fantastic."

"*Gern gschehne*. We're so glad you could join us." *Mamm* gave Emily a grin before they both disappeared into the house, shutting the door behind them.

Emily met Chris's gaze, his face partially hidden in the shadow of the porch roof.

"May I join you?" she asked.

He shoved over to the far side of the glider and then patted the seat beside him.

Emily swallowed against her dry mouth and switched on two lanterns as she made her way across the porch. She sat on the seat beside him. When his leg brushed hers, heat crawled up her neck.

"Are you angry about what you called my dirty trick?" she asked, breaking the silence between them.

"No. Of course not." He angled his body toward her and gave her a breathtaking smile. "I had a great time."

"*Gut*." She gave the glider a little push with the toe of her shoe and enjoyed the comforting motion.

Chris rested his elbow on the arm of the glider. "I was hoping to get a moment alone with you to talk."

"Oh? Do you need to discuss something with me?"

His eyes were dark blue in the low light of the lantern. "No, nothing in particular. I just want to steal some of your attention for a little bit."

"Oh." *You always have my attention.* Emily looked down to where their hands were only millimeters apart. She longed to lace her fingers through his, but she didn't want to appear too eager and ruin any possibility of deepening the relationship blossoming between them.

"You looked like you were having fun playing softball earlier," she said.

"*Ya*, I had a lot of fun. John is really *gut* at it, and he's so funny." Emily saw him grin. Was he recalling something amusing John had said? "Mike is a really nice guy. He's easy to talk to."

Emily took in Chris's eyes, yearning to understand him better.

"What are you thinking right now?" he asked.

His question caught her off guard as he looked at her. He was so close that she couldn't help but once again take in his musky male scent, now blended with the aroma of moist earth coming from the pasture. "Why didn't you want to come tonight?" Emily whispered the question as if his response frightened her.

Would Chris say he only liked her as a friend and didn't want to give her the wrong impression? Or worse, would he say he came only because of the chance to spend time with John, as if seeing her didn't matter?

Chris rubbed his chin, and Emily's shoulders tightened with dread.

"I meant it when I told you I was afraid I was intruding. I didn't want to worm my way into your family time."

"Worm your way in?" She clicked her tongue. "I invited you, Chris. I wanted you to come. My family wanted you to be here too. Isn't it obvious that we like you?"

Something cryptic flashed in his eyes. *Please talk to me*, she silently pleaded with him. "How have you been sleeping?"

"All right." He gave a noncommittal shrug, and she was certain he wasn't telling her the whole truth.

"Have you tried warm milk again?" She moved the glider with her toe.

She thought she saw him fighting a grin. Was he going to laugh at her?

"I'll have to give it another try," Chris said.

Emily looked toward the pasture as darkness crept over the green grass, and a comfortable silence fell over them.

"I really like your *dat*," Chris suddenly said. "He's funny and encouraging."

"*Ya*. He is great."

"You're blessed to have him." Sadness flickered in his eyes. Was he comparing Emily's father to his?

"Would you come to my youth group meeting with me Sunday night?" The question escaped her mouth without her permission. She held her breath while he held her gaze for a moment.

"I don't think so," he finally said gently.

"Oh." Emily tried to smile through her disappointment.

"I'm sorry."

"It's fine." She could hear the tremble in her voice. Why did she have to wear her emotions on her sleeve? She turned her attention back to the darkening pasture to avoid his gaze. She couldn't reveal how much his rejection stung.

"Emily." Chris's hand covered her elbow. "Emily, please look at me."

She faced him, and the intensity in his eyes shocked her.

"It's not that I don't want to spend time with you," he said, his tone nearly as gentle as his hand. "I just don't think I'd feel comfortable."

"It's okay." Her voice was soft and reedy. "It's not a big deal."

Chris didn't look convinced as he released her arm. "I should probably go. It's getting late."

"*Ya.*" She pointed toward the lanterns. "Do you need a light to guide you back home?"

Chris looked at her for a moment. "No, *danki.*" He stood and then held out his hand. She took it, and he lifted her to her feet as if she were weightless. He held her hand. "*Danki* again for inviting me. Actually, I should thank you for sending John to get me."

"*Gern gschehne.*" She enjoyed the comforting, soft touch of his skin. "*Gut nacht.*"

Chris gave her hand a tender squeeze before releasing it. "I'll see you soon." He headed down the porch steps and off into the darkness.

Emily stood on the porch and stared off into the dark, watching his silhouette float toward Hank's house. She ached to understand Chris and his confusing behavior. The intense way he looked at her and held her hand served as evidence he liked her, yet he seemed so hesitant at the same time.

Regret settled heavily on Emily's shoulders. Why had she invited him to youth group? She should've listened to her intuition instead of her mother and sisters and let the relationship progress at his pace instead of trying to force him to take it to the next level.

Emily turned off the lanterns and then hugged her sweater to her chest as she walked toward the back door. As she entered the house, Emily hoped she'd be able to solve the puzzle of Christopher Hochstetler.

CHAPTER 13

CHRIS DRAGGED HIS LONG LEGS OVER THE SIDE OF THE bed and took deep, ragged breaths as sweat soaked through his T-shirt and sluiced down his back.

This was the fourth night the nightmare had repeated in Chris's mind as if it were a movie playing over and over again at one of those *Englisher* cinemas. At first it began like most of the other dreams that had plagued him—Chris was in the pasture and heard Gabriel screaming for help. But this dream took a different twist as Chris ran fast enough to reach the back of the pasture before Gabriel was killed. When he arrived, however, Chris's boots were cemented in place, and he was stuck in mud less than ten feet from where Gabriel stood screaming for help.

To Chris's horror, he was forced to watch Mischief repeatedly kick Gabriel in the head, and all Chris could do was scream and cry as his brother died right before his eyes. Tonight he'd woken up sobbing in a cold sweat, just as he had the previous three nights.

Once his breathing slowed to an almost normal pace, Chris looked at the clock. It was only nine-forty-five. He'd barely slept thirty minutes and the nightmare had left him gasping for breath and crashing back to reality.

Chris shoved himself from the bed and pulled on a pair of trousers, socks, and a clean, plain white T-shirt. He quietly headed downstairs, where he drank a glass of water while leaning his back against the counter and reflecting on the day.

Today had been an off Sunday without a church service in his uncle's district, and Chris had turned down the offer of visiting friends along with *Onkel* Hank and *Aenti* Tillie. Instead, he had spent all day alone, perusing leatherworking books in his room and thinking about how much his life had changed during the past few months. Although Chris had chosen to spend the day in solitude, the loneliness had nearly suffocated him. He missed Emily, but he imagined she was having a good time with her friends at the youth gathering.

Chris took a long draw from the glass and then set it on the counter. He could still feel the sting of the painful disappointment in Emily's eyes when he'd turned down her invitation to go to the youth gathering with her. If he missed her so much, why had he turned down her invitation?

Because he didn't feel worthy of her youth group. Emily had such a solid faith, while Chris wasn't certain where he stood in God's eyes.

How could God forgive Chris for letting his brother die?

Chris ran his hand down his sweaty face as the dream filled his mind's eye again. He could still hear Gabriel's bloodcurdling screams and then the gruesome *crack* as the horse's hooves shattered Gabriel's skull. Gabriel went silent forever, leaving Chris to sob as he stood in the merciless mud.

He took another shaky breath and swallowed back a moan. He had to find something to occupy his mind and push away the nightmares. While looking through his uncle's leatherworking books, Chris had researched how to add designs to his projects, and he was itching to get started. Since it was Sunday, he wasn't permitted to go to the harness shop and continue working on his coin purse project. But he could walk the perimeter of the pasture. Surely the cold October night air would help clear his head.

In the mudroom he pushed his feet into his boots, pulled on a jacket, took a lantern from a peg on the wall, and walked out onto the back porch. He breathed fresh air into his lungs and closed his eyes, willing himself to forget the horrible dream that had left him emotionally stumbling.

When he opened his eyes, he turned toward the Fisher home. The house was dark, but a lone lantern glowed on their back porch.

Curiosity shoved Chris off the porch and propelled him down the rock path. He was stunned to see Emily sitting on the glider, pulling a black sweater tighter around her green dress and slight frame. As he drew closer, the soft glow of the lantern sitting on the porch railing made her hair look more golden and her eyes a deeper shade of blue.

"Chris?" Emily's tone was hushed, but her eyes widened. "What are you doing here?"

"I couldn't sleep." He raked his hand through his hair. Why hadn't he combed it? He hoped he didn't look as disheveled as he imagined himself to be. "May I join you?"

"*Ya, ya.*" She patted the glider beside her just as he had Friday night when they sat there together. It seemed as if their conversation then had taken place weeks ago instead of only forty-eight hours earlier.

He climbed onto the porch and sat down onto the seat beside her, placing the lantern on the floor next to the glider.

"Did you go to the youth gathering tonight?" He was acutely aware of the scent of her shampoo. It had to be strawberry, but he couldn't bring himself to ask and risk embarrassing both of them.

"*Ya.*" She sighed as she stared out toward the dark pasture.

"The youth gatherings don't normally end until around ten back in Ohio. Do they end earlier here?"

"They end around ten here too. I came home early." She examined her hands in her lap, and her pretty faced crumpled with a frown.

"Did something happen?"

She lifted one shoulder in an apathetic shrug. In the short period of time he'd known Emily, he had never seen her unenthusiastic about anything. Something had to be wrong.

"Do you want to talk about it?" he asked gently, hoping not to come on too strong.

Emily sniffed and gave another shrug.

Chris held his breath, hoping she wouldn't cry. If she cried, how would he restrain himself from pulling her into his arms and consoling her?

Whoa. Where did that boldness come from?

"I'm a horrible person," Emily whispered, her voice quaking.

"That is impossible," Chris said, a smile teasing his lips. "You're the sweetest person I've ever met."

"I'm serious." Her gaze sharpened as it met his. "I'm terrible, and you shouldn't make fun of me."

The misery on her face pushed away his humor. "I'm sorry. I wasn't making fun of you. I just can't imagine you doing anything terrible. What happened, Em? You know you can talk to me."

"I should have stayed home tonight." She focused her attention on her lap once again. "I spent the entire time thinking about my *schweschdere*, and . . . and . . ." She made a small sound that resembled a hiccup. Or was it a sob?

"Em?" Chris leaned over and touched the tip of his finger to her cheek, finding it wet. "Emily, you're crying." Alarm rushed through him. "Did someone hurt you?"

She wiped the back of her hand across her cheeks before sniffing once again. "No, no one hurt me." Her voice was thick with emotion.

"Please talk to me." Chris rested his hand on her arm. Seeing her cry was nearly his undoing. An overwhelming desire to help her overtook him. "I've poured my heart out to you, so you don't need to feel embarrassed. I'm your *freind*, right?"

A bleak smile played at the corner of her lips, and his shoulders relaxed slightly.

"You're using my words against me." She sniffed again. "Very *schmaert*, Chris. Is that your dirty little trick?"

"No, I'm not trying to play a trick on you. I just want you to tell me what's wrong. It's killing me to see you cry." He angled his body toward her, and the glider shifted under them.

"I don't want you to think I'm a bad person."

"I could never think that about you. What happened tonight?"

"I spent the whole time at the youth gathering thinking about the happiness my *schweschdere* have." Her eyes glistened with fresh tears. "I kept thinking about Veronica and her *boppli* and then Rachel and her wedding. They both have found the loves of their lives, and they are *froh*, really and truly *froh*." Her lower lip trembled. "And I'm *froh* for them, Chris. I really am."

"I know you are."

"I've never told anyone this." She paused and took a deep breath as another tear traced down her pink cheek.

Chris wiped the tear away with the tip of his finger. "Emily, you can tell me anything, and I will listen without judgment."

"Okay." She swallowed and worried her bottom lip. "I'm

jealous of *mei schweschdere*. I'm so jealous I can taste it sometimes, as though I think God has shown them his favor and not me. Maybe it's okay to want what they have, but I know jealousy is a sin. I also know God isn't withholding his blessings just because he hasn't answered the desires of my heart yet."

She shook her head. "God knows what he's doing, and I should only be *froh* for them. After all, Veronica's first fiancé died in a terrible accident at the shed store where he worked. She's so blessed to have Jason. They are perfect for each other, and now they are starting a family."

Emily paused. "Rachel's ex-boyfriend cheated on her with her best friend. She found out when she heard them talking at Veronica's wedding. She was completely crushed, but then she met Mike when she started teaching at John's school. Now they're getting married and starting a life together, which is a blessing too. I don't have the right to be jealous when my *schweschdere* have been through so much. They deserve all the happiness they can find.

"But sometimes . . . sometimes"—she looked down at her lap and took a deep breath—"I get so jealous when I see Mike look at Rachel as if she were the most *schee maedel* in the world. And my body tenses up when I hear Veronica talk about how sweet and thoughtful Jason is."

She jammed her eyes shut for a moment, as if her words were too painful to say aloud. "I've never had a boyfriend and sometimes I wonder if I ever will. I'm not picky, but I want a boyfriend who will listen to me and let me share my feelings. I want someone to cherish me and look at me as if I were the most special *maedel* in the world. I want God to give me what my *schweschdere* have. That's selfish and wrong, isn't it?"

Chris looked at her. Were the boys in her youth group blind?

How could they not appreciate how special Emily was? "Emily, you have—"

"I know what you're thinking." Her voice quavered as she interrupted him. "You think I should be thankful for everything I have. There are so many blessings in my life. I have a *wunderbaar* home with supportive parents. I know I should be patient, waiting for God to answer my prayers for the right man and marriage at the right time. I'm terrible to dwell on what my *schweschdere* have."

She sniffed. "Besides, after Rachel leaves, my parents will need me to do my chores, help out in the harness shop, make quilts, and host dinners more than ever. It would be terrible if I left home now too, right? That's probably what God's thinking."

Emily looked up and her misty blue eyes seemed to beg Chris to tell her she wasn't horrible.

Chris attempted to respond, but shock choked back his words. Emily had no idea how lovely she was—inside and out. Her worst sin was feeling jealous of her sisters? To him, that only proved she truly was angelic, just like that painting he'd seen in that *Englisher* church. If Chris had only met her before Gabriel's accident, he would've made it his business to scoop Emily up and find a way to convince her to marry him and start a family with him. Maybe that's what God would have wanted.

Who was he kidding? He never would have courted Emily last spring. Back then, he would've been too self-centered and immature to realize how special Emily was. It took losing Gabriel to force Chris to realize what was most important in life. Now his life was in shambles.

Emily blinked as more tears flowed down her cheeks. "You do think I'm terrible. I never should have told you anything. I'm going to bed." She stood and started for the door.

"Emily, wait." Chris grabbed her arm and tugged her back toward him.

She stumbled and then righted herself, coming to a stop in front of him with her right leg leaning against his left leg. Her breathing came in shallow puffs, and her eyes were cautious.

"I promised to listen to you without judgment. That means you have to promise not to jump to conclusions before I have a chance to share my feelings. Okay?" Chris held her arm to make sure she wouldn't bolt into the house.

After a beat, she finally nodded. "All right. That's fair."

"*Gut.*" He gave her a hopeful smile. "Would you sit, please?"

Emily slowly sat down beside him, and he released her arm. Her shoulders stiffened as she folded her hands in her lap and sat with her shoulders rigid and her back ramrod straight, looking as if she were ready for a church service to begin instead of talking with a friend.

She angled her body toward him and licked her lips, and his mouth dried. He tried to quickly gather his thoughts before she tried to dart for the house again.

"Emily, you are the sweetest, kindest, most generous, and most amazing *maedel* I have ever met."

Her eyes widened as she gaped at him.

"I could never, ever think you were horrible. You're being too hard on yourself."

"But jealousy is a sin, Chris."

"I realize that, but I also think it's natural to feel this way."

"Were you ever jealous of Paul?" Emily looked at him as if he held the answers to all of her deepest questions.

"*Ya.*" That was an understatement. "I think I've been jealous of Paul's expertise as a horse trainer ever since I realized I was expected to learn the trade just as well. It meant he had *mei dat's* approval, and I wanted that too." He heard the thread of self-deprecation in his words.

"Were you envious when he moved out and got married?"

"*Ya*, I was." Chris rubbed his jawline. "And I was envious of his *wunderbaar* relationship with his *fraa* and also when they had their first child. I know jealousy and envy are sins, but sometimes I don't think we can help ourselves."

Emily's eyes sparkled in the soft light of the lantern, and he hoped she wouldn't cry again. "I'm going to miss Rachel when she moves out. Did you miss Paul when he moved out of your parents' *haus*?"

"*Ya*, I did."

A memory slapped him, knocking him off balance for a moment. He recalled standing with Paul in the hallway outside their bedrooms in their parents' house. Paul was twenty-two, and Chris was nineteen. It was late in the evening the day Paul had married Rosanna.

Paul had a duffel bag slung over his shoulder as he grinned at Chris. "Well, this is it. I'm taking my *fraa* to our new *haus*." He shook Chris's hand. "You know, Chris, we may argue sometimes, but we're still *bruders*. I'll miss you. Take *gut* care of Gabriel."

"Chris?" Emily's sweet voice brought him back to reality. "Are you all right?"

"*Ya*." His voice trembled with the grief of the memory. Did Paul miss Chris? He'd never seemed to blame Chris for Gabriel's death like *Dat* did, but was he disappointed Chris hadn't taken good care of Gabriel?

"I upset you. I'm sorry. I should've kept all this to myself, but tonight it all came bubbling to the surface. I've been holding it in for so long, and I just—"

"It's all right. You've been a shoulder for me to cry on, and now it's my turn."

A genuine smile appeared on her face, and the muscles in her shoulders visibly loosened. His Emily was back. Relief flowed through him.

"You need to stop beating yourself up, okay?" He was careful to keep his words gentle. "You're such a special *maedel*, and the right man is going to find you and cherish you for the rest of his life. It may seem like Veronica and Rachel have everything you want, but when it happens to you, it will be just as special." He paused. Why was his voice shaking so much? "Just be patient."

She nodded slowly, as if digesting his words. "You're right. I need to wait for God's perfect timing. *Danki* for listening to me. Now it's your turn."

"What do you mean?"

"I just poured my heart out to you, so now it's your turn to tell me something you've never told anyone else." She touched his arm. "I'll listen without judgment. But remember, you have to let me share my opinion without drawing your own conclusions before I'm done. All right?"

"No," Chris said quickly. "I never agreed to that." His secrets were much worse than hers.

Emily tipped her head to the side and seemed to stare right through him. *"Was iss letz?"* Her eyes warmed, reminding him of the clear summer sky. "Are you afraid of losing my friendship?"

Chris grasped the back of his neck with his hand, massaging the tight muscles there. How did Emily know him so well after such a short period of time? *"Ya.* Maybe."

"Chris, I've just shared my deepest secrets with you. I promise you nothing you tell me will scare me away."

"Your idea of a terrible secret and my idea of a terrible secret are completely different." Chris shifted on the glider, and it began to swing again.

"I'm listening." She was challenging him.

As he took in her eager eyes, something deep inside of him crumbled, like a brick wall tumbling down. He couldn't disappoint her.

Chris took a deep breath through his nose as he looked out toward the dark pasture. "I haven't told you everything about Gabriel's accident." The memories of that day hit him with full force, and he choked back his words for a moment. "I told you I wasn't with Gabriel when the horse kicked him, and when I found him he was already dead."

"Yes. Go on." Her words were tender but supportive, giving him the strength he needed to continue.

"I told you I was distracted, right?" He kept his eyes trained in the direction of the pasture.

"*Ya*, I remember that."

"I wasn't just distracted." He folded his arms over his chest in an attempt to stop his body from trembling with agony and remorse. "I was trying to flirt with a *maedel*. Salina Chupp stopped by to talk to *mei mamm* about a recipe or something. I don't remember exactly what she needed, but she was standing outside the barn when Gabriel and I were leading Mischief to the pasture. I told Salina *mei mamm* was at the grocery store, and Salina seemed grateful she was gone."

He paused to take a ragged breath. "Deep down I knew Salina had had a crush on me for years. She went out of her way to make it obvious to me by giving me valentines in school and talking to me at youth group gatherings. I never paid much attention to her.

I . . . I've never been good with relationships. But suddenly that day, I was braver than usual, and I decided to, well, respond."

Chris looked down at his lap. "I told Gabriel to lead the horse to the pasture and I would be there in a minute. By the time I got there, Gabriel was . . . he was—" His voice hitched as the grief and regret he'd been trying to keep at bay suddenly overcame him.

Emily shifted in his peripheral vision, and he was certain she was going to dash into the house, leaving him to sob alone on the porch. Instead, she laced her fingers through his and gave his hand a gentle squeeze.

He glanced up in surprise. Her eyes were warm and supportive. Why wasn't she running away from him?

"Go on. Get it all off your chest. I'm not going anywhere." She squeezed his hand again, and the gesture gave him the courage to continue.

Chris kept his eyes locked on hers. "I let my younger *bruder* take a dangerous horse out to the pasture by himself while I talked to a *maedel* I didn't even like. I was attempting to flirt with a *maedel* while my younger *bruder* was dying in the back pasture."

"You didn't know. It wasn't your fault."

"It *was* my fault," Chris insisted, finding fortitude in the caress of her skin against his. "I never should've convinced Gabriel to get the horse. I deliberately disobeyed *mei dat*. I don't know how I could have been so irresponsible."

"But you told me you were only trying to win your father's favor," Emily said. "You said you wanted to show him you could train that horse so he would finally see how *schmaert* you are. You disobeyed him, but you only had the best intentions in mind."

"That doesn't matter in *mei dat's* eyes. One of my first memories is of *mei dat* lecturing Paul and me about how we had to be the model sons. We were supposed to be the example for the community to follow."

"Why?"

"Because he's the bishop."

Emily's eyes widened. "He's the bishop?"

"*Ya*," Chris said, his voice trembling with a combination of embarrassment and fury. "*Mei dat* has a successful business, and he's never struggled financially. His oldest son, Paul, who is his second big success, has followed in his footsteps and made *Dat* proud."

Chris looked down, hoping to escape her intense gaze. "But I've been nothing but a disappointment to him. I never measured up to Paul. I haven't shown interest in horse training, and in *mei dat's* eyes, that's failure. My worst mistake of all was trying to flirt with a *maedel* while my younger *bruder* died just on the other side of a row of thick trees."

More humiliating tears flowed down his hot cheeks. Why did he have to lose it in front of Emily again? She probably considered him the most cowardly man she'd ever met.

"Chris." Her hand gently shook his shoulder, and the scent of strawberries permeated his senses. "Please, Chris, look at me."

He peeked up, and she traced the tip of her finger down his cheek, sending quivers swirling up his back. When she rested a hand on one side of his face, he leaned into her touch. "You're not terrible for flirting with a *maedel*. You need to stop punishing yourself."

"God is punishing me too." He whispered the words.

"What do you mean?" Emily's eyes darkened.

"I don't have insomnia." He closed his eyes and pinched the bridge of his nose. "I've never told anyone this."

"You can trust me."

He opened his eyes to see her leaning in close. She laced her fingers through his again.

"I have nightmares about Gabriel's accident. I wake up sobbing almost every night, and then I can't go back to sleep." He frowned. "That's not exactly true. I probably could go back to sleep if I wanted to, but I don't want to relive the nightmares."

A weight lifted from his shoulders, and he longed to share more. She looked at him intently as if her life depended on his next words.

"The nightmares always end the same way—with Gabriel dead in the pasture and me crying over him. Sometimes they start differently, but I can never save him. For the past four nights, I've had the same dream. In fact, I had it right before I came out here. I was going to go for a walk, but when I saw your lantern on I came over here instead."

"What was your dream?"

He told her, and she blinked, her face full of sympathy.

"*Ach.*" Emily's eyes glimmered with tears. "That's terrible."

"It's my punishment. I deserve it. If Gabriel can't live, then I should live with the daily memory of his death."

"No, no, no," Emily said emphatically. "That's not true. You don't deserve it."

"I do."

"God wouldn't punish you. God forgives and heals. You need to forgive yourself."

"I can't." Chris looked down to avoid her eyes.

"Chris." Emily placed her fingers under his chin and tipped his face up to meet her affectionate eyes. "As a dear friend recently told me, you are too hard on yourself."

A smile overtook Chris's face. "There you go using my words against me."

She gave a little laugh, and her eyes twinkled in the low light. "*Ya*, I am, but I'm telling you the truth." Her fingers slipped from his chin. "God forgave you a long time ago. Now you have to forgive yourself."

Emily made it sound so easy, but he didn't know how to forgive himself. He didn't know where to even begin.

"And you're not a failure. You're a kind and gentle man. We all make mistakes. That's what makes us human. Chris, you hardly mention your *mamm*. Is your relationship with her good?"

"*Ya*."

"Have you called her since you got here?"

"No, I haven't." He waited for her eyes to show signs of disappointment, but they remained supportive. "*Mei mamm* called *Aenti* Tillie, and apparently *Mamm* said she wants to hear from me. I haven't gotten around to it." *Actually, I'm just a coward . . .*

"You'll call her when you're ready. Just don't wait too long to call her. I'm sure she wants to hear your voice and know you're okay."

Chris turned his attention to the sky to avoid her sweet face. He could feel the intensity of her stare as he took in the stars. They were silent for a few moments, the only sound coming from the distant hum of a car engine and a barking dog. He turned back toward her. "*Was iss letz?*"

"Nothing." She blushed. "In this light, your eyes are green again. It must have something to do with the way the lanterns are reflecting the light."

Her smile faded. Something in the air shifted between them, and the atmosphere sparked with electricity.

Chris leaned closer to her and pushed back a wisp of her hair that had escaped her prayer covering. When his fingertips brushed her cheek, a slight gasp escaped her mouth. He leaned closer, and just before his lips brushed hers, the back door creaked open.

"Emily?"

CHAPTER 14

CHRIS SHIFTED BACK, HITTING HIS SPINE AGAINST THE arm of the glider. It rocked roughly, nearly knocking Emily off of it.

What had just happened?

Emily grasped the arm of the glider and shifted away from him, her cheeks flushing bright pink as she turned toward the door.

"Oh, hi, Rachel." Emily lifted her hand in a little wave. "I was just . . . well, I mean . . . we were just talking."

Rachel craned her neck and her eyes focused on Chris. She pulled her robe around her. "Oh, hi, Chris. I didn't realize you were out here visiting. I came down to get a glass of water and I heard voices and saw the lantern. I'm sorry. I didn't mean to interrupt."

"Oh, it's no problem. I was just leaving." Chris stood and looked down at Emily. *"Danki* for talking with me. I hope to see you soon."

"Ya." Emily smoothed her hands down her sweater. "I'll bring you lunch tomorrow."

"Sounds great." He gave her a nervous grin. "I'll see you then." He grabbed the lantern from the floor next to the swing and then looked at Rachel. *"Gut nacht."*

Chris loped down the porch steps and ambled toward *Onkel* Hank's house. His thoughts and emotions spun like a cyclone as his boots moved him down the rock path. He had almost kissed

Emily, and he wasn't sure if he should admonish or thank Rachel for interrupting them. Though he wanted to kiss Emily, he was certain it would have been a mistake.

But it had happened so quickly. One moment he was looking at the stars to pull himself away from her hypnotizing stare. The next moment she complimented the color of his eyes again, and he was drawn in by her loveliness and sweetness. That invisible magnet was wreaking havoc on his self-control.

Emily continued to astonish him with her unfailing empathy and forgiveness. Chris had expected her to reject and reprimand him when he admitted the truth about where he'd been when Gabriel died. Instead, she'd held his hand and consoled him, promising him God had already forgiven him. Emily seemed almost too good to be true. Why hadn't one of the young men in her youth group already snatched her up?

Chris's feelings for her were deepening with every step he took. And why was he torturing himself by imagining what it would be like to have Emily as his girlfriend, or possibly his wife? A shiver danced across the nape of his neck.

As he approached the back porch, he recalled Emily's words about calling his mother. *"Just don't wait too long to call her. I'm sure she wants to hear your voice and know you're okay."*

Chris stopped at the bottom porch step and turned toward the phone shanty. It seemed to silently beckon him to approach.

Stop being a coward, Chris, and call your mother!

He stepped into the shanty and dialed his parents' number. He ground his teeth together when *Dat's* recorded greeting sounded over the phone. Even over the phone, Wilmer Hochstetler's authoritative voice caused Chris to cringe as if he were six years old again.

"You have reached the Hochstetler family farm. For Hochstetlers' Belgian and Dutch Harness Horses, please press one. For the Hochstetler family, please press two. Thank you."

Chris pressed two, and when the beep sounded, he leaned back in the seat and ran his free hand down his face as he gathered his thoughts. *"Mamm,* this is Christopher. *Aenti* Tillie told me you called. I just wanted you to know I'm fine. I'm working in *Onkel* Hank's harness shop, and I really like it." He paused, longing to sound more confident. "So you don't need to worry about me. I hope you're doing well. Give my love to Mamie and Betsy. I'll talk to you soon. Bye."

Chris hung up the phone and then headed toward the porch. He hoped his message would give his mother solace and convince her he was just fine.

"I didn't think Chris was going to go to the youth group meeting with you." Rachel lowered herself down onto the corner of Emily's bed.

"He didn't go with me." Emily couldn't stop grinning. She had floated into the house, and then Rachel trailed her up the stairs so they could talk without risking waking their parents. She dropped down on the bed beside Rachel and flopped back on her pillows.

"I don't understand." Rachel tipped her head, her eyebrows pinched together. "If he didn't go to youth group with you, then how did he wind up on the porch with you tonight?"

"He said he couldn't sleep, so he came outside to go for a walk. When he saw the lantern on our porch, he came over. We sat and talked for the longest time." Emily hugged her arms to her middle. Chris had listened as she shared her deepest secrets, and he'd consoled her when she cried. And then he'd opened himself up completely, allowing Emily to see him at his most vulnerable. It was difficult to believe this was the same man who had been rude to her the first time they met. Their friendship had come such a long way.

"I'm so *froh* for you, Em!" Rachel leaned back against the pillows beside her. "You've finally found a special man you can talk to. It's so *gut* to see you *froh* and falling in love. I'm just so sorry I interrupted you. I didn't mean to barge in."

"Falling in love?" Emily made a face. "No, I don't think it's like that. We're only *freinden*."

Rachel gave a sardonic snort. "Please, Em. I'm not blind. You two were having a pretty intense conversation when I opened the door."

A quiver danced over Emily's skin as she recalled that moment when Chris almost kissed her. She'd never been kissed, and she could only imagine his lips brushing against hers. Kissing before marriage was forbidden, but Emily couldn't stop her longing for his affection. She was thankful Rachel had interrupted them before it went too far.

"It's okay." Rachel placed her hand on Emily's arm. "I know you're confused, but just take your time and get to know Chris. Everything will work out."

Doubt curled low in Emily's belly, and she gnawed her bottom lip.

"*Was iss letz?*" Rachel asked.

"But what if he moves back to Ohio?" Emily's question held a hint of her dismay. "Chris came here because he's been having problems with his *dat*, but what if he works things out and goes home?"

Oh, that sounded terrible!

"I'm not saying I don't want him to work things out with his family. I've encouraged him to call his *mamm* and talk to her. And it would be a blessing if he can work things out with them. At the same time—"

"Calm down." Rachel placed her hand on Emily's shoulder and gave it a gentle squeeze. "I understand what you mean, Em. We all want Chris to work things out with his family, but you'll be heartbroken if he leaves and doesn't come back."

"Exactly." Emily sighed. "I know God has the perfect plan for all of us, so I need to just take it day by day, right?"

"Right."

The grief in his eyes when he talked about his younger brother and the nightmares that plagued him haunted her. She longed to do something special for him to help him see how much she and her family cared about him. An idea struck her and she sat up.

"Chris's birthday is a couple of weeks away. Would you help me plan a surprise party for him?"

"*Ya.* That sounds like fun. What do you have in mind?"

THE FOLLOWING AFTERNOON, THE BELL ABOVE THE HARNESS shop door chimed. Chris stopped working on a coin purse and stepped into the showroom.

"Good afternoon." He greeted an older couple dressed in jeans and matching T-shirts featuring horses and buggies on them. "How may I help you?"

"Hi." The woman grinned, accentuating the wrinkles around her brown eyes. She turned to the man. "I told you it was an authentic Amish store, George. They wouldn't put a tourist trap on the same land as a real farm."

"What can I say, Brenda?" The man shrugged. "You're always right."

Brenda turned back to Chris. "We're looking for souvenirs. What do you have?"

Chris made a sweeping gesture toward the round displays. "We have key chains, doorknob hangers, and pouches. What exactly are you looking for?"

Brenda perused the key chains and then moved to the doorknob hangers and finally the wallets and coin purses.

"Hmm," she finally said, turning toward Chris. "Do you have anything with horses and buggies on it?"

Chris reflexively tapped his trouser pocket where he had concealed the drawing he'd planned to use for the coin purse project that had haunted him since last week. "No, we don't. Is that what you're looking for?"

"Yeah." Brenda picked up a horse key chain, examining it closely. "I guess I'll take a few of these."

"All right." Chris rang up three key chains and put them in a paper bag for her. After she paid him, he handed Brenda the change.

When the customers left, Chris retrieved the drawing and sat at the worktable again. Silence filled the harness shop as Chris examined his sketch. He had been alone in the shop since shortly after lunch when Emily went home to do laundry and Leroy and *Onkel* Hank left to buy supplies.

Chris traced the drawing with the tip of his finger and heaved in a deep breath. Today's customers had confirmed what Chris had been thinking—the harness shop needed to branch out and include some touristy souvenirs if they wanted to expand their business. Chris had read his uncle's leatherworking books on

Sunday, and he'd written down the steps for hand carving a design in leather.

Back in his room last night, Chris had been too hyped up to sleep after his emotional conversation with Emily. He'd found a pencil and notebook and drawn horses and buggies until he figured out the best design for a coin purse.

Now he stared at the drawing as doubt slithered into his thoughts like an unwelcome visitor. He wondered what *Onkel* Hank and Leroy would say if the drawing wasn't good and Chris messed this up. He worried that they would demand he pay for the supplies and then fire him since he was an employee and therefore had no right to design new merchandise without permission.

Will they be disappointed in me, like Dat *is?*

Chris squeezed his eyes shut. He desperately needed to evict his father's words from his mind once and for all. If only he knew how to do it.

He suddenly remembered Emily sitting beside him on the glider last night.

"And you're not a failure. You're a kind and gentle man. We all make mistakes. That's what makes us human."

Chris shoved aside his insecurities and self-doubt and turned his attention to the tracing paper. He could do this. Well, at least, he would give it his best shot.

Chris dampened the leather with a wet sponge and then set the tracing paper on top of it. He began to trace the design.

Once the design was transferred, he traced the design with a swivel knife. He was careful to keep his hand steady, and he did his best not to push too hard. He quickly lost himself in his work, and his shoulders relaxed. He said a silent prayer, telling God about his hopes that both *Onkel* Hank and Leroy would be happy with his work.

He suddenly realized this was the first time since Gabriel's death he had prayed other than at meals. It felt right, and perhaps he had Emily's encouragement—and God's faithfulness—to thank.

"IS ANYONE HOME?" *ONKEL* HANK TEASED, ENTERING THE store later that afternoon.

"*Ya*, I'm still here," Chris said as his uncle crossed to the work area.

"How were things?" *Onkel* Hank hung his hat on the peg at the far end of the work area.

"*Gut*." Chris shrugged. "I had a few customers. I sold some key chains and took an order for a few saddles."

"Great. I told Leroy you could handle the store just fine." *Onkel* Hank's eyes moved to the worktable, and the muscles in Chris's neck tightened as apprehension nipped at him.

"What do you have here?" *Onkel* Hank picked up the coin purse Chris had finished. He ran his fingers over the horse and buggy design, and his eyes widened.

Anxiety and fear writhed in Chris's gut. He prepared himself for the criticisms and reprimand. He imagined himself packing up his clothes and purchasing a bus ticket to Ohio.

"Christopher, did you make this?" *Onkel* Hank turned his gaze on Chris.

Chris nodded, willing himself not to grimace in anticipation.

Onkel Hank dropped onto the stool beside him. "Did you draw the horse and buggy freehand or did you trace it?"

"I, uh, drew it."

"This is fantastic. You're a natural!"

Chris gaped. *I'm a natural?*

The bell over the door chimed as Leroy entered the shop.

"Leroy!" *Onkel* Hank hollered. "Get over here and see what Christopher made."

Leroy sidled up to Hank and they both stared down at the coin purse with their eyes wide.

"Wow!" Leroy looked at Chris. "Did you make this today?"

"*Ya.*" Chris moved his hand over the edge of the worktable as he spoke. "A couple of customers have asked for souvenirs featuring horses and buggies on them, so I thought I could add a design to the coin purse and then maybe try it on a wallet. I was also thinking about designing a key chain."

"How did you learn to do this?" *Onkel* Hank asked. "Tell the truth, now. Did you already know how to do leatherwork, but you didn't want to tell me?"

"No, no." Chris shook his head. "I didn't know anything about leatherwork until I came here, but I found a couple of your leather-working books on the shelf in the *schtupp*, and I looked at them on Sunday." He pointed to the piece of paper. "I copied the instructions and I thought I would give it a try."

Leroy and *Onkel* Hank examined the coin purse again and then exchanged glances. Chris held his breath. Even if they liked what he'd done, he'd still acted without asking if it was okay.

"This is brilliant," *Onkel* Hank said. "Why didn't you ever think of this, Leroy?"

He shrugged. "I thought you were the brains of this operation, but apparently Chris is."

"Do you realize how many of these we're going to sell?" *Onkel*

Hank set the coin purse on the worktable and then squeezed Chris's shoulder. "I'm so glad you came to work for us."

Surprise seized Chris's words, and he stared dumbly at his uncle.

"Are you all right, son?" *Onkel* Hank asked. "You look perplexed."

"I didn't think you'd approve because I didn't ask permission."

Onkel Hank's bushy eyebrows drew together. "Why would I be angry with you for using your creativity to help boost sales?"

Chris gave a half-shrug.

"Christopher, I trust you to help us make decisions that will improve sales." *Onkel* Hank's smile returned. "How many of these can you make before the end of the day?"

Relief eased the tension in Chris's back. "I don't know. Maybe four?"

"Well, we'd better get started," Leroy chimed in. "Why don't you draw another copy of that horse and buggy so Hank and I can help you?"

EMILY'S THOUGHTS LINGERED ON HER CONVERSATION WITH Chris as she hung the laundry on the clothesline. Although she was excited about finishing his quilt and planning his birthday party, she also wanted to do something else nice for him. What could she do to make his week better? What could brighten his day and help him cope with his grief and the issues with his father?

As she pinned a pair of her father's trousers to the line, an idea filtered through her mind. Chris had told her more than once that his father was critical of his work on the horse farm. She could leave him encouraging notes at the shop. Her notes could help

Chris realize he was worthy of praise and capable of being a productive contributor to her father's business.

She smiled as she moved the clothesline and then lifted another pair of trousers from the large basket. She would find her favorite stationery and start writing notes this afternoon. Certainly this would help Chris's self-esteem and show him how much he meant to her.

"ARE YOU GOING TO JOIN US FOR SUPPER?"

Chris jumped with a start when *Aenti* Tillie's voice sounded beside him. He gave her a bashful smile as he looked up. "I'm sorry. I didn't even hear you come in."

"I didn't mean to sneak up on you. You were so engrossed in your project I didn't know if I should say anything or just leave." She lifted one of the completed coin purses from the table and gasped. "Hank is right. The new coin purse design is gorgeous."

"He told you about it?"

"*Ya*, he's been raving ever since he came in for supper." She hopped up on the stool next to him. "How long are you going to work tonight?"

"I just want to finish this one. I promised *Onkel* Hank five, and this is the last one." Chris turned his focus back to his work.

"You do realize you can finish this tomorrow."

"I don't want to let *Onkel* Hank down." He worked in silence for a few moments, but he could feel his aunt observing him. He could almost hear her thoughts. He finally peered up at her brown eyes. "Why don't you just tell me what you're thinking?"

Aenti Tillie gripped the side of the stool with her hands and leaned forward. "Hank told me you were worried he'd be upset with you because you decided to try designing something new without asking him first."

"That's right. This isn't my business, and I didn't pay for the supplies. I didn't want to waste his budget on a dumb idea."

"Why would you think it's a dumb idea?"

Chris set his beveller on the table. "I don't know. I'm new at this business, and I figured my ideas might be things *Onkel* Hank and Leroy tried in the past but failed miserably. I didn't want to upset *Onkel* Hank and then lose my job."

"Did you really think your *onkel* would fire you?"

Chris didn't respond.

"Christopher, there's something I've wanted to ask you for a while."

"All right."

Her eyes were hesitant. "I've gotten the impression that you've fallen out with your *dat*."

Chris swallowed and took in her eyes, unsure of where she was going with this conversation.

"I'm right, aren't I?"

He gave her a slight nod. "*Ya*. That's true."

"I don't know what happened, and you don't have to tell me unless you want to. I just want you to know that Hank and I are *froh* you're here. We couldn't have any *kinner* of our own, so we cherish the time we can spend with you. Don't be afraid to speak your mind or offer your suggestions to Hank. He thinks the world of you."

"*Danki*." Chris's tone was strained with both surprise and appreciation.

She touched his arm. "You should come eat now. It's almost six thirty. You can finish that tomorrow."

"I'm almost done. I won't be much longer."

Aenti Tillie stood. "All right. I'll reheat your food when you come in."

"*Danki*," he said as she walked toward the door. "*Aenti* Tillie?"

"*Ya?*" She spun to face him.

"I left a message for *mei mamm* last night. I let her know I'm okay."

"*Gut.* I'm glad to hear that. She'll be *froh* to hear your voice." She pushed open the door and then looked over her shoulder at him. "Don't work too late."

The door clicked shut behind her, and his aunt's words rolled through his mind as Chris continued working on the coin purse. He was overwhelmed by her compliments about his leatherworking talent, and for the first time he started believing that maybe he wasn't a disappointment after all.

Chris smiled. And maybe, just maybe, leatherworking was his true calling.

CHAPTER 15

Tuesday morning Chris yawned as he entered the harness shop. He nodded a greeting to *Onkel* Hank as he spoke to a customer at the front of the store. Then he continued to the work area, sat on his usual stool, and opened his tool case. A pink envelope with his name written across the front in neat, slanted handwriting sat on top of the tools. He immediately recognized the penmanship from the record books. He opened the envelope and read a note written on matching, light pink paper.

> Chris,
>
> Don't forget you are *schmaert* and talented. You can do any-thing you set your mind to doing. Have a *gut* day. I'll see you soon.
>
> Sincerely,
>
> Em

Chris smiled as he read and reread the note. Then he put the letter back into the envelope, folded it, and slipped it into his pocket. The words echoed through his mind as he spent the morning creating more coin purses with the horse and buggy design. Gratitude filled him as he imagined Emily writing such a thought-ful note. Her friendship was a blessing, and he was thankful he came to Bird-in-Hand.

WEDNESDAY MORNING CHRIS FOUND ANOTHER NOTE SIT-
ting on his stool. He opened the pink envelope and peered down
at Emily's pretty handwriting.

> Chris,
>   You are a gifted leatherworker, and *mei dat* and your *onkel*
> are grateful to have your help at the harness shop. I look for-
> ward to seeing you soon.
>
>   Sincerely,
>   Em

His insides warmed as he read the words again, committing
them to memory.

"What have you got there, son?" Leroy sat down on the stool
beside him.

"Oh, it's just a note." Chris quickly slipped it back into the
envelope and pushed it into his pocket.

"Emily said she had something for you. She asked me to put it
on your stool this morning. She said it was important."

Important. Chris let the word roll around in his mind for a
moment. Yes, Emily was important to him too. "*Danki.*"

"*Gern gschehne.* So can I help you make more coin purses?"

"That would be great." Chris touched his pocket before he
started working.

THE FOLLOWING FRIDAY AFTERNOON CHRIS STEPPED OUT OF
the harness shop and headed for *Onkel* Hank's house. He breathed
in the cool autumn air and smiled. Emily had left him notes for the
past four days. He found them either in the toolbox or on his stool.

Each morning after reading the new note, he tucked it into his pocket and mentally recited it during the day. Her words gave him confidence that he could do a good job for his uncle and Leroy.

This morning's note was just as encouraging as the others.

Chris,

Don't forget I believe in you, and don't forget to believe in yourself. Your leather creations are a blessing to your customers. I'm grateful to be your *freind*.

Sincerely,

Em

Chris touched his pocket where the note was securely stowed. When he went to his bedroom later this evening, he would add it to the pile he kept tucked in the top drawer of his bureau. Some nights when he awakened from a nightmare, he'd retrieve the notes and reread them while imagining Emily's sweet voice reciting them to him. Her sentiment and confidence in him touched him deeply.

He'd spoken to Emily briefly yesterday afternoon when she came to the shop to work on the accounting books, but he didn't have the confidence to mention her thoughtful notes. He'd wanted to thank her, but he wasn't certain how to put his appreciation into words. How could he possibly express how much her encouragement and confidence in him had affected him? He had to thank her the next time he saw her so she'd know how much her notes meant to him.

Chris climbed the porch steps, and as he yanked open the door, he heard Emily in the distance.

"Chris!" Emily rushed down the rock path toward him.

"Hi, Em." He let the door click shut and then met her at the bottom of the steps. "How are you?"

"I'm fine." She rested her hand on the porch railing. "I've been so busy this week I haven't seen you much, and I wanted to join you for lunch today. But I had to help my mother prepare for a dinner tonight. Did you have a *gut* day?"

"I did." Chris touched his pocket where today's note was stashed. Then he took a deep breath. "*Danki* for the notes you've left me."

She smiled. "You like them?"

"I do. I like them a lot." He leaned against the railing. "They mean a lot to me. I've kept every one. *Danki* for thinking of me."

"*Gern gschehne.* I didn't want you to forget you're doing a *gut* job. *Mei dat* thinks a lot of you." She paused. "I think a lot of you too."

His pulse dashed as he looked into her deep blue eyes. "I think a lot of you too, Em."

"Emily!" Mattie appeared on her back porch. "The group is here already." She waved. "Hi, Chris!"

Chris returned the wave before Mattie disappeared into the house. A van steered into the driveway and parked by the Fishers' back porch, and disappointment wafted over Chris. "You have to go."

Emily sighed with a frown. "I was hoping to have more time to talk." Her face brightened. "I can bring you lunch at the harness shop next week. Does that sound *gut*?"

"That sounds perfect." He touched her arm. "I look forward to it."

"Great. I'll make something nice, and we can talk then."

"I can't wait." Chris beamed as Emily hustled back down the rock path. He couldn't wait to have a chance to talk to her again.

EMILY SET THE PICNIC BASKET ON THE WORKTABLE MONDAY afternoon and then perched on the stool next to Chris. "I have some really important questions for you, Chris. I've been thinking if we're going to be good *freinden*, then I need to know more about you."

He arched an eyebrow as a playful smile teased the corners of his lips. "All right, Em. What do you want to know?" He looked charming. She loved when he played along with her silly banter.

"Well, let's see." She pretended to contemplate important questions as she pulled out two roast beef sandwiches, potato chips, and bottles of water. Chris's birthday was Friday and she'd been planning his surprise party for two weeks. She only needed one small piece of information—his favorite kind of ice cream. "I don't know what your favorite color is."

"Blue." His eyes challenged her. "What else?"

"I don't know what your favorite season and month are."

"Autumn and October." He folded his arms over his muscular chest. "Anything else?"

"Hmm. I need to think." She pretended to count down a real list on her fingers. "I don't know much about your food preferences."

"I love anything you bring me for lunch. I'd eat dirt if it meant I could spend time with you."

"Eww." She scrunched her nose in disgust, and he laughed out loud. Oh, how she enjoyed his laugh! "I promise I will never bring you dirt for lunch."

"That's fine, but you look cute when you make that face." His smile was bright, and his eyes were blue-green today.

"What is your favorite meal?"

"Hmm." He tapped his chin. "I'd say chili."

"Chili? Do you like it super spicy or just medium spicy?"

"Medium is fine."

"Uh-huh." She made a mental note. She could bring him chili for lunch on Friday.

"What else do you want to know about me?" he asked, his eyes still challenging her.

For a moment, Emily was lost in those eyes, and lost in thought. She wished she'd had more time to be with Chris this week.

"Em?" Chris looked at her intently.

Heat blazed a trail up her neck to her ears. "*Ya?*"

"Do you want to pray before you ask me more questions?"

"*Ya*, that sounds *gut*." She bowed her head in silent prayer. After the prayer, she handed him a sandwich and then passed the bag of chips.

"I'm on the edge of my stool waiting for your next question," Chris teased, unwrapping his sandwich.

"Okay." She snatched a chip from the bag. "Cake or ice cream?"

"Both."

He was making this easy. "What kind of ice cream?"

"Oh, that's a tough one because I love ice cream in general." He ran his hand down his opposite arm as he peered up at the ceiling. "I would say my favorite ice cream flavor is cookies and cream."

"Do you like chocolate cake with chocolate icing?"

He paused before answering, and she held her breath, hoping he wouldn't figure out the true reason for her questions.

"*Ya*, chocolate cake with chocolate icing." He lifted his sandwich and took a bite.

Emily beamed. She could handle making a chocolate cake with chocolate icing, but now she had to determine what to get him for a gift. She'd ask Tillie for suggestions later today.

"Now I get to ask you the same questions." He sipped from his bottle of water. "This is *appeditlich*, by the way."

"I'm glad you like it." She took a bite of her sandwich.

"All right." He set the bottle down on the table. "Favorite color?"

"Pink," she said easily, grabbing another chip.

"Season and month?"

"Hmm." She silently debated if she enjoyed fall or spring more. "That's a tough one, but I'll go with autumn and October."

"Why did you pick the same season and month I did?"

"I'm sitting here with you and it's currently October." She shrugged. "That makes it my favorite season and month."

He grinned. "*Danki*. So what was next? Ice cream or cake?"

"Strawberry ice cream and—"

"Strawberry?" His handsome face held an ambiguous look. He opened his mouth to say something and then closed it.

"What?"

"Nothing." He shook his head. "Now, what about your favorite cake?"

"Wait a minute." She held up her hand. "What were you going to say?"

A slight blush tinted his cheeks. "You said you like strawberry ice cream."

"*Ya*, I know." Emily searched Chris's eyes. What was he hiding?

"Your hair," he began. "It smells like strawberries. At least, that's what I think it smells like, but I was too embarrassed to ask you if you use strawberry shampoo."

Emily laughed. "You were afraid to ask me about my shampoo?"

He gave a shy shrug.

"You should've asked me, Chris." She playfully smacked his shoulder. "*Ya*, I do use strawberry shampoo. Do you like the scent?"

"Very much." They sat close enough that Chris could inhale the scent of her hair now, and when he did his smile showed that he liked it. Did that mean he was attracted to her? The question sent a shiver of excitement through her.

"So where were we?" He lifted the sandwich again. "That's right. Your favorite meal."

"I suppose it's meat loaf. I love *mei mamm's* recipe."

"All right. What about cake? What's your favorite cake?"

"I would say vanilla cake with vanilla buttercream icing." She bit into her sandwich.

"Yum." He raised his eyebrows, and she giggled.

A comfortable silence fell over them as they continued to eat. What was he thinking? She hoped he didn't suspect she was planning anything for his birthday. Gift ideas rolled through her mind. She considered clothing, such as suspenders, shoes, or a winter coat. She could also get him something for his room—a lantern or a candle. How about something more personal, like a shaving kit?

"I left a voice mail message for *mei mamm*," he suddenly said.

"Really?" Emily was pleased. "When did you call her?"

His smile was bashful. "The night you told me I should. I thought about what you said about how she would want to hear my voice and know I'm okay, and I realized you were right."

"That's fantastic, Chris." Emily wiped her mouth with a paper napkin. "Have you heard back from her?"

Chris nodded. "*Ya*, she left me a message last week, telling me how everyone is doing. She said my *bruderskinner* are outgrowing their clothes and the horse farm has been busy. Everyone is fine."

He sidestepped the subject of his father, but she didn't want to press him. He had made tremendous progress with his family just by calling his mother. "I'm so *froh* to hear that."

His brow creased. "I didn't mention *mei dat* in the message I left for her, but she mentioned he's doing well too."

"Oh." So there it was—the topic was out in the open. Emily couldn't bear the anger in his tone.

"She didn't say he'd asked about me, but I'm sure he hasn't." Chris grabbed a few chips from the bag. "I'm sure he's *froh* I'm gone since what happened to Gabriel was my fault."

"Chris, you have to stop saying that about yourself. It's not true."

He huffed before eating a chip.

"Did you like the note I left for you today?"

Chris met her gaze and his brow relaxed. He wiped his hand on his napkin and lifted the pink envelope from his pocket. "*Ya*, I did. *Danki*."

"*Gern gschehne*." She could feel herself beaming as she retrieved a ziplock plastic bag from the basket. "I made you some *kichlin*. Chocolate chip."

"*Danki*." He took one from the bag.

Emily glanced across the table and spotted a leather wallet with a horse and buggy design carved on the front. She took in a quick breath as she picked it up and ran her fingertip over the horse and buggy. "Did you make this?"

His eyes were guarded, as if he worried she wouldn't approve of his work. "*Ya*. It's my first one."

"This is amazing, Chris." She turned the wallet over in her hand and examined the horse and buggy. The detail was breathtaking. "Did you draw this freehand?"

"*Ya*."

"I had no idea you could draw." She looked up again, and he shrugged. "You have a talent you kept from me."

The tightness returned to his jawline, and a muscle worked there. Clearly he was still not comfortable with compliments about his work. She wondered why the notes she left him hadn't helped to restore his confidence. She needed to find a way to convince him he was worthy of praise for his accomplishments.

"Have you always liked to draw?"

Chris's eyes walled up, resembling two blocks of ice. Gone was the affable, gentle Chris. Instead, he once again resembled the angry, belligerent Chris who had walked into the harness shop for his first day at work and frowned at Emily.

Emily's stomach muscles cramped, and she longed to take the words back. "I'm sorry. I didn't know—"

"It's all right." He turned his attention to the cookie crumbs dotting the paper napkin on the table. He pushed them around with his finger as he spoke. "It was a bone of contention between *mei dat* and me. He once caught me drawing and told me it was sinful. But it was a stress reliever for me. I like to draw mundane things like a tree or a farmhouse with a barn behind it. I wasn't creating a graven image, but he didn't seem to understand. After that, I hid my drawings so he wouldn't find them and criticize me again. He wouldn't want anyone to know one of the bishop's sons had done something prideful."

Emily gaped. She hadn't meant to bring up another painful subject. When would she learn to tread lightly when she spoke to him? "I'm sorry."

The muscles in his jaw relaxed. "Em, my problems with my father are not your fault." He swept the crumbs into his hand and brushed them into the wastebasket beside him.

"*Mei dat* told me you've single-handedly boosted sales. You're doing a great job."

"*Danki*." He picked up two cookies and handed one to her. "I just thought I'd give it a try and see how your *dat* and *mei onkel* liked the wallets. I wonder if they will be as popular as the key chains and coin purses."

"I imagine they will all sell." She bit into her cookie. "You'll probably have to work late some nights to keep up with the demand."

Chris chewed the cookie and swallowed. He paused as if contemplating something, and his eyes warmed. "I've gone two nights without a nightmare."

Emily clapped. "That's *wunderbaar* news!" She squashed the desire to hug him as excitement rushed through her. "Oh, I am *froh* to hear that."

"Thanks." A shy smile overtook his lips again. "I was afraid to tell you because I thought maybe it was a fluke, but I actually slept through the night last night for the first time in months."

Chris shifted closer to her and placed his hand on top of hers, and heat swept through her. "*Danki*."

"Why are you thanking me?"

"You've helped me tremendously just by listening to me and leaving me the encouraging notes." Chris laced his fingers with hers. "I can't thank you enough."

As she stared into his blue-green eyes, she glimpsed her future. She envisioned herself starting a life with him. Warmth flooded every cell in her body. Was Chris the man for whom she'd been waiting? Had God sent Chris here to heal his battered heart and fall in love with her?

A blend of excitement and fear overtook her.

Maybe this was happening too fast. She recalled how Veronica had worried she'd fallen in love with Jason too quickly. But that had turned out all right, hadn't it?

Emily's mind spun with confusion. Maybe she was imagining this sudden and powerful feeling.

The bell chimed above the door. She instinctively pulled her hand away from his, sat up straight on the stool, and smoothed her hands over her gray dress. She hoped her cheeks would cool down.

"Lunchtime passes by too quickly, doesn't it?" Hank's question boomed through the small building.

"*Ya*, it sure does," Chris agreed.

The phone rang, and Hank moved behind the counter to answer it.

"I better get back to work on the dresses for Rachel's wedding." Emily busied herself with cleaning up the remnants of their lunch to avoid passing out from humiliation. Holding Chris's hand got her so worked up.

"*Danki* for lunch." Chris tossed the used napkins into the wastebasket. "It was *appeditlich*."

"*Gern gschehne*." Emily kept her eyes focused on packing up the basket. Once the basket was closed, she stood. As she took a step toward the front of the store, Chris caught her arm, forcing her to peek up at his worried eyes.

"Is everything all right?" he whispered. "Did I say something to offend you?"

"Everything is fine," she insisted, and he released her arm. "I have to get home, but I will see you tomorrow."

Chris tilted his head, suspicion lingering in his eyes. "Are you sure you're okay?"

"I'm fine. I'll let you get back to making those fantastic wallets so you can continue to impress *mei dat*."

His smile removed the worry from his face. "Have a *gut* afternoon."

"You too." Emily hefted the basket onto her hip and gave Hank a little wave as she exited the store. Instead of going straight home, she walked up the rock path to Hank and Tillie's house. And just before she knocked on the back door, she got an idea.

Tillie wrenched open the door. "Emily! It's so *gut* to see you."

"Hi, Tillie. Do you have a minute?"

"*Ya, ya*. Come in."

Emily followed Tillie into the kitchen and set the basket on the table.

"Have a seat," Tillie said. "Would you like something to drink?"

"No, *danki*." Emily sat in a chair. "I want to ask for your help and advice."

"Oh." Tillie's brown eyes twinkled as she sat down across from Emily. "What do you need?"

"As I'm sure you know, Chris's birthday is Friday, and I'm planning a surprise party for him." Emily touched the basket handles. "I was wondering if we could have the party here. I'll bring the cake after supper so he won't suspect anything."

"That's a great idea. Do you need me to make anything to go with the cake? Do you want me to pick up ice cream?"

"That would be great. He told me his favorite is cookies and cream."

Tillie picked up the pencil and notepad on the table and wrote that down. "I'm going shopping Friday afternoon, so I'll get it then."

"*Danki*. Now I need your advice." Emily sighed as her fingers continued to rub the smooth wooden handles. "I've had no idea what to get Chris for his birthday. Do you have any thoughts?"

"Oh. I don't know. I was going to give him some money."

"Well, on the way over here, I got the idea of getting him a set of leatherworking tools. I thought he might want his own tools since he's excelling at the work. Does that sound *gut* to you?"

Tillie looked at Emily for a moment. "You realize the tools are very expensive, right?"

"I was going to ask *mei dat* where the best place is to buy them." When Tillie didn't answer, Emily kept talking. "I can't think of anything else, and I don't want to ask him and give away the surprise. I'm making him a quilt, but I've been so busy with Rachel's wedding preparations that I've only had time to sneak in some work on it before bed every night. I'm going to have to give him the quilt for Christmas."

"You're making a quilt for him?" Tillie's eyes widened.

Emily shrugged. "*Ya*. It's a lap quilt. I'm glad I chose a small size and easy pattern since I don't have much time."

"You really care about Christopher."

"Well, *ya*. We're *gut freinden*." Emily tried to keep her words nonchalant.

Tillie's eyebrows drew together. Was it disapproval or maybe concern? The uncertainty stirred apprehension in Emily's chest.

"I think tools would be a nice gift, but I don't think you can afford a set by yourself," Tillie finally said. "What if Hank and I chip in to help you pay for them?"

"No, *danki*. I'm going to check with *mei dat*." Emily appreciated the offer, but she wanted to give Chris a gift from just her. "Does Chris like a particular snack? I need ideas for what to tell my family to get him if they ask me."

Tillie touched her chin. "I've noticed he likes to get into Hank's roasted peanuts, and I've seen him pick up packs of Skittles at the grocery store. I think he enjoys sweet-and-sour candy."

"Oh, *gut*. That helps me a lot." Emily's mind ticked off a list of things she'd have to accomplish for the party. "Do you think I can bring the cake around six?"

"*Ya*. That's perfect."

"I'm going to invite Veronica and Jason, and I'll tell Rachel to call Mike." Emily rubbed her hands together. "I'm so excited. I think Chris will be surprised."

"I think so too."

"*Danki*," Emily said. "I need to go, but I will see you Friday if not before."

Emily said good-bye to Tillie and then hurried home. Rachel and *Mamm* sat in the sewing room, working on the dresses for the wedding. They both greeted Emily when she entered the room.

"You look excited about something," Rachel observed. "How was your lunch with Chris?"

"It was *gut*." Emily sat down on the chair across from the sewing table. "I talked to Tillie about the surprise party Friday, and she said we can have it at her *haus*. After everyone gets here, we'll go over there and surprise Chris."

"You're going to have a surprise party for Chris?" *Mamm* looked up from the dress she was pinning.

"*Ya*, I thought I told you." Emily went over her plans. "I'm going to ask *Dat* where I can get Chris some tools. He's doing so well with his leatherwork and I imagine he wants his own set. Tillie said they are expensive, but I thought maybe *Dat* would know where I can get a used set."

"That's a *gut* idea." Rachel nodded before returning to pinning the skirt on a dress.

Emily bit her thumbnail as trepidation sent questions whirling through her mind. She wondered if Chris would appreciate getting tools for his birthday or if he would prefer something else. If he didn't like drawing attention to himself, he may not want to have a party at all. On the other hand, his feelings might be hurt if she didn't give him a party.

Then her thoughts turned to Tillie and the expression she'd given Emily. Why did Tillie look anxious when Emily mentioned she and Chris were friends? Emily had known Tillie her whole life, and Tillie had always been supportive of Emily and her sisters. It didn't make sense that Tillie wouldn't want Chris to have a friend here after all he'd endured over the last few months.

"Emily, stop biting your nail. That's a disgusting habit." *Mamm's* comment tugged Emily back to the present.

"Oh." Emily dropped her hand into her lap and stood. "What would you like me to do?" she asked Rachel. "I can take over for *Mamm* if you'd like."

"Sit, Emily," *Mamm* said. "Tell me what's wrong."

She sat back in her chair. "Nothing is wrong. I'm just thinking about the party. I need to make a list of everything I need to do. Chris told me his favorite food is chili, so I'll take that to him for lunch on Friday. Also, he likes chocolate cake. I need to go to the grocery store."

Rachel peered up from her sewing. "Are you sure that's all that's on your mind?"

Emily started to lift her thumb to her mouth again and then folded her arms over her chest to prevent herself from biting her nails. "I've been thinking a lot about Chris and how I feel about him."

Mamm and Rachel simultaneously lifted their eyebrows.

A grin slowly spread across Rachel's face. "Are you in love?"

"I think so," Emily whispered. "I'm not sure, but something happened today at the shop. It was as if I suddenly realized I'm meant to be with Chris. It was overwhelming and confusing."

Rachel squealed as she reached over and squeezed Emily's hand. "That's fantastic!"

Mamm beamed. "Did he tell you he loves you?"

"No." Emily shook her head. "He hasn't said it to me, but he said I've been a tremendous help to him with everything he's gone through with losing his *bruder*."

Mamm's blue eyes were suddenly full of concern. "Just take it slowly with him. Let him tell you how he feels when he's ready and don't rush it."

"I won't." Emily looked at the dresses. She needed to change the subject so she could take her time to sort through all the confusing feelings swirling inside of her. "Now, what can I do to help?"

CHAPTER 16

"Happy birthday!" Emily sang as the bells above the door chimed.

Chris looked up from the cash register and grinned as a customer who was on his way out of the shop held the door open for Emily. "Thanks."

"You're welcome! I hope you're hungry." Emily looked positively radiant as she stood in the doorway holding two cupcakes with chocolate icing in one hand and the picnic basket in her other. A delicious spicy aroma permeated the store. Was that chili? Emily thanked the customer as she stepped into the shop, and Chris couldn't stop smiling at her.

"Aw. Is it your birthday?"

Chris hadn't noticed another customer had come up to the counter until she spoke.

"Yeah, it is." Chris gave the middle-aged woman a diffident smile.

"It looks like your girlfriend is going to make it special for you," she said with a smirk.

"I'll set everything out on the table." Emily's cheeks blushed bright pink as she walked to the back of the harness shop.

My girlfriend? I should be so blessed to call Emily my girlfriend.

Chris told the woman the price before slipping her four wallets and four coin purses into a bag.

The woman paid him and took the bag. "These wallets and coin purses are going to make fantastic gifts for my family back home. I'm so glad I stopped here."

"Thank you," he said. "Have a nice day."

"You too. Happy birthday!" The woman disappeared out the door.

Chris sauntered to the back of the shop where Emily had cleared off one side of the worktable and covered it with a blue tablecloth. She set out two bowls of chili, the two cupcakes, and two bottles of water. The delicious aroma of the chili wafted over him and made his stomach gurgle with delight. "Did you make chili for me?"

"*Ya.*" She gave him a shy smile, and his spirit soared.

"So you played another dirty little trick on me, huh?" he teased.

"What do you mean?" Her brow creased as she glanced over her shoulder at him.

"On Monday you said you wanted to know more about me and you started out by asking me what my favorite color is." He pointed toward the table. "What you really needed to know was what my favorite food is. That was a dirty little trick."

Emily's eyes sparkled with teasing. "I did what I had to do to get the information I needed." She gestured toward the stools. "Are we going to sit and enjoy your birthday lunch?" She hopped up on a stool and patted the one beside her.

"*Ya.*" He sat down beside her and inhaled the delicious smell. "This is too much."

"Don't be *gegisch*. It's your birthday."

"*Danki.*" Chris's body surged with a rush of confusing emotions. He hadn't expected Emily to remember it was his birthday. He was grateful when his aunt and uncle wished him a happy birthday at breakfast this morning, and he hadn't expected anything beyond their kind words. Yet here was sweet Emily sitting beside him with a special lunch made just for him. Her thoughtfulness was overwhelming.

"Shall we pray?"

"*Ya,*" he agreed, and she bowed her head. Chris followed her lead, closing his eyes. He was certain *Mamm* had remembered his birthday, but had *Dat* thought of him today? Did Paul remember the significance of the date?

A pang of longing crashed through Chris. He missed his family.

Emily shifted on the stool, and Chris opened his eyes. He moved a spoon through the bowl of chili as sadness and regret clawed at his shoulders, clenching his muscles.

"I hope you like the chili. I used *mei mammi's* recipe. Veronica has all *mei mammi's* recipe cards, but I copied this one before she moved out. Did I tell you the story about how Veronica found recipe cards in *mei mamm's* hope chest in the attic, and she—" Emily stopped speaking, and he could feel her gaze boring into him. "Are you okay?"

"*Ya.*" He forced a smile before shoveling a heaping spoonful of chili into his mouth. He relished the spiciness on his lips. "It's *appeditlich. Danki.*"

Emily placed her spoon in her bowl. "*Was iss letz,* Chris?" When he didn't respond, she furrowed her brow. "Did you want to spend your birthday alone? Am I intruding?"

"No, no, no." He touched her arm. "That's not it at all."

"So then what is it?"

Chris rested his arms on the table and then shrugged. "I was just thinking about my family."

"You're wondering if they remembered how special today is." She finished his thought for him.

Why was he so transparent? He looked up at her tender eyes. "Exactly."

Emily angled her head to the side. "I'm certain they're thinking of you and missing you today. I'm sorry I'm your only guest for your lunch party." She lifted a cupcake. "Would you rather eat dessert first?" She raised her eyebrows.

Chris couldn't stop a chuckle. "*Danki*, Em. You're exactly what I need today."

Something flashed across her face, and her eyes warmed. His pulse thumped and then raced through his veins at near breakneck speed.

"We can eat our chili first," he finally said. "It's fantastic. Tell me the story about your *mammi's* recipes."

"Oh, okay. So I mentioned to you that Veronica's first fiancé, Seth, died in an accident. A couple of months later, Veronica was cleaning the attic and came across a box of recipes in *mei mamm's* hope chest."

Chris grinned as Emily launched into a story of how her oldest sister found a raspberry pie recipe and then opened a bake stand. He enjoyed the excitement in her eyes and the charming lilt of her voice.

After they finished the chili, Emily sang "Happy Birthday" to him, and then they enjoyed dessert. Chris relished the moist sweetness of the cupcake.

"This was the best party ever," Chris told her. "*Danki*." The word wasn't enough to tell her how much her friendship meant to him. Her kindness had helped relieve some of the sadness that had settled in the pit of his stomach when his thoughts turned to his family.

"*Gern gschehne.*" She began packing up the empty bowls and used utensils. "I have to get home. Rachel wants to start on the table decorations today. I'm hoping I can come see you later."

"It's all right. I know you're busy."

Emily quickly looked away before folding up the tablecloth. Once all of the remnants of lunch were packed, she stood. "I hope you have a *gut* afternoon."

Why was she in such a hurry? *Onkel* Hank and Leroy hadn't returned to the store, and she never left before they returned. "All right."

She gave him a little wave and started for the door.

"Em," he called after her, and she stopped in the doorway, the bell chiming above her. "Is something wrong?"

"Why would you ask that?" Emily pushed the ties to her prayer covering over her shoulders. What was she hiding?

"You seem to be in a rush to get out of here."

"What?" Her eyes shimmered with what seemed like panic for a brief moment. "Oh no. I'm not in a rush. I just promised Rachel I'd help her, and I know she's waiting. You know how she gets. She's the most impatient person I know." She gave a little laugh that seemed forced.

"Oh." He decided to let her off the hook. "Tell her hi for me."

"I will. Bye!" Emily pushed through the door in a hurry. The door clicked closed, and Chris beamed. Emily was only trying to be the best sister she knew how, and she knew just when to come and brighten his day. She knew him so well and yet she hadn't rejected him. She truly was an angel. A blessing.

As he returned to the task of making more wallets, Chris's thoughts turned to making sure her birthday was just as special in January, if he was still living in Bird-in-Hand then. If he was, what would his relationship with Emily be like? Would she want to be more than his friend? His pulse accelerated.

Leroy and *Onkel* Hank joined Chris in the work area.

"Did you have a nice lunch?" Leroy asked.

"*Ya*, it was nice," Chris said.

"Christopher." *Aenti* Tillie's voice sounded from the front of the store. "Have you thought about what you want for supper?"

Chris cringed. He'd completely forgotten Tillie had asked him this morning to choose something special for his birthday supper. When he said it didn't matter, she said she'd give him until lunchtime to decide since she planned to go grocery shopping this afternoon.

"You forgot?" *Aenti* Tillie placed her hand on her hip in mock irritation. "Just because it's your birthday doesn't mean you—"

"It's your birthday?" Leroy asked.

"Yeah," Chris said.

"Happy birthday!" Leroy patted Chris's shoulder. "How old are you now? Forty?" He chuckled, and Chris joined in.

"No, I'm not quite forty." Chris touched the piece of leather he'd been working on. "Only twenty-four."

"You're still a child," Leroy teased. "I hope you have a happy birthday, son."

A strange look passed between Leroy and *Onkel* Hank. What did that mean?

"So what do you want for supper?" *Aenti* Tillie asked again.

"I don't know." Chris shrugged. "Surprise me."

"How about steak?" *Onkel* Hank offered. "You like steak, right?"

"That's so expensive," Chris countered, shaking his head. "I don't expect you to spend that much."

"Don't be *gegisch*," *Aenti* Tillie said. "Steak it is."

A memory suddenly struck Chris. He was nineteen or twenty as he sat in the kitchen enjoying a steak for his father's birthday. Gabriel sat across from him, laughing when Paul shared a story about a confused customer who didn't understand why Amish horses weren't a separate breed. A renewed feeling of melancholy rushed through him.

"Has *mei mamm* called today?"

Aenti Tillie's smile waned slightly. "No, I haven't heard from her, but I'm certain she'll call before the day is over."

"Oh. Did anything come for me in the mail?" He despised the desperate edge to his words.

"No. I'm sorry."

Mamm *didn't even send me a birthday card.* Chris's chest tightened. He'd at least hoped his mother would send him a card to let him know she hadn't forgotten him.

What did you expect? You left your family. That inner voice sliced through his soul with a dose of reality.

"I'm heading to the store. I'll be back soon." *Aenti* Tillie looked at Chris. "We'll have a really nice birthday supper for you."

As *Aenti* Tillie headed out the door, Chris pushed away his disappointment in his family and marveled at the generosity his aunt and uncle had shown him since he'd come to live with them. His parents may have forgotten him, but he was still blessed beyond measure, thanks to his aunt and uncle.

EMILY PUSHED THE ICING AROUND ON THE CAKE LATER THAT afternoon. She glanced up at the clock, and her frown deepened. "I should've started baking earlier. I'm running out of time."

"Everything will be fine," Rachel sang out as she wrapped the set of tools Emily had picked up at a store Tuesday afternoon. "Just calm down."

Emily growled as the icing looked lopsided. She'd wanted this cake to be perfect. She wanted everything to be perfect, but she'd struggled with everything she touched all afternoon. First she ruined a seam in Veronica's dress, and then she lost track of time and put the cake in the oven too late. Now she couldn't get the icing to smooth out over it. She was ready to scream as frustration tightened her stomach.

"Your *schweschder* is right." *Mamm's* hand was gentle on her shoulder. "Everything will be fine. You have fifteen minutes, and that is plenty of time."

Emily gritted her teeth. "This cake looks terrible."

"It looks fantastic, but as usual, you are being too critical of yourself," *Mamm* said. "Why don't you go change your dress while I finish icing it?"

Emily couldn't tear her eyes away from the cake she'd made for Chris. It might be a disappointment, but it was her creation and she should ice it.

"Emily," *Mamm* said slowly. "You need to learn to let go. We don't expect you to do everything for everyone else all the time. Go and get ready, and Rachel and I will finish up here. You have less than fifteen minutes to get ready, and I know you want to fix your hair and change your dress."

Emily sighed. *Mamm* was right. It was time she learned to accept help from someone else. "*Danki.*"

She rushed upstairs and changed into her favorite blue dress. She brushed out her waist-length hair, put it into a bun, and re-pinned her prayer covering. She hurried down the stairs and was grateful to find Veronica, Jason, Mike, and John in the kitchen. Relief flooded her. They were on time!

Everything was going to be okay. She took a deep breath and silently counted to ten in an attempt to calm her anxiety.

"The gifts are wrapped." Rachel held up the wrapped tool kit and John held up two gift bags.

"The cake is ready too." *Mamm* pointed to the cake saver on the counter. "And it's perfect. It isn't lopsided like you thought earlier."

"*Danki.* Are you ready to go?" Emily lifted the cake saver.

"It's going to be fine, Em." Veronica gave Emily's shoulder a squeeze. "You need to relax."

Emily looked up at her eldest sister, taking in her comforting blue eyes. She was grateful her family was concerned about her and knew when to tell her to calm down. She'd be lost without her sisters and mother.

"Let's go." As Emily led her family out the back door and down the porch steps, she hoped Chris would be happy about the party and not irritated that she'd planned it without his knowledge.

CHAPTER 17

"CHRISTOPHER!" *AENTI* TILLIE'S VOICE RANG FROM DOWN-stairs. "Would you please get the door?"

"*Ya*. Just a minute." Chris pulled a fresh, mint-green work shirt over his plain white undershirt. He'd just finished taking a long, hot shower. He was full after the delicious meal of steak and pota-toes, and he longed for a few minutes to sit and relax. His back and neck were sore after working in the harness shop all day and then mucking stalls.

He pushed his hand through his thick, damp hair as he headed down the stairs toward the kitchen. He didn't mind answering the door for his aunt, but it seemed a strange request when he was on the second floor and she was on the first. Besides, who was com-ing to visit after supper?

Chris reached the bottom step, and his aunt and uncle stood in the doorway leading to the family room, smiling at him. Why had his aunt called him downstairs to answer the door when she was standing two rooms away from it?

He eyed them with suspicion. "What's going on?"

"Go answer the door." *Onkel* Hank smirked. "It's for you."

With a mental head shake, Chris crossed the kitchen and walked toward the mudroom. Why was everyone acting so strangely today? Emily had rushed back home after lunch. Leroy seemed a little odd when he acted as if he didn't know it was Chris's birthday, which was improbable since Emily had baked cupcakes in his house. Now his aunt and uncle were grinning at him as he answered the back door. Had they all lost their minds today?

Chris wrenched the door open. Emily stood on the porch, flanked by her family.

"Surprise!" they yelled in unison.

"Happy birthday!" Emily held up a cake saver. "We're here for your party."

"My party?" Chris asked, shocked. "I didn't know I was having a party."

"That's what makes it a *surprise* party." Emily winked at him and then stepped past him, heading into the kitchen.

"Happy birthday." Veronica walked into the house behind Emily.

Jason echoed the wishes as he followed her.

"Happy birthday, Chris." Leroy patted him on the shoulder on his way through the door. "I knew it was your birthday, but I was warned not to give away any of the surprise. I didn't want Emily upset with me."

"Happy birthday." Mattie followed Leroy.

"You look really surprised." Rachel grinned. "Happy birthday."

"It's *gut* to see you." Mike came in behind Rachel. He stayed in the mudroom as Rachel went into the kitchen. "Happy birthday."

"*Danki*," Chris said, finding his voice. He'd never expected this. "I'm a little overwhelmed right now."

"You look it," Mike said. "Emily has been planning this for a couple of weeks."

"She has?" Chris asked with more surprise. "I had no idea."

"Well, that was the idea." Mike chuckled. "She was really

stressed earlier, hoping everything would come together the way she planned."

"Oh." Chris suddenly understood why she was acting unusual earlier. Renewed admiration for Emily flowed through him. She was such an amazing *maedel*.

Why would she go to all this trouble for me?

"Will you play ball with me after we have cake and ice cream?" John asked. "It's been too long since our last game."

"We'll see, buddy," Mike told him. "Let's wait and find out what Emily has planned, okay? We don't want to upset her. She worked hard to coordinate this party."

"All right." John frowned.

"I'm sure we can make some time," Chris promised. "It's my birthday, so I get to pick what I want to do."

"Yes!" John said.

"Chris?" Emily called. "Are you ready for us to sing to you?"

Mike pointed toward the kitchen. "You better go."

"*Ya*, you're right." When he entered the kitchen, the smell of coffee washed over him. The family was gathered around the kitchen table, and a large, beautiful cake with chocolate frosting sat in the middle of the table. He stood in a puddle of mixed emotions as everyone in the room looked at him.

"Are we ready to sing?" Emily asked.

The family began a loud and wonderfully off-key version of "Happy Birthday," and Chris beamed as sentiment churned inside of him. He'd never imagined Emily and her family would throw a surprise party for him. He wasn't a member of their family, but they treated him as if he were. What had he done to deserve their generosity?

As they sang, Chris's eyes locked with Emily's. She was glowing with her bright smile and her blue dress that complemented her gorgeous eyes. He was spellbound with his focus frozen on her.

When the song ended, Emily began cutting the cake. Tillie scooped ice cream and Rachel filled coffee cups.

"So how does it feel to be twenty-four?" *Onkel* Hank sidled up to Chris.

"Well," Chris began with a shrug, "I think it's pretty much the same as twenty-three."

"Wait until you hit fifty," Leroy teased. "You'll feel a difference between forty-nine and fifty."

"*Ya*, that is true," *Onkel* Hank agreed, and the two men laughed.

"Chris, were you really surprised?" Veronica shoved a plate with a large hunk of cake and a scoop of cookies and cream ice cream into his hand. After he took it, she gave him a spoon. He was pleased to see the cake under the frosting was chocolate too.

"*Danki. Ya*, I was completely surprised." He pushed the spoon through the moist cake and took a bite. It was beyond delicious. It was positively delectable!

"I told you he'd be surprised, Em," Veronica said over her shoulder. "You were so worried, and it was perfect."

Chris looked over at Emily. "This cake is amazing, Em. I think it's even better than the cupcakes."

"*Danki.*"

As soon as Chris had taken the last bite of cake and ice cream, John pushed two gift bags toward him. "You need to open your presents."

"Presents?" This was just too much.

Veronica laughed as she handed Hank a piece of cake. "It's your birthday, Chris. How could we not bring you presents?"

"Open them." John held the bags up higher.

"Okay." Chris set his plate on the table and took one of the bags. He pulled out a card signed by Rachel, Mike, and John. Inside he found a variety of sweet-and-sour candies. His favorite. How did they know? Emily must have done research. He looked up at Mike and then Rachel. "This is perfect. *Danki.*"

"Open this one now." John thrust the other gift bag toward Chris.

He opened the card, signed by Veronica and Jason. Inside the bag were two jars of roasted peanuts. "*Danki,*" he told Veronica and Jason. "I love these."

"Here's another one." Mattie handed him a card. "This is from Leroy and me."

"*Danki.*" Chris opened the card and found money. "This is too much."

"No, no. Don't be *gegisch.*" Mattie waved it off. "Enjoy it."

"I've been waiting all day to give you this." *Aenti* Tillie gave him another card. "You probably thought we weren't going to give you anything, but I wanted to wait until the party." She glanced at Emily.

Chris opened the second card, which also contained money. "*Danki.*"

"And now mine." Emily lifted a package wrapped in bright blue paper from the counter and handed it to Chris. He remembered now that Jason had carried it into the house. Emily's smile was tentative, holding a hint of worry. Was she concerned Chris wouldn't like her gift?

Chris removed the blue envelope taped to the front and opened it, revealing a card with a serene scene of a lake with sailboats on the front. He opened the card and under the printed words "Happy Birthday" was a note in neat handwriting.

Dear Chris,

I'm so grateful to have the opportunity to spend your birthday with you. I hope you enjoy the gift and use it in *gut* health. As I've written in the notes earlier, you are very talented, and I'm honored to be your *freind*.

Always & forever,

Em

He ripped open the paper to find a hard plastic case. He unlatched it and flipped it open. Inside was a complete set of leatherworking tools. He gaped. Emily had to have spent close to a hundred dollars—maybe more—on this beautiful set. He ran his fingers over the tools as his mind reeled.

"Emily." His voice trembled with a combination of awe and admiration. "This is too much. I can't accept this."

"It wasn't too much." She stepped closer and her scent— strawberries and chocolate—sent his senses spinning. *"Mei dat* helped me find this set, and they're actually gently used." She shrugged as if it weren't a big deal. "I thought you should have your own tools. Every talented leatherworker needs his own set, right?"

Chris swallowed as he took in her sweet face. If they weren't standing in a room full of people, he would be tempted to pull her to him for a warm hug.

Their gazes locked, and the rest of the room faded away. It was as if they were the only two people there. Time seemed to stand still, and her closeness made it hard to breathe.

"Who else wants cake and ice cream?" Rachel suddenly asked, a little too loudly.

Could Rachel sense his thoughts? Did she know how desperately he wanted to speak to Emily alone?

Conversations buzzed around the room as Rachel and *Aenti* Tillie made sure everyone had cake and ice cream.

Emily broke their trance and looked down at the tool set. "The tools aren't top of the line, but *mei dat* said this is a *gut* starter set. You can buy better tools when you're more experienced."

"Em," he whispered. "They're perfect. I'm really over-whelmed. You shouldn't have spent so much money on me. You didn't need to. And I—"

"Stop," Emily said, a smile tugging at the corners of her mouth. "I wanted to get these for you. You never know how to accept a compliment, and sometimes a compliment comes in the form of a gift. When someone tells you how capable you are, you either shut down or change the subject. Chris, you have absolutely no idea how special you are. I wanted to do something nice for you because you're *mei freind*, and I'm so grateful to have you in my life."

She pointed to the tool set. "Do me a favor. Accept the tools and enjoy them. Keep creating *wunderbaar* items that customers will buy." She bit her lip, and her cheeks reddened. "And maybe think of me every once in a while when you're working. That's all I ask."

"That won't be difficult." Affection flooded through Chris. "*Danki*, Em."

John tugged on his sleeve. "Chris! Can we play ball now?"

"John, that was rude," Mike said, chastising the little boy. "Chris and Emily were talking."

"It's okay," Emily said. "You can go have fun. It's your birthday."

Torn, Chris looked back and forth between John and Emily. He longed to stay with Emily, but he didn't want to disappoint John.

"We can talk later. I promise." Could she read his thoughts?

"It's fine," Chris told Mike before looking down at John. "I'll play, but you have to let me pitch first. Sound *gut*?"

"Oh yeah." John clapped and then looked at Jason. "Are you going to play ball with us?"

Jason turned toward Veronica.

"Go on." She waved toward the door. "Have fun. I'm fine."

Chris looked at Emily. "I'll see you in a little bit."

"I'll be here," she promised.

As Chris followed the others out the door, his spirit soared. He'd never expected a birthday like this, and his heart was overwhelmed.

CHRIS CLIMBED HIS AUNT AND UNCLE'S BACK PORCH STEPS two hours later. The pasture and the harness shop were shrouded in darkness, and a cold breeze caused him to tremble under his coat. The scent of wood-burning fireplaces drifted over him as he beamed. It had been such a wonderful evening that he thought his soul might overflow with happiness.

After spending an hour playing ball with John, Mike, and Jason, he sat on the porch and talked with all the men before having a second piece of cake.

When Jason and Mike announced it was time for them to leave, Chris walked to the Fishers' house with everyone while Emily stayed behind to help his aunt clean up.

As Mike went into the house to pick up some cupcakes Emily wanted them to take home, Veronica waved Chris over to their buggy.

"*Danki* again for the roasted peanuts, Veronica. And the party was fantastic."

"*Gern gschehne.*" Veronica paused before she continued. "I wanted to talk to you for a moment." Her blue eyes were serious. "Emily worked hard to plan that party. I just want you to know she cares deeply for you. She pours herself completely into everything that's most important to her. Please be careful with her heart."

Chris swallowed as the sentiment of her words flowed through him. "I will."

"*Danki,*" Veronica said. "I'm sure we'll see you soon."

After saying good-bye to everyone, he headed back to his uncle's house. Veronica's words rang through him as he went into the kitchen once again. *Aenti* Tillie was washing dishes and Emily was drying them. He smiled, and for the first time since he'd come to Bird-in-Hand a few weeks ago, he completely relaxed. *This is home. It's truly home. Just like my aunt and uncle, I'm a member of Emily's family, and I belong here.*

Contentment stole over him, and he grinned. He owed it all to Emily and her generous spirit. Something unfamiliar took root in his soul. What was that feeling?

Emily spun and gasped, facing him. She clutched a hand to her black apron. "I didn't hear you come in. How long have you been standing there?"

"Only a few minutes." He crossed the kitchen to her.

"I asked Veronica and Mike to take a few of the leftover cupcakes I had at the *haus*. Did they take them?" Emily dried a dish.

"*Ya*, they did." He retrieved a dish towel from the counter. "Do you need help cleaning up?"

"No, no." *Aenti* Tillie waved them off. "You can both go. I can handle this."

Emily gave her a pointed look. "I don't expect you to clean all this up. The party was my idea."

"And I'm *froh* to help." *Aenti* Tillie pointed toward the cake saver. "Do you want to take the rest of the cake home?"

Emily shook her head. "Oh no. That's for Chris."

"*Danki*," he said. "I will enjoy it."

"You can go," *Aenti* Tillie said again. "Hank will be back in a minute, and he can dry for me."

"*Danki*, Tillie." Emily hesitated and peered up at Chris, her eyes expectant.

"May I walk you home?" he asked, and her face relaxed. He'd read her thoughts for once.

"That would be nice." Emily turned toward his aunt. "*Danki* again for everything."

"I enjoyed it. *Gut nacht.*" *Aenti* Tillie waved.

Chris grabbed a lantern from the mudroom and headed out to the porch, propping the door open for Emily.

She shivered as her shoes hit the porch. "The temperature has dropped in the past few hours."

Chris shucked his coat and draped it over her shoulders. "Here."

"No, no," she protested, pushing it off her shoulders. "You need it."

He raised his eyebrows. "You don't ever think of yourself, do you?"

Emily blinked, her face full of surprise.

"Keep it. I don't need it."

"Okay." She pushed her slim arms through the sleeves and hugged the coat to her middle.

Chris grinned, imagining the coat would smell like her when she returned it. He reached over and took her hand in his. To his surprise, she laced her fingers with his and smiled up at him. Her skin was warm and soft, despite the cold evening air.

"The party was *wunderbaar*," he said as they walked side by side toward her house. "I can't thank you enough."

"I'm so glad you enjoyed it. I was worried you'd be upset with me."

"Why would I be upset?"

Emily glanced at the path ahead of them. "I meant what I said earlier about how you have trouble with compliments, and you don't seem comfortable being the center of attention. I was worried you might prefer to spend your birthday alone."

"Who would want to spend their birthday alone?"

She shrugged. "I don't know."

"Well, that's not what I wanted, so *danki* very much."

"*Gern gschehne.*"

"And the gift you gave me. You spent way too much, Em."

"You deserve your own tool set." She squeezed his hand. "You've earned it, Chris."

"*Danki.*"

When they reached her house, Chris set the lantern on the edge of the porch. He looked down at her, and her eyes were warm blue pools in the light of the lantern. He longed for another mile to walk beside her.

"I told you blue was my favorite color, right?"

Her brow creased. "*Ya*, you did."

"Do you know why it's my favorite color?"

She shook her head.

"It's because of your eyes. I could never get tired of looking into your eyes. In fact, I lose myself in them."

An almost inaudible gasp escaped her pink lips as she stared up at him.

Chris didn't want to leave her. He wanted to sit on the porch with her all night long. He missed her when they were apart, and he cherished every moment they were together. He looked forward to hearing her voice and staring into her eyes. He awoke in the morning thinking of her, and she filled his thoughts during the day. She was also his last thought before he fell asleep at night. Since Chris met Emily, his nightmares had become sporadic, and he'd dreamed of her more than once.

Exhilaration roared through him like a summer storm as he stared down at her. The air around them seemed to spark with their attraction.

"Chris?" Her eyes gleamed with tenderness. "Are you okay?"

"*Ya.*" His response was thin and reedy. "I'm better than okay."

Chris placed his hands on her arms and leaned in close. Her body shivered at the contact, and her warm breath danced along his cheek. He closed his eyes, enjoying the feel of it. Dipping his chin, he brushed his lips over her cheek.

"I'll see you tomorrow," he whispered against her ear. "*Danki* for everything, Em." *I love you.*

When he released her, she started to pull off his coat, but he held up his hand to stop her. "Just keep it until tomorrow."

"All right." Emily smiled up at him, her eyes glimmering. "*Gut nacht.* Happy birthday."

"It was the happiest." He said a silent prayer, asking God to help him keep Emily in his life so he could cherish her forever.

CHAPTER 18

EMILY WAVED AT CHRIS BEFORE DISAPPEARING INTO THE house. Chris was walking on clouds as he made his way back to *Onkel* Hank's place. He was approaching the steps when he heard the phone in the shanty ringing. His shoulders clenched with apprehension. Phone calls late at night usually meant bad news. Had something happened to his parents?

He rushed into the shanty and snatched the receiver from the cradle. "Hello?"

"Christopher?" *Mamm's* voice was soft and unsure in his ear.

Fear shot through his body, freezing him in place. "*Mamm*? Is everything all right?"

"*Ya*, I want to wish you a happy birthday. I didn't want to bother you earlier, so I thought I'd give you a call before heading to bed."

"Oh." Chris blew out a sigh of relief as he sat down on the bench inside the shanty. "*Danki*."

"Did you have a nice birthday?" Her words were hesitant.

"*Ya*, I did." Chris leaned his elbows on the small desk where the phone sat. "*Mei freind* planned a surprise party for me, and I wasn't expecting it. I just walked her home."

"Her? What's her name?"

"Emily Fisher. She lives next door."

193

"Oh, that's so nice. I was praying you would find some happiness in Bird-in-Hand."

Chris was almost certain he heard a hitch in her voice. Was *Mamm* crying? "*Mamm?*" He sat up straight as alarm swept through him. "Are you all right?"

"*Ya, ya.*" She sniffed. "I've been so worried about you. It's so *gut* to actually speak to you and have a conversation. Tell me about Emily."

"Ah, well." Heat drenched his cheeks. "She's *schee*, and she's *schmaert*. She makes quilts and cooks, and she also works in the harness shop."

"Are you in love?"

Chris cringed, unsure how to respond to the question.

"I had a feeling God sent you to Bird-in-Hand for a purpose. I suppose it was to fall in love. I'm so *froh* for you."

Chris gnawed his lower lip. Was *Mamm* right? "How is everyone?"

"*Gut, gut.* Paul and Rosanna visited today and brought the *kinner* over. Betsy is trying to talk more, and Mamie wanted to help me cook." *Mamm* chuckled a bit. "They are so sweet. Everyone asked about you, and they told me to tell you happy birthday."

"Even *Dat?*" He immediately regretted the question. Why did he have to ruin this good conversation?

Mamm hedged. "We all miss you. It's not the same without you."

She was avoiding the question, and his temper flared. "Did *Dat* say he misses me, or are you assuming he does?"

Mamm sighed, and he could picture her face in his mind. "Christopher," she began, her words measured, "you are our son, and we both miss you very much."

"If *Dat* misses me, then why hasn't he called me?" He longed to curb his emotions, but his voice shook as he asked the question.

"I could ask you the same question. Why haven't you called your *dat* and tried to talk to him?"

Chris was stumped.

"You both are very stubborn. The only way you can work out your problems is to sit down in a room together and take turns talking. That would mean keeping quiet while your *dat* talked and then he would have to do the same for you. Is there any chance this could happen?"

"I doubt it." Chris shook his head as if she could see the motion through the phone line. "He never listened to me." He was defensive, but it was the truth.

"That's what you both say." She clicked her tongue. "Let's not argue, all right?" She sounded drained, as if the conversation was physically exhausting, and guilt swamped his frustration. "So how is *mei bruder* doing?"

Chris was grateful for the subject change. "He's doing great." His mood brightened. "I really enjoy working in his shop. In fact, I've designed products that are selling well." He launched into telling her about his work and thirty minutes passed quickly.

"I suppose I should let you get to bed," *Mamm* said. "It's getting late."

"*Ya*, I guess so." Disappointment and regret washed over him. He longed to talk to her some more. "*Danki* for calling."

"*Gern gschehne*. It's so *gut* to talk to you."

"You too, *Mamm*. Please give everyone my love."

"I will." She paused, and he could almost feel her contemplating something. "Christopher, would you consider coming home?"

He sucked in a breath.

"I'd love to see you," she added quickly. "We all would like to see you even if you only came for a short visit. You left so quickly, and I feel as if there is so much to be resolved. If you came home to talk to your *dat*, I know you two could work things out."

Chris swallowed and silence stretched between them like a great chasm. He didn't want to hurt his mother's feelings after the pleasant conversation they'd shared, but he also didn't believe a simple discussion in the barn or over coffee would erase the pain his father's accusations had caused.

"I don't know," he said finally. "I'll have to think about it."

"All right. Will you at least promise to call me again soon?"

"Of course I will. Take care, *Mamm*."

"You too, Christopher." *Mamm* sniffed. "*Ich liebe dich*."

Chris's eyes squeezed shut as homesickness wafted over him. "I love you too, *Mamm*." They both said good night and disconnected the call.

He carried the lantern into the house as regret, longing, and homesickness roared through his mind. His attachment to Emily was blossoming, and he didn't know if he should laugh or cry. He was relieved to have spoken to his mother but also frustrated with her request for him to come home and talk to *Dat*. He hung his hat on the peg on the wall in the mudroom and yanked off his boots.

Chris entered the kitchen and was surprised to find *Aenti* Tillie and *Onkel* Hank still up. They were sitting next to each other at the table. "Hi. I thought you had gone to bed."

"We were just talking." *Onkel* Hank pointed to a chair on the other side of the table. "Have a seat, son. Join us."

"Okay." Chris dropped into the chair across from them.

"Did you enjoy your party?" *Onkel* Hank asked.

"*Ya*. It was fantastic. I was really surprised." Chris looked at his aunt. "*Danki* for all you did to help plan it."

"*Gern gschehne*," she said. "All I did was pick up the ice cream and give Emily suggestions for gifts."

Another wave of astonishment rushed through him. Emily had gone to great lengths to plan this party for him. "*Danki*." He paused for a moment. "I just talked to *mei mamm*."

"Really?" *Aenti* Tillie's eyes widened.

"*Ya*." Chris's fingers traced the hem of the blue tablecloth as he spoke. "The phone was ringing when I came back to the *haus*. She said she wanted to wish me a happy birthday. We talked for quite a while. She said everyone is doing well."

"That's great." *Onkel* Hank glanced at *Aenti* Tillie and a silent conversation passed between them. He turned back toward Chris. "There's something we want to discuss with you."

Although his aunt and uncle's faces were pleasant, apprehension stiffened the muscles in Chris's back, causing him to sit up straight. "What's on your mind?"

"Tillie and I have both noticed your friendship with Emily has grown lately." *Onkel* Hank folded his hands on the table.

"It's apparent you care deeply for her," *Aenti* Tillie said. "And I know the feelings are mutual. I could tell when she visited me earlier this week and asked for my help with the party. She was both excited and nervous about planning this party for you. It meant a lot to her."

"I care very deeply for her." A weight lifted from his shoulders when he admitted the truth aloud. His happiness, however, deflated like a balloon when both his aunt and uncle frowned in unison. Something was very wrong.

"While we're *froh* you've become *freinden*, we're also concerned." *Onkel* Hank folded his hands on the table.

"*Was iss letz?*" Chris asked. "Why are you concerned?"

"Christopher," *Aenti* Tillie began, "you're our nephew, and we love you very much, but we've also known Emily all her life. We've watched her and her *schweschdere* grow up, and they are all steadfast in their faith."

Chris swallowed against a swelling lump as dread clamped down on him. Where were they going with this conversation?

"Emily is baptized," *Aenti* Tillie said slowly. "Are you?"

Stunned, Chris stilled, shock stealing his words for a moment. This was not where he'd imagined the conversation would steer. "No."

"I didn't think you were, because your *mamm* mentioned you weren't baptized when I spoke to her a few months ago." Her tone was gentle but firm. "You do realize Emily is forbidden from having a relationship with you since you aren't baptized. In fact, she could get into trouble if anyone finds out you and Emily are seeing each other."

Bile rose in his throat. Of course he was aware it was forbidden for a baptized member to date a nonbaptized member of the church. Emily was probably already baptized since most Amish youth were baptized by the time they turned twenty. Chris had been living in a fantasy world where he believed he could have a relationship with Emily without even considering his status in the church.

He should have known having a relationship with Emily was too good to be true. Why had Chris allowed himself to become so attached to her?

Because she's beautiful and perfect in every way.

"We're not officially seeing each other," Chris said lamely. "I haven't asked her to be my girlfriend."

"Were you planning to ask her?" *Aenti* Tillie's dark eyes challenged him.

"*Ya.*" Chris ran his hand down his face as his body shook. His life was coming apart at the seams.

"I've been concerned all week, but I didn't know how to approach you about this," *Aenti* Tillie continued, seemingly oblivious to his inner turmoil. "I almost said something to Emily on Monday, but I didn't know what to say. I also didn't feel it was my place to tell her you're not baptized."

"Have you told her?" *Onkel* Hank asked.

Chris shook his head. "No, I haven't. It hasn't come up in our conversations."

"You need to tell her," *Onkel* Hank said gently. "And you have to tell her as soon as possible."

Chris frowned. "I know."

"It was apparent tonight that you and Emily have become attached to each other," *Aenti* Tillie continued. "I spoke with Mattie earlier, and she's delighted Emily met you. She told me Emily has always put her sisters' needs before her own and never made an attempt to date. Now that Emily has become your *freind*, she seems much happier than ever before. Mattie is elated to see those changes in Emily." She frowned. "I didn't feel it was my place to tell her you're not a member of the church. It's your business, and you need to be the one to tell Emily. But you need to tell her soon, Christopher. You can't let this friendship go any further. She has to know the truth."

Chris swallowed a groan as he placed both hands at the back of his neck. This was going to hurt Emily deeply. Veronica asked him to be careful with Emily's heart. He squeezed his eyes shut. Veronica would be disappointed with him too. Why had he allowed his friendship with Emily to go this far? Why hadn't he been smart enough to push her away?

Because I fell in love with her.

"Christopher," *Onkel* Hank said. "It's not the end of the world."

Chris opened his eyes to his aunt and uncle looking at him with sympathy.

"You realize you can fix this problem easily, right?" *Onkel* Hank gave him a tentative smile. "You can join the baptism class in the spring in our church district. Join the church and then date Emily. Your *aenti* and I have plenty of land. We can help you build a *haus*, and maybe someday you and Emily can make it your home together."

"No." Chris shook his head. "I'm not ready for that."

"What do you mean?" *Aenti* Tillie tilted her head to the side.

"I'm not ready to join the church," Chris said. "It's not the right time."

"I don't understand." *Aenti* Tillie squinted at him. "Joining the church is a personal and private decision, but I have to ask you why. You live like an Amish man. You haven't gone out into the world to live like an *Englisher*. Why don't you want to join?"

Chris licked his dry lips, considering his answer. Chris's relationship with his father had been precarious for a long time, and since his father was the bishop, he'd never felt comfortable joining the baptism class in their church district.

Then when *Dat* told Chris he was responsible for Gabriel's death, Chris began doubting his relationship with God. And that made Chris wonder, would he have to confess his sins before the church district before the members would allow him to join the church? He couldn't imagine standing in front of the congregation and detailing all the mistakes he'd made that day that led to Gabriel's accident. It would be too painful.

Onkel Hank and *Aenti* Tillie stared at him, their brows wrinkled. Chris didn't know how to explain his complicated feelings to them.

"I'm not sure when I'll be ready or if I will ever be ready to join." Chris spoke softly, then cleared his throat against a dry knot as his trembling fingers pulled at a loose thread at the seam of the tablecloth. "I will tell Emily I'm not baptized, and I'll tell her we have to stop seeing each other."

He looked up to see that *Aenti* Tillie's eyes had misted, and Chris held his breath, hoping she wouldn't cry.

"Christopher, I don't understand why you won't join the church." She twisted a paper napkin as she spoke. "*Onkel* Hank and I are so *froh* you came to live with us. We'd love to see you make a life here. Emily is a *wunderbaar maedel*, and you two would be so *froh* together."

"I know she's *wunderbaar*." *But I'm not good enough for her. Or the church.* He only deserved to be alone.

Aenti Tillie's face darkened. "Does this have something to do with your father?"

Chris felt as though his stomach plummeted. He did not want to discuss this with them.

"It's late. I think we need to get to bed." Chris pushed his chair back and stood. "*Danki* again for everything. I'll see you in the morning." He collected his birthday cards and gifts and exited the kitchen. He heard his aunt and uncle speaking in hushed tones as he climbed the stairs to his bedroom.

Chris changed into shorts and a T-shirt and then dropped onto the bed. In the low light of the lantern, he stared at the birthday card from Emily, running his fingers over her neat handwriting.

Cold knots of despair and shame tightened like a rope around his chest. Since he'd arrived in Bird-in-Hand, Emily had weathered his rudeness and his moods just to be his friend. Emily had broken down all the walls he'd built up around his heart, and she coaxed Chris out from behind them with their meaningful talks and her encouraging notes. She'd shown him love when he didn't deserve it. Now he would repay her kindness with the bitter pill of his honesty, which would shatter her precious heart and her trust.

A dull ache pierced his temples. Why hadn't he even considered the issue of his baptism? The answer was clear—he'd been too blinded by Emily's unwavering friendship and acceptance of him that he never took a step back to consider where their relationship might lead or how the rules of their community affected their future.

And now Chris had to find a way to tell Emily the truth. He couldn't bear to see pain in those beautiful blue eyes when he admitted he wasn't baptized—and wouldn't be anytime soon. She didn't deserve the heartache he was going to cause her.

Chris rested the card on his chest and closed his eyes. He was certain he wouldn't sleep tonight. All his wonderful memories of time with Emily would torture him, as would imagining what life could have been like if they'd married and started a family.

CHAPTER 19

Emily draped Chris's jacket over her arm and hugged it to her chest as she rushed down the rock path leading to the harness shop. Heat thrummed through her veins as she remembered the feel of his tender lips against her cheek last night. She'd fallen asleep replaying their conversation in her mind, and she'd dreamed of Chris walking her around the pasture while holding her hand and talking to her. She awoke this morning imagining their future together. She couldn't wait to see him again.

When she reached the harness shop, Emily yanked the door open and hurried inside. She waved at her father, who was talking to a customer, and then continued to the work area, where Chris and Hank sat side by side.

"*Gude mariye*," Emily sang as she hung the jacket on a peg on the wall beside his hat. "I brought your jacket."

Chris glanced up, and his blue-green eyes were dull with purple circles outlining his bottom lids. He looked almost ill. "Hi, Emily."

"Chris," she gasped. "*Was iss letz?*" The light she'd seen in his eyes last night was gone, and he reminded her of the cold and distant man she'd seen when they first met. Had his nightmares returned? She longed to ask him, but she didn't want to bring up such a private topic in front of his uncle.

Chris turned to Hank. "Would it be all right if Emily and I went for a walk?"

"*Ya, ya.*" Hank nodded. "Take your time, son."

"*Danki.*" Chris stood, put on his coat and hat, and gestured toward the front of the shop. "Let's go for a walk around the pasture."

His eyes remained stoic, and worry rushed through her. Had something bad happened after he'd gone home last night?

Dat drew his eyebrows together as she followed Chris out the door.

"What's going on?" she asked as they walked together toward Hank's pasture.

"We need to talk." His tone was flat, causing her to shiver.

The gray clouds above them mirrored the look that contorted his handsome face, and the air smelled like rain.

"What is it? Did you have a bad nightmare?"

"No. Yes." He shoved his hand through his hair as his mouth formed a thin line.

"Chris, you're not making sense." She stopped and reached for his hands, but he quickly shoved them into the front pockets of his trousers. Was this the same man who threaded his fingers through hers as they'd walked from Hank's house to hers last night? She looked into his tired eyes.

"I didn't sleep at all last night."

"You were so *froh* last night. What happened after I left?"

He gestured toward the pasture. "Let's walk over there."

Emily held her breath as they approached the fence. She couldn't shake the foreboding that had taken hold of her.

Chris leaned forward against the fence, resting his forearms on the top rail and facing the horses frolicking in the field in front of them. His shoulder muscles stiffened as if he carried the weight of the world on them.

"Chris." Her voice trembled. "I can't bear seeing you like this. Please talk to me. What's going on? Have I done something to upset you?"

"You?" His gaze swung to hers. "No, Emily. You could never do anything to hurt me."

"Then what is it?" Her voice rose with frustration. "Why are you so cold and distant after the intimate conversations we've shared? We've become close over the past few weeks, but you're still shutting me out. I deserve your trust." She reached for his face but stopped short, her fingers frozen in midair. "Tell me what's going on. I can't take this silence from you. Why couldn't you sleep?"

He squeezed his eyes shut and then opened them again. "I need to tell you something."

She swallowed, and anxiety simmered inside of her. *This is going to be bad—really, really bad.*

"I should have told you in the beginning." He paused for a beat, keeping his eyes focused on the horses. "I'm not baptized."

"Okay." She held her breath, waiting for him to continue speaking, but he remained silent. "Is that it?" Relief loosened the knot forming in her stomach.

He turned toward her. "You know what that means, right?"

"Of course I do. We can't date until you're baptized. You can join the baptism class in the spring, and after you're baptized in the fall, we can officially be together." Her words were presumptuous, but she was certain he wanted to date her after the way he'd kissed her cheek last night. Still, she hedged. "I mean, only if you want to date me. I didn't mean to sound so arrogant."

When his face became pained, her eyes widened with renewed fear. This was bad, very bad. Her hands trembled with her worry.

"We can't be together at all," he said.

"Why?"

"I'm not going to be baptized. I'm sorry, but I can't be with you."

"I-I don't understand," she stammered. Confusion grabbed her by the shoulders and shook her. Had she misread her friendship with Chris? Had everything they'd shared been a lie? "Do you care about me, Chris?"

"*Ya.*" His voice hitched.

Emily looked into his eyes, searching for any trace of a lie and coming up short. This didn't make any sense at all, and she yearned to comprehend it. Why was he talking in circles?

"Please be honest with me." Her words wobbled with renewed anguish. "I want the truth and only the truth. Tell me how you feel, no matter how much it might hurt me. Do you have any feelings for me at all?"

Chris rubbed his chin and then nodded. "I care deeply for you, Emily."

"If that's true, then why would you choose not to be with me?"

"I can't be baptized." He took a deep breath in through his nose, and his bottom lip trembled. "I'm stuck between two worlds. I don't belong in the *English* community, but I'm not a member of the Amish community."

"You're not making any sense." She furrowed her brow. "You're an Amish man." She pointed toward his clothes. "You live and act like one. You were raised in an Amish household, and your father is a bishop. You live in the Amish community and work in an Amish shop. If you care about me, why don't you want to join the church so we can start a life together?"

"It's not that simple. The faith doesn't come as easily to me as it does to you. I don't belong to this community, and I don't belong to the one back home."

Exasperation shoved away her emotional pain and then surged through her entire body. "That's not true," she said, her voice rising to a shout. "Your *mamm* reached out to you. Your family loves you, but you're too stubborn to see it."

Chris heaved a deep sigh. "You're not listening to me."

"*Ya*, I am listening to you, but I don't like what I'm hearing. You're so blind you don't see what's right in front of your eyes."

He shook his head. "No, it's more than that. Your parents are loving and supportive, and all *mei dat* has done is tear me down since Gabriel died. The truth is I think he's always thought of me as a failure, and I only made it worse. You know who you are and what you want. You probably knew from the time you were a little girl that you wanted to be a member of the church. I have no idea who I am or where I belong."

"How can you say that?" She nearly spat the words at him as vehemence jolted her body. "Doesn't our friendship mean anything to you?"

"Of course it does." He wore a wounded expression. "It means everything to me, Emily."

"Then why don't you want to join the church? Are you going to let your *dat's* cruel words restrain you from living a *froh* life?"

Chris sucked in a breath as tears flooded his eyes and then spilled down his cheeks. She repressed her urge to wipe away his tears and comfort him. For a moment she couldn't speak. She felt as though a hole had been punched through her rib cage.

"I don't understand." Suddenly her tears fell like rain, soaking her black sweater. "You're standing here crying with me. If it hurts so much to push me away, then why aren't you holding me close instead? Why are you punishing yourself and me?"

"I'm not punishing you." His face was a mask of suffering and pain. "I'm saving you from the misery of being stuck with me for the rest of your life."

"The misery of being stuck with you?" Emily gave a sardonic laugh. "The misery I feel now is from not being able to be with you, Chris." Despair squeezed her lungs, making it hard to breathe. "Don't you understand how I feel about you? Aren't my emotions written on my face when I look at you?"

His eyes darkened. "I'm not worth your time."

"Is that what your *dat* told you? That you're not worth anyone's time?" She paused, but when he hesitated, she continued. "If he did, then your *dat* is wrong, and you're wrong too."

Chris wiped his hands down his cheeks. "You have no idea what you're talking about, Emily."

"Yes, I do." Fury pushed away her grief. "The moment I saw you, I knew you needed a *freind*, and I've tried my best to help you. I see now that I've done all I can do for you. Now you need to reach out to God."

"Emily, I don't think—"

She held up her hand to silence him. "If you come to God broken, he will heal you and make you whole again." A renewed confidence gripped her as she continued. "You need to stop feeling sorry for yourself and open your eyes, Christopher. There is a whole community out here who loves you, but you won't give us a chance. You choose to separate yourself from God and from the rest of your community. You have to stop pushing away all the people who care about you."

When his eyes showed he remained unconvinced, she pointed toward her parents' house. "Don't you remember how John immediately took a liking to you? And I've seen you talk to *mei dat*, Jason, Mike, and your *onkel*. We've all accepted you into our community. It's become your community. Why can't you see that?"

Chris gaped at her but remained silent, and his silence sliced at her soul. After their romantic talk last night, Emily imagined he'd ask her to be his girlfriend today. She never imagined he'd tell her they couldn't be together.

"If you've changed how you feel about me, then just tell me," she said, her tone tight with betrayal as her hands shook. "Please don't blame it on my community."

Chris closed his eyes and shook his head. "Emily, I'm trying to tell you that you are not the problem." He tapped his chest over his heart. "I'm the problem. I don't belong here, and I don't belong with someone as special as you."

"But I'm telling you I want to be with you, Chris." Her words radiated with her desperation. "I think God sent you here for a reason, and maybe that reason was for us to find each other."

Something enigmatic flickered across Chris's face, but then his somber look prevailed. "I'm sorry. I can't be with you."

Emily swallowed a sob. "So that's it? It's over?"

Chris gave her a curt nod. "*Ya.* I'm sorry for hurting you."

"I'm sorry too," she managed to say before turning to run home.

HOT TEARS FLOWED DOWN EMILY'S CHEEKS AS SHE THREW herself up the stairs and into the sewing room. *Mamm* and her sisters looked up from their sewing projects as Emily dropped onto a chair by the door.

"Emily!" *Mamm* gasped, leaning over to her. "What happened?"

"What's wrong?" Veronica demanded.

"Are you okay?" Rachel chimed in.

Emily opened her mouth to speak, but a sob stole her words. She covered her face with her hands as her body shook under the weight of her despair. A chair scraped the floor and then tender, protective arms encircled Emily and pulled her close.

"*Ach, mei liewe,*" Mamm whispered against her ear. "Calm down and tell us what happened."

"We're here for you, Em," Rachel whispered, her voice thick.

"Please tell us what happened, sweet Emily," Veronica said.

Emily took deep, quivering breaths as she tried to calm her body. She opened her eyes and Rachel handed her a box of tissues. Emily wiped a tissue across her cheeks and then blew her nose.

"I just went to see Chris." Her body shook with her frustration and grief. "He looked as if he hadn't slept last night, and he told me he hadn't. He said he wanted to go for a walk to talk in private." She told them what Chris said, and her mother's and sisters' faces darkened as she spoke. "I tried to convince him to join the church, but he said he can't. And he said we can't be together."

A sob broke free from deep inside of her, and tears began anew. Her heart shattered as she recalled the pain in his eyes.

"I don't understand," Rachel said. "It was so obvious how *froh* he was last night."

Veronica reached over and squeezed Emily's hand. "I'm so sorry, Em. I thought you and Chris would be the next ones to get married."

"I did too," Emily said softly, her voice shaking through her tears. "I thought he was the one. We seemed to relate so well. He was my best *freind*. But now all my dreams are dashed. I don't understand. I thought he loved me too."

Mamm's eyes glimmered with tears. "I can't stand to see you in so much pain, Emily. I'm so sorry, and I know how you feel. I promise you things will get better. You feel as if your world is falling apart right now, but God has the perfect plan for you. It may not make sense in the moment, but everything will fall into place."

"Maybe you need to just give him time," Veronica said. "He's been through a lot with losing his *bruder*. You also mentioned he has problems with his *dat*. Maybe he needs to work through all those issues before he can completely focus on his place in the church and his relationship with you."

Emily sighed. "I don't think so. He was adamant. I think I've lost him." Her focus moved to the dresses on the sewing table. She needed a distraction. "How can I help with the dresses?"

"No, Em." Rachel's eyes were fierce. "You are not going to take the focus off of yourself. We are here to support you, right?" She looked from *Mamm* to Veronica, and they both nodded in agreement. "If you want to talk about Chris, then we will listen. We're completely devoted to you."

Emily appreciated her sister's support, but she didn't want to discuss her crushed dreams. "It's okay, Rach. There's nothing else to say. Chris has made his decision, so I'd rather talk about your wedding and work on the dresses."

Rachel arched a dark eyebrow.

"I don't want to talk about it anymore. Really." Emily pointed toward the sewing table. "Tell me how I can help you."

Rachel paused, and then her shoulders relaxed. "All right. I could actually use your help with this one seam. It's not lining up the way I want it to."

Emily moved over to the sewing table. As she worked, Chris's face filled her mind.

Would the ache in her chest ever go away?

CHAPTER 20

DESPONDENCY BOGGED CHRIS'S STEPS AS HE REENTERED the harness shop and slowly walked toward the work area. He was grateful the only other person there was *Onkel* Hank, and both the customer and Leroy were gone. He sat on his stool and stared down at the wallet he'd been creating before Emily arrived.

Although his eyes were focused on the wallet, his mind was stuck on the torment and betrayal he'd witnessed in Emily's eyes before she took off running toward her house. He shuddered. How could he hurt her that way? She didn't deserve it. It would've been better if he'd never met her at all. He'd broken her heart. He'd been nothing but a detriment to her and her family.

I'm nothing but a failure.

Chris closed his eyes and sucked in a shuddering breath as agony dug into his shoulders and clamped down on his chest.

"Leroy went to get supplies." *Onkel* Hank broke through Chris's mental tirade. "He won't be back for a while."

Chris cleared his throat and took a tremulous breath.

"We sold the last of your wallets and coin purses earlier. That means we have to get busy making more."

"Oh." Chris's voice was shaky.

"Christopher."

He turned toward his uncle, who was looking at him, sympathy in his brown eyes.

"Talk to me, son." *Onkel* Hank placed his tools on the table.

"Emily didn't take it well."

Onkel Hank gave him a bleak smile. "I didn't expect her to take it well. It's obvious she cares about you. I would even go so far as to say she loves you."

"I never meant to hurt her." Guilt soured in Chris's stomach like curdled milk. "I was just honest with her and explained I can't be with her. I'm not worthy of her." He stared at his hands. "I didn't tell you and *Aenti* Tillie this last night, but I don't think I'm worthy of the church either, and that's why I can't be baptized. I don't know where I belong." He hated the desperation resonating through his distraught tone. He stared down at the unfinished wallet, hoping he could keep his threatening tears at bay.

"I understand how you feel."

Chris's gaze flicked up to meet his uncle's. "What do you mean?"

Onkel Hank touched his long beard as a faraway look overtook his eyes. "I met Tillie when I was nineteen, and I wasn't yet baptized. She'd been baptized for two years. I was feeling pretty lost and confused until I met her and my life fell into place. I was baptized, and we married a year later."

Chris let his uncle's story filter through his mind. It was too easy, too straightforward. "What do you mean, you felt lost?" He touched the piece of leather on the worktable.

Onkel Hank leaned an elbow on the table. "I don't think I've ever told you I have an older *bruder* who left the Amish church and was shunned."

"*Ya*," Chris said. "*Onkel* Naaman. He lives in Baltimore and works as a police officer."

"That's right." *Onkel* Hank's bushy brown eyebrows rose. "I'm surprised *mei schweschder* shared that with you."

"Why wouldn't she tell me about your *bruder*?" Chris asked, still tracing his fingertips over the leather.

"I know how strict your *dat* is, and I assumed he wouldn't want to discuss someone, especially a family member, who had left the faith."

"That's true. I don't think *Dat* has ever mentioned his name, but *Mamm* has." Chris tilted his head. "What did *Onkel* Naaman have to do with your confusion?"

"I always looked up to Naaman, so it was a real shock to me when he left the church. Even though my two younger *schweschdere* had been baptized, I wasn't certain if I should join the church or follow Naaman to the *English* world. When I met Tillie, I realized I belonged here with her." He paused, looking at Chris for a moment. "Do you feel Emily pulling you toward the church?"

Chris shrugged. "I don't know what I feel. I'm sort of numb."

"Do you love Emily?"

Although his heart responded with a resounding yes, Chris couldn't say the word aloud. "I'm not sure."

Onkel Hank sighed. "You're confused, and you shouldn't be baptized if your heart isn't right with God."

"I know." Chris ran his hand down his face as misery took root deep in his gut. He'd come to Bird-in-Hand to start a new life, but now he was just as tormented as he had been back home in Sugarcreek.

"That doesn't mean I think you should give up on the

community, Emily, or yourself. You're still young, Chris. You still have time to be baptized."

His uncle's encouraging words did little to stop the pain twisting in Chris's gut.

The door to the harness shop opened, and Leroy's voice sounded from the front of the shop. "How about you two get off your behinds and help me unload this truck?"

Onkel Hank chuckled. "We'd better go help him."

"All right." Chris stood, and *Onkel* Hank patted his shoulder.

"It will all work out, son. And you're always welcome here with us. You can stay as long as you like, even if you decide not to join the church."

Chris followed his uncle out to the driveway, still agonizing over what his future would bring and where he belonged.

"How are you feeling?"

Emily peeked up from the quilting magazine she'd been thumbing through. Rachel was clad in a white nightgown, her thick, dark hair hanging loose to her waist as she stood in the doorway. Her pretty face and dark eyes were tense with concern.

"I'm all right." That was a bald-faced lie, but she didn't want to add to the anxiety already stiffening Rachel's shoulders. Emily had spent the day trying to come to terms with her loss, but her chest and head still ached with the reality of Chris's painful words. After dinner she'd taken a shower and then headed to her room, where she'd looked through magazines by the light of her lantern and a pumpkin spice–scented candle.

Rachel pointed at Emily's bed. "May I join you?"

"*Ya.*" Emily patted the quilt beside her.

Rachel climbed in next to her, and they both snuggled down and stared at the dark ceiling. The shadow from the candle flame danced there, and the scent of pumpkin sweetened the air, mocking Emily's grim mood. Memories of staying up late while talking to her sisters engulfed Emily, and the reality of Rachel's wedding punched her in the gut.

"I can't believe you're moving out soon." Emily's words were thick with the grief flourishing inside of her.

Rachel turned toward her with a sad smile. "*Ya*, that's true. It's coming fast."

"Too fast." Tears stung Emily's eyes, and she tried in vain to swallow them. She'd lost her first love and now her second sister was going to move out. It was too much for her to process at once.

"I won't be far away." Rachel touched Emily's arm. "I promise we'll visit all the time." She grinned. "You're a better cook and seamstress, and I'll need your help all the time."

Emily gave her a watery smile. "You know I'll always help you."

"I'm going to miss seeing you every day."

"Nah." Emily shook her head. "You won't. You'll have Mike and John to keep you busy, and I imagine you'll have more family members soon."

"I hope so."

"You will." Emily squeezed Rachel's hand.

They stared at the ceiling in an amiable silence for a few moments. Despite Emily's efforts to keep her thoughts focused on her sisters, her mind betrayed her, and she recalled the feel of Chris's warm lips as they brushed her cheek last night. Why had she allowed him to get so close and then steal her heart?

"I think he loves you," Rachel said as if sensing her thoughts.

"What?" Emily rolled to her side and looked at Rachel. "Why?"

"It was so obvious at the party last night. I could tell by the way he smiled at you and the pure adoration in his eyes when he opened the tool set you gave him. It was written all over his face."

Emily should have been thrilled by her sister's words, but instead they seemed to drive the knife deeper into her soul. She flopped onto her back and looked up at the ceiling.

"Em? I didn't mean to upset you."

"It's not that." Emily rubbed her eyes with the heels of her hands. "I just don't know what to do. Really, there's nothing I can do. If he doesn't join the church, we can't be together. I thought I found the man I would marry. Now I'm worse off than before I met him because all he's given me is a broken heart coupled with broken dreams. I never imagined this would happen."

"I'm sorry, Em."

Rachel was silent for a few moments as the shadow of the candle's flame sputtered across the ceiling.

"What do you think *Mammi* would say about this situation?" Rachel asked.

Emily turned toward her again. "I don't know. What do you think?"

Memories of *Mammi* rushed over Emily. She recalled sitting at her grandmother's kitchen table with her sisters, eating grilled cheese, drinking chocolate milk, and talking. She could almost smell the aroma of her grandmother's house now—vanilla infused with freshly baked bread . . . and happiness.

More tears threatened Emily's eyes. Life was so simple when she was a little girl. She didn't have to contend with the pain of broken relationships and confusing feelings.

"Well, I think *Mammi* would tell you to pray for Chris," Rachel said. "She'd say only God can heal Chris's heart and help him see he not only needs the community, but he belongs in the community. If we pray, maybe Chris will realize he's already a part of the community even though he doesn't see it yet."

A tear traced Emily's cheek as she looked at Rachel. "You're right. *Danki.*"

"*Gern gschehne.*" Rachel squeezed her hand, and Emily silently thanked God once again for her sisters.

CHRIS LEANED HIS ELBOW ON THE ARM OF THE CHAIR AND stared out across his uncle's pasture as he sat on the porch Sunday afternoon. He slumped back, breathed in the brisk fall air, and then yawned. He hadn't slept much at all last night, but it wasn't nightmares about his brother that had kept him awake. Instead, it was the haunting memory of the pain in Emily's eyes. An icy shudder moved up his spine as he recalled their conversation yesterday morning. He hated that he'd hurt her so badly, but he couldn't accept her insistence that he belonged in this community. She had to be wrong. She just had to.

Instead of facing her at church this morning, he'd told his aunt and uncle he wasn't feeling well, and he stayed in his room all day, flipping through books and trying to nap.

You're a coward, Christopher Hochstetler.

He scowled and ran his hands down his face. As usual, his gruff inner voice was right. He was a coward, but running away was the only way he knew to deal with his heartache.

Chris rubbed his eyes with the heels of his hands as confusion clouded his thoughts. His heart told him to listen to Emily and talk to her bishop about joining the spring baptism class. His head, however, told him to stay away from Emily and allow a more deserving man to ask for her hand in marriage and build a life with her.

Which answer was the right one? Where did he belong?

An ache started behind his eyes, and he pinched the bridge of his nose. He was a mess. He was no closer to figuring out his life than when he'd first arrived in Bird-in-Hand.

Chris heaved a deep sigh that seemed to bubble up from his toes. He had just looked out toward the pasture again when the phone rang in the shanty. He frowned. The phone continued to ring, and he stared at the shanty for a few moments longer.

Finally, inquisitiveness shoved him out of the chair and pushed him down the porch steps. Once in the shanty, he picked up the phone's receiver and held it to his ear. "Hello?"

"Christopher? Is that you?"

"*Ya, ya.*" Chris dropped onto the bench. "*Mamm.* How are you?"

"I was hoping to reach you." Her voice wobbled. "I was afraid you were at church or visiting."

"No." Chris shook his head as if she could see his face. "I stayed home today, but *Aenti* Tillie and *Onkel* Hank went."

"Oh." She paused. "Are you ill?"

"No." He needed to change the subject. "Is everything all right?"

"No." Her voice was thick. "Paul had a fire at his *haus* last night."

"What?" Horrific images slashed through him. "Is he all right? How are Rosanna and the *maed*?"

"They're all fine. Praise God. I can't imagine losing them after . . ."

Chris swallowed hard, following her train of thought. He shoved a shaky hand through his hair.

"Rosanna had a pot on the stove when she heard Mamie scream and rushed to see what was wrong. It turned out the girls had gotten into some markers and Betsy was chewing on one. She had green marker all over herself, head to toe." *Mamm* clicked her tongue. "Rosanna was cleaning her up in the bathroom when she remembered the pot. Back in the kitchen she found flames already spreading to the curtains above the sink. She thinks she dropped a potholder too close to the burner when Mamie's scream scared her."

"*Ach*, no!" Chris gasped.

"She got the *kinner* out and screamed for Paul. He ran out of the barn and called nine-one-one. Thankfully, no one was hurt, but the *haus* is a mess. They're going to stay with us for a while. The men in the community are going to start helping with the *haus* tomorrow. They have to replace two exterior walls in the kitchen, along with the appliances and cabinets. There's also quite a bit of cleanup, and repainting is needed because of smoke damage."

"It sounds like a lot of work." An image of his brother's large, white clapboard house filled his mind. The two-story home included five bedrooms, a spacious kitchen, and a large family room, evidence of the success his brother enjoyed from his growing horse business. He imagined smoke pouring from the kitchen at the back of the house.

What a nightmare for Paul and Rosanna, and their little girls must have been terrified. Sadness slid over him as he imagined his nieces sobbing in their parents' arms as the firefighters put out the blaze.

"While the men work, the women are going to have to wash all the linens and clothing," *Mamm* continued. "It may take some time, but your *dat* and Paul think they should be back in the *haus* by Christmas. It could've been much, much worse. Thank God they are safe and the damage is minor."

"I'm so relieved to hear that."

"I wanted to call you last night, but it was so late. I thought you might have been in bed already, and I didn't feel right leaving you a message and running the risk of worrying you. I thought it would be better if I talked to you so I could explain that Paul, Rosanna, and the girls are okay."

"*Danki*. You called at a *gut* time. I was just sitting on the porch when I heard the phone ring."

"Is everything okay, Christopher?"

"*Ya*," he said, a little too quickly.

She was silent for a few moments, and he imagined her winding the phone cord around her finger while contemplating what to say to get him to open up to her.

"Why did you stay home from the church service?"

The question was simple, but the answer was too painful for him to share. "I just felt like being alone today."

"Is everything all right with your *freind* Emily?"

Chris cringed, wondering if *Mamm* could read his emotions over the phone. "*Ya, Mamm*," he fibbed. "Everything is fine."

"Oh, *gut*."

They were both silent for a few moments, and an ache radiated through his rib cage. He missed his family.

"I'll let you go, Christopher. I just wanted to tell you about the fire and let you know everyone is okay."

"I'm glad you called." The words sprang from his lips.

"It's always so *gut* to talk to you. I'll call you soon. Give my love to Hank and Tillie."

"I will. Good-bye." Chris hung up the phone and then leaned back in the chair, resting his head against the wall of the shanty. He closed his eyes and visualized the men in the community working on Paul's large farmhouse.

And then he recalled Paul standing in the hallway outside their bedrooms the night of his wedding. *"You know, Chris, we may argue sometimes, but we're still bruders. I'll miss you."*

The urge to help rebuild Paul's house clamped down on his shoulders, digging into his muscles like a hundred sharp knives.

I need to go home and help. I need to be there for mei bruder.

The notion caught Chris off guard. He tried to push it away, but the idea remained, echoing through his mind. Yes, he did need to help Paul, because if the situation were reversed, Paul would help him.

Was that why *Mamm* called? Did she expect him to come home and help?

Or is Mamm *hoping this event might be the catalyst to bring me home?*

Chris stood and exited the shanty, and his gaze moved to the Fisher family's house. A vise clamped over Chris's stomach and twisted. He needed to go home as soon as possible.

Was this the sign Chris needed to find the strength to walk away from Emily and give her the chance to find a man who deserved her love? Emily didn't need Chris, but his family back in Ohio did.

But if that was true, why did the idea of leaving Emily cut him to his core?

CHAPTER 21

"I'm surprised Chris wasn't in church today."

"*Ya*," Emily said as she and Rachel climbed the porch steps later that afternoon. She looked toward Hank's house. She'd hoped she would see Chris today and maybe even get a chance to speak to him, but his absence only drove home what she'd feared most—their friendship was over.

"Do you think he's ill?" Rachel held the back door open for Emily to step through.

"No. I think he's avoiding me."

Rachel frowned. "I was thinking the same thing, but I didn't want to say it."

"You can be honest with me. I can handle it." Emily hung her sweater on a peg in the mudroom. She could tell Rachel had more on her mind but was hesitant to express it. "What else do you want to say?"

Rachel hung up her sweater. "Nothing, nothing." She stepped into the kitchen. "Would you like some tea?"

"Rachel." Emily followed her. "Don't be afraid to tell me how you feel. You'll probably say something I've already been thinking."

Rachel started filling the kettle with water. "He might be avoiding you, but maybe he needs a day or two to think things over. It may not be a bad thing, you know?"

"*Ya*. Maybe he just needs some time." The feeling of dread that had burned in her belly yesterday continued to smolder.

Emily moved to a cabinet and pulled two mugs from the bottom shelf as Rachel set the kettle on a burner. Her gaze moved to the window, and she saw her parents walking together out of the barn. Although they both had serious looks on their faces, they were holding hands. She sighed. She longed to find a strong relationship like her parents had. Would she ever have a husband who would support her emotionally, no matter what they faced together?

Her knees felt weak as she recalled the pain and anguish contorting Chris's handsome face when he told her he didn't think he was worthy of the church or the community. She'd prayed for him and his family during the church service this morning. She begged God to change Chris's mind and lead him back to the church . . . and to her.

In a moment of renewed strength, Emily longed to march over to Hank's house right now and again tell Chris how wrong he was. She wanted to convince him to reconsider and give the community another chance, but she had to step back and let Chris come to her. She couldn't force him to change his mind. Only God could convince him.

Tears filled her eyes, but she didn't want to cry again. She'd cried herself to sleep last night, and she didn't want to spend today crying too.

"Em? Are you all right?"

Emily turned to where Rachel stood observing her, two tea bags in her hand. "*Ya*, I'm fine." She set the mugs on the table and then pointed to the cookie jar. "There should still be some *kichlin* left from the batch I made Thursday."

"Oh yeah." Rachel set the cookie jar between the mugs.

"Chocolate chip. My favorite. After I'm married, will you sneak *kichlin* over to *mei haus* so I can tell Mike I made them for him?"

Emily laughed, a true, genuine laugh, releasing some of the sorrow and despondency haunting her. "You really think you can pass off my baking as yours? Rach, you do realize Mike is much smarter than that."

Rachel giggled. "You're right, Em. Mike knows you're the much better cook, but it was worth a try."

Emily laughed some more and then wiped her eyes.

Rachel gave Emily's arm a squeeze. "It's so *gut* to see you laugh. I promise you everything is going to be okay. Just give Chris time."

"I'll try."

"*Gut.*"

Rachel pulled her into a warm hug, and Emily rested her cheek on her sister's shoulder. She hoped Rachel was right and Chris would come back to her soon.

"I NEED TO TELL YOU SOMETHING." CHRIS SAT DOWN ON A chair across from his aunt and uncle later that evening. They were in the family room. A pang of sadness crept up on him, but he tried to shove it out of the way and instead focus on his family and how much they needed him. "I got a call from my mother earlier. She had some bad news."

"Oh?" *Aenti* Tillie's eyes widened as she looked at *Onkel* Hank. "What happened?" *Onkel* Hank asked.

When Chris told them about his brother's house fire, his aunt and uncle both gasped. "*Mamm* said everyone is fine, but the *haus* sustained quite a bit of damage."

"Praise God they're all right," *Aenti* Tillie said, squeezing his uncle's hand.

"*Ya*." *Onkel* Hank frowned. "I'm so thankful they are okay. What a horrible scare for Rosanna and the *kinner*."

"I know." Chris took a deep breath. "I want to go home to help them rebuild the *haus*." His tone strained against his churning emotions. "I feel like I should. I know Paul would do it for me."

"Oh." This time *Onkel* Hank's eyes grew wide. "I understand. When do you want to leave?"

"Tomorrow." Chris rested his forearms on the arms of the chair. "I called the bus station, and there's a bus leaving in the morning. Could I contact your driver and get him to pick me up first thing?"

"*Ya*." *Onkel* Hank looked at him, his eyebrows raised, but he kept his thoughts to himself.

Aenti Tillie tipped her head to the side. "Are you ready to work things out with your *dat*, or do you think you'll come back here?"

Chris rubbed one of his tense shoulders with his opposite hand. Conflicting emotions took hold of him. "I don't know if I can ever work things out with *mei dat*, but I feel like Paul needs me."

"That's a *gut* start." To his surprise, she smiled. "I'm glad to hear it."

"I am too," *Onkel* Hank added. "We will miss you, son, but you are always welcome here."

"That's right," his aunt said. "If you decide you want to come back and stay here or if you want to come and visit, your room will always be waiting for you."

"*Danki*. I'm going to go finish packing." As he stood, he felt as though a ball of ice had formed in his chest. He was about to walk away from Bird-in-Hand and sweet Emily.

He climbed the steps, then made his way into his room. He saw the tool kit Emily had given him sitting on the dresser. He ran his fingers over the cool plastic case as he recalled the excitement in her eyes when he'd opened it. He was afraid she would ask for the tools back when he told her they couldn't be together. But he was glad she hadn't. He wanted to take them back to Ohio with him in case he never returned but found a leatherworking opportunity somewhere else.

And because he would always treasure her thoughtfulness.

Chris crossed the room to the window and looked over at her house. He longed to see Emily's beautiful blue eyes and breathe in her scent of strawberries and cinnamon. He'd never had such a strong bond with anyone in his life. But their relationship was forbidden. If he pursued her without being baptized, he would get her into trouble, possibly even shunned. He couldn't risk that. Yet he longed to be with her. She consumed his thoughts.

The little voice in the back of his mind instructed him to go to Emily and tell her good-bye, but he couldn't get his legs to move. Instead, he stood cemented in place, staring at her house and wondering if he would ever see her again.

Chris sank down onto the edge of the bed, and it creaked under his weight. By Tuesday evening, he would be back in Ohio with his family, and Bird-in-Hand would soon be a distant memory.

But would the pain slicing through his soul ever fade?

EMILY CARRIED THE PICNIC BASKET AS SHE WALKED DOWN the path leading to the harness shop Monday afternoon. Although she'd promised herself she'd let Chris come to her, she couldn't shake the overwhelming feeling that he needed her. She'd spent most of the night tossing and turning as she worried about him.

When she finally pushed herself out of bed that morning, she was consumed with the urge to take him lunch. After the breakfast dishes were done and the laundry was hung on the line, she packed ham and cheese sandwiches, along with pretzels and cookies, and then headed out to the harness shop.

Unease cramped Emily's stomach muscles as she approached the door, and she sent up a silent prayer to God, asking him to use this lunch to help Chris realize Emily still wanted to be his friend.

She wrenched the door open and walked through the showroom. Hope blossomed in her chest as she approached the work area. She was thankful there weren't any customers in the shop, and she hoped she and Chris could get some time alone to talk and possibly even work things out.

She was surprised to find only her father and Hank working. She crinkled her brow as both *Dat* and Hank looked up and their eyes widened.

"Where's Chris?" Emily shifted the basket on her arm.

Dat's gaze moved to her basket and then up to her face. "You brought Chris lunch?"

"*Ya*, I did." Why was *Dat* surprised? She'd brought him lunch before. "Where is he?"

Hank frowned. "Chris didn't talk to you last night?"

"No. I haven't spoken to him since Saturday morning."

Hank's face contorted to a deep frown. "You don't know."

"I don't know what?" Unease swelled up in her chest. "What do you mean?" She looked back and forth between them and her unease exploded into frustration. "What's going on?"

Dat frowned. "Chris left this morning."

"He left?" Emily tipped her head to the side. "I don't understand. Where did he go?"

"He went back to Ohio," Hank said. "He went back to be with his family."

"What?" Emily squinted. They weren't making any sense. Then reality crashed into her, and her breath came out in a rush. "He left? For good?"

"Possibly. I'm really not sure, *mei liewe*," Hank said. "His *bruder* had a *haus* fire. Everyone is okay, but the *haus* needs a lot of work. Chris said he needed to go home to help him rebuild. Tillie and I told him he's always welcome to come back, but he said he wasn't sure what he'd do after the *haus* was fixed." He paused. "I'm so sorry, Emily. I thought Chris told you. He got the call while we were at church yesterday, and I assumed he went to see you before he told Tillie and me he was leaving."

"He left." This time it was a statement, and her body was shaking like a leaf caught in a windstorm. "He left me without saying good-bye." Knots formed in her stomach and became balls of lead. "I can't believe it." She dropped the basket, and it landed with a clatter on the floor.

"Emily." *Dat* shot to his feet and touched her arm. "Are you all right?"

"I'm fine." A torrid tide of tears burned her eyes. She took a step backward and smacked her spine against the wall, sending stinging pain cascading down her back. She had to get out of there before she started to cry. "I need to go."

"Emily, wait." *Dat* held up his hands as if to calm her. "I'm sure there's a perfectly good explanation for why he didn't tell you he was leaving."

"*Ya*, there is." She gave a derisive snort. "He didn't care enough about me to tell me he was leaving. Our friendship meant nothing to him."

"No, no," Hank insisted. "That's not true. He told Tillie and me that he cares for you very deeply, but he's not ready to join the church."

She didn't want to hear this. Nothing Hank could say would heal her crushed and dejected soul.

Emily wiped tears from her eyes with the back of her hand and pointed to the basket. "You can have the lunch. I'm going home." Her voice sounded foreign to her, and her throat ached when she spoke.

Dat started to speak, but before he could respond, she rushed out the door and ran up the path to the house. She exploded through the back door, through the mudroom, and into the kitchen. *Mamm* was standing at the sink and, startled, turned to Emily.

"He left!" Emily cried, her whole body trembling. "Chris went back to Ohio today and he didn't even say good-bye to me. He's gone!" She leaned her head against the wall and dissolved into tears, hugging her arms against her aching chest as grief spilled out of her.

"*Ach*, no!" *Mamm* exclaimed.

Her mother's arms pulled her into a warm embrace, and she buried her face in her mother's shoulder as sobs racked her to her very core. A door clicked shut somewhere close by and then footsteps entered the kitchen.

"Is she all right?" *Dat's* question was soft and tender.

Emily could feel *Mamm's* head move from side to side as a silent response.

"*Ach*, no." His voice was closer.

A strong hand caressed her stiff back. It was *Dat's* hand, and the gesture warmed her soul. Oh, she was so grateful for her supportive parents.

When the tears subsided, she wiped her eyes with a napkin *Mamm* handed her. As she blew her nose, both of her parents looked at her with worried faces.

Mamm pointed to a kitchen chair. "Sit."

Emily complied, and *Dat* sat down beside her as *Mamm* brought her a glass of water. Emily took a long drink, but the water did little to soothe her parched throat. *Dat* rubbed her shoulder, and the pain in his dark eyes was enough to make Emily sob all over again.

"I'm so sorry," *Mamm* finally said, coming to sit down across from her. "Did he say why he left?"

Dat told her about the fire, and *Mamm* shook her head.

"I understand that he wants to help his *bruder,*" Emily began, her words soft and thin, "but why didn't he say good-bye? Why didn't he tell me he was going to leave? Did our friendship mean nothing—" Her voice hitched, and she stopped speaking, afraid she'd start crying again.

"*Ach, mei liewe,*" *Dat* said. "Maybe he was afraid to face you."

Emily looked at her father. She'd never seen him so emotional. It was as if *Dat* could feel her pain. Was that what it felt like to be a parent?

"Why would he be afraid to face me?" Emily asked. "We were *freinden.*"

Dat sighed as he continued to massage her shoulder. "I think it's more complicated than that. Sometimes people don't know how to handle their emotions, and instead of facing things head-on, they run and hide."

He looked at *Mamm,* and something imperceptible seemed to pass between them. It was as if they were having a silent discussion with their eyes. But Emily dismissed her curiosity as more tears filled her eyes.

"Chris's behavior doesn't make sense. I thought we were close. I was certain he cared about me. He said he did." A dull ache started behind her eyes and her lip trembled.

But then guilt squeezed her lungs. She had no right to try to keep Chris from his family, but she longed for him to have told her he was leaving. His running off without a word made her feel insignificant.

"Would you like something to eat?" *Mamm* offered. "How about a sandwich or maybe some tea?"

Emily's stomach roiled. "No, *danki.*"

Mamm went to the sink anyway, filled the kettle, and placed it on the stove. Somehow *Mamm* always knew what her daughters needed even when they protested.

"Emily." *Dat* angled his body toward her. "I know you're hurting, sweetie, and I'm so sorry about that. If I could take away your pain, I would." His voice hitched, and tears threatened Emily's eyes again. Seeing her father this emotional was almost too much for her. He'd always been a pillar of strength for each of his daughters.

Dat continued. "I think the reason he's so confused is that he's going through some complicated issues with his family. Maybe Chris feels he needs to go home to not only help his *bruder* but also work things out with his *dat.*" He paused and rubbed Emily's arm. "I know this is difficult for you, but I believe you should give him a little bit of time. Don't give up on him yet."

Emily worried her lip. "Do you really think he cares about me?"

"*Ya*, he does care about you," *Mamm* suddenly chimed in. "I could tell when you were together. Have faith."

Emily swallowed a groan. Why had she invested so much of herself in him?

Dat touched Emily's cheek. "The pain will go away, *mei liewe*. I know it hurts now, but it will get better. I promise, sweetie."

"*Danki, Dat*." She forced a smile for his benefit. "You can go back to work now. I'm sorry I upset you."

"*Ach*, no, no, no," he insisted. "You are much more important than my work. I wanted to make sure you were okay, and I'll stay here as long as you need me."

She took a deep breath against the heavy weight forming inside her rib cage. "I'll be fine."

"All right." He turned toward *Mamm* and raised his eyebrows, as if asking her if she believed it was okay for him to leave. *Mamm* gave him a little nod, and he stood, looking at Emily again. "I'll see you later. Come and get me if you need me, all right?"

"I will. *Danki, Dat*."

He started for the door and Emily turned to *Mamm* just as the kettle began to whistle.

"Let's have tea," *Mamm* said.

As *Mamm* headed to the stove, Emily put her head in her hands and wondered if her splintered soul would ever heal.

CHAPTER 22

CHRIS'S STOMACH TWISTED AND HIS HANDS TREMBLED AS he stepped out of the taxi and hefted his duffel bag back onto his shoulder Tuesday night. After the long and tedious bus ride, he'd finally arrived home. His shoulders and back stiffened as the taxi turned around and motored toward the main road. Chris looked over his shoulder and bit back the urge to run after the car and beg for a ride back to the bus station.

Coward!

Instead, he stood at the end of the rock driveway and stared dumbly at his parents' house as the cold wind bit at his cheeks and nose. The sprawling, two-story white house boasted a generous wraparound porch and nearly a dozen windows. Although the grass was brown in the cold autumn weather, the fence surrounding his father's two dozen acres of pasture was pristine and most likely recently painted.

Everything looked the same as it had when he'd left. He'd only been gone for a month, but it felt as if he'd been gone for a year. So much had changed for Chris during those weeks. He had learned how to do leatherwork, and he'd fallen in love.

He squeezed his eyes shut and his breath hitched in his chest. Emily had to know by now that he had left. Was she upset when she heard the news? What a stupid question. Of course she was upset. If he returned to Bird-in-Hand, she most likely would never speak to him again. He cringed as a poignant ache took hold of him, clenching his stomach even tighter.

The front door to the house opened and Rosanna stepped onto the porch. Chris took a deep breath and started toward the house, his boots steering him down the rock driveway.

"Chris?" Rosanna called. "Is that you?"

He waved in response, and Rosanna stepped back into the house. He envisioned her announcing to the rest of the family that he was home. He braced himself for the welcome or for the rejection. What if no one but his mother wanted him back?

"Chris!" Paul appeared on the porch and then jogged down the steps to meet Chris on the walkway. Paul was almost as tall as Chris, and his light brown hair and matching beard were the same color as Chris's hair. But Paul's eyes were blue like their mother's.

Sometimes Chris wished their differences ended there.

"I didn't know you were coming home today." He gave Chris a hug, smacking him on the back and grinning. "It's so *gut* to see you. How are you?"

Chris held back a sigh of relief. "I'm all right." He let his duffel bag drop to the ground with a thump. "*Mamm* called me Sunday and told me about the fire. I came as soon as I could. How is everyone?"

"Christopher!"

Chris's eyes darted toward the porch and his heart squeezed as *Mamm* rushed toward him. Her eyes were watery as she held out her arms. He leaned down to her, and she pulled him into a warm embrace. He was relieved to see her light brown hair was still threaded with only a few silver strands. He knew he had worried her.

"I'm so thankful you're home," she whispered, her voice shaking. "My family is back together again."

Chris heaved a trembling sigh. "I want to help Paul."

Mamm cupped a hand to his cheek. "*Danki* for coming." A tear trickled from one of her eyes, and Chris swallowed as a warm knot formed in his chest.

"*Onkel* Chris!"

Mamie hurried out of the house, followed by Rosanna, who had Betsy in her arms. Mamie reached him and held up her arms. Her brown hair hung to her shoulders in thin braids, and her brown eyes flashed with excitement. She reminded Chris of a mini version of Rosanna, coloring and all.

Chris lifted her into his arms and a smile overtook his lips as his soul warmed. He adored Paul's sweet girls. "Hi, Mamie."

"Welcome home." Mamie kissed his cheek. "*Mammi* said she really missed you. We're *froh* you're back."

"*Danki*." Oh, how he had missed this little girl.

Rosanna touched his arm. "It's *gut* to see you."

"*Danki*," Chris said. "It's *gut* to see you too."

Betsy clapped her hands. She looked like her mother too, but she had inherited Paul's blue eyes.

"Are you hungry?" *Mamm* took hold of Chris's arm and tugged him toward the house. "Come inside. We have chicken potpie."

"One of your favorites, Chris." Paul heaved Chris's bag to his shoulder and started toward the house.

Still holding Mamie in his arms, Chris allowed his mother to steer him up the steps and into the house. His shoulders relaxed slightly, but his stomach remained tight. Was *Dat* home, deliberately avoiding him?

When they stepped into the foyer, Paul and Rosanna headed

toward the kitchen. Mamie squirmed, and when Chris lowered her to the floor, she took off after her parents. *Mamm* held on to Chris's arm, signaling for him to linger back by the door with her, giving them a little privacy.

"I was hoping you'd come." *Mamm's* eyes were still misty but also sparkling with happiness. *"Danki."*

Chris's intuition had been right; his family needed him. But his soul still ached for Emily.

"Where's *Dat*?" The moment he asked the question, he wanted to pull it back.

Mamm frowned. "He'll be down in a minute."

Ah. So *Dat* was avoiding him.

He inhaled through his nose as doubt coursed through him. Nothing would ever change between *Dat* and him. Coming home was a mistake.

No. You're here for Paul, not Dat.

"Just give him time." *Mamm* squeezed Chris's arm. "You both are stubborn, and one of you has to make an attempt to clear the air before you can work this out."

"He's impossible to talk to," Chris snapped, and *Mamm* blanched as if he'd struck her. "I'm sorry. I didn't mean for it to come out that way."

"Chris," Rosanna called from the kitchen. "I'm warming up your potpie. Would you like some bread? It's still warm."

"That sounds fantastic," he called back to her.

"Let's go to the kitchen, Christopher. We can talk later."

Chris followed *Mamm* into the kitchen, washed his hands at the sink, and then sat at his usual spot at the long table. It was obvious that they had all just finished eating when he arrived. He kissed his nieces good night before they went upstairs with

Rosanna for a bath, and Paul sat down across from him. *Mamm* brought his food and then started clearing the table.

The aroma of chicken potpie combined with freshly baked bread caused his stomach to gurgle. He hadn't eaten since early that morning. After a silent prayer, he dug into the potpie, relishing the delicious taste.

"So how was Pennsylvania?" Paul buttered a piece of bread for himself. "*Mamm* said you've been working in *Onkel* Hank's harness shop."

"It was *gut*." Chris took a piece of bread from the basket in the center of the table. "But I want to hear about your *haus*. How is the work going?"

Paul set the bread on a napkin and rubbed his tired eyes. "It's a lot of work, but it's going all right. I've got a crew of men helping to take out the walls in the kitchen. We have to replace two of them. We're going to get the kitchen rebuilt before we start painting upstairs. It's going to be awhile." He smirked. "The *kinner* are sleeping in your room, but we can move them if you want your bed back."

"No, no. It's no trouble. I can sleep in the sewing room." Chris buttered his own piece of bread.

"You can sleep in Gabriel's room," *Mamm* said.

Chris stilled for a moment and then looked up, meeting her gaze. "What did you say?"

"Gabriel's bedroom is the same as he left it." To Chris's surprise, *Mamm's* face remained cordial, without any trace of bereavement. "I just have to put clean sheets on the bed, but that won't take long at all. You should stay in there."

"No, thanks. I'd rather stay in the sewing room." He couldn't fathom sleeping in Gabriel's bed when his grief was still so raw.

Mamm's brow creased. "But there's only a single bed in there."

"It's fine," Chris said. "I'll be okay."

"Rosanna can move the *kinner* to Gabriel's room. It's not a problem." Paul shrugged.

"I don't want to put her through any trouble," Chris said. "I'll stay in the sewing room."

"Fine. It's settled." *Mamm* stood. "I'll make the bed. When I get back, we can have cake and celebrate your return home. I'm so glad I baked a chocolate cake earlier. Now I know why I had the urge to make one. It was for you, Christopher. It will be your belated birthday cake." She walked out of the kitchen humming, and Chris's chest squeezed again.

Paul met Chris's gaze. "She's so *froh* you're back."

"*Ya*, I could tell." Chris forked more of the potpie into his mouth. His whirling emotions left him feeling wrung out—as if he'd been forced through a wringer washer.

"She told me she called to tell you about the fire, and she hoped you'd come and help." Paul broke the piece of bread in half. "I appreciate that you're here, but you really didn't have to feel obligated to come back for me. You know the people in the community always pull together to help each other. We had it under control, and *Mamm* said you were *froh* in Pennsylvania."

"I wanted to come," Chris insisted. "You're *mei bruder*, and you would do the same for me."

"*Ya*, that's true. *Danki*. Do you think you'll go back to Bird-in-Hand, or are you here to stay?" Paul took a bite and chewed.

Chris swallowed a forkful of potpie. "I don't know." His heart wanted him to hop on the next bus to get back to Emily, but his mind had accepted he would never be satisfied with being only her friend.

They ate in silence for a few minutes, and Chris looked up when he heard heavy footsteps in the hallway. He glanced toward the doorway as *Dat* appeared. He stood at a muscular six feet, and his dark hair and beard were streaked with gray.

His hazel eyes assessed Chris from across the room. "Christopher. You're home."

Chris gritted his teeth as he nodded a reply. In his peripheral vision, he saw Paul shoot him a warning glance.

Dat looked at Chris a few more moments, and the air was thick with tension. Finally, *Dat* turned and disappeared from the doorway. His footfalls echoed as he continued back down the hallway.

"Don't let him get to you," Paul said after *Dat* was gone. "Just give it time, and you two will eventually work things out."

Chris looked at his brother. How could he offer Chris any valuable advice when he had never done anything to disappoint *Dat*? He was sure Paul couldn't fathom being branded a disgrace in their father's eyes.

"What?" Paul snatched another piece of bread from the basket. "Why are you looking at me as if I've sprouted a second nose?"

"What makes you think *Dat* and I will ever resolve our problems?" Chris placed his fork on the table next to his plate and leveled his gaze with his older brother's. "You've always been *Dat's* example of how the perfect son should behave. You've spent your entire adulthood enjoying *Dat's* praise while I have lived in your shadow."

Paul gaped as Chris continued.

"*Dat* has rubbed the fact that I can't train a horse as well as you can in my face." Chris spoke slowly to drive his point home. "He said I should try to be more like you so I can take over this farm someday. I always feel like a failure because I didn't take to horse training like you did, and Gabriel's death only deepened the rift between us."

Paul held up his hands to silence Chris. "I'm only trying to help."

"If you really want to help me, then tell me something I can do to make it better." Chris held his breath as Paul stared at him. "That wasn't rhetorical. I honestly don't know what I can do to fix it." He pointed toward the door. "You saw his reaction when he saw me. He's not *froh* I'm back. He's probably disappointed I didn't stay away for *gut*." He despised the tremor in his voice. Why did discussing his father always rip him apart inside?

"You can't possibly believe *Dat* doesn't want you here with the rest of our family." Paul's blue eyes held sympathy. "We're his sons, and we're the only sons left."

Chris rubbed his chin as tears threatened his eyes.

"Gabriel's death was not your fault. You need to stop blaming yourself for that." Paul paused, looking at Chris. "Is that the reason you left?"

Chris looked down at his half-eaten potpie as guilt poured through him like a tidal wave. His hands trembled as he gripped his fork.

"You can't really believe it was your fault, no matter what *Dat* has said. I told him not to buy that awful horse, but he's always so stubborn. He wanted to prove he could train it, but I knew he couldn't. That horse never should've been in *Dat's* stable. That horse killed Gabriel, and you didn't."

Chris looked up at Paul's deep frown. "But I was the one who told Gabriel to take the horse out to the pasture. I wanted to try to train it to prove to *Dat* that I was as *gut* as you." He pointed a shaky finger toward his chest. "It's my fault because Gabriel was listening to me. He looked up to me the same way I still look up to you."

Paul's frown crumbled, and his blue eyes misted. "That doesn't make it your fault."

Chris scowled. "I still don't see how *Dat* and I can work this out. We've been estranged for too long."

Paul folded his arms over his chest. "You and *Dat* are both very stubborn and headstrong."

Chris rolled his eyes. "Now you sound like *Mamm*."

"Oh *ya*?" Paul grinned. "I suppose that's where I get my intelligence from, then."

Chris couldn't stop his smirk. "And your modesty too."

Paul chuckled. "I think you should try to talk to *Dat* calmly. Somehow try to keep your fiery temper in check and just talk to him. Explain that you want to work things out for the sake of the family. Maybe that will work. Whenever I've had problems with him, I have had to take a step back and try to speak calmly to him. If I fly off the handle, he gets defensive."

"I know. I've seen his defensiveness more than once." Chris couldn't envision his father ever truly listening to him, but maybe it was time for him to give it a try.

Suddenly he realized what Paul had said.

"Wait. You've had problems with *Dat*?"

"Of course I have. Do you really think you're the only one who ever comes up against his stubborn and critical nature? It's true that we have our love of horses in common, but I guess you've missed all the times he's tried to tell me I don't know what I'm talking about."

"No, I didn't know. I guess I was too wrapped up in myself, too afraid I was the only son he thought ever failed him."

Paul sighed, and his eyes softened again. "I'm really sorry."

"For what?"

"I'm sorry he's compared you to me. I had no idea." He leaned forward, resting his hands on the table. "I can't imagine how awful that's been for you. I'm surprised you don't hate me."

"I could never hate you. You're *mei bruder*."

"Thanks." Paul looked toward the door. "*Mamm* has been gone for quite a while now. She must be helping Rosanna put the girls to bed." He pointed toward the counter where a cake saver sat. "I'd hate to see that fresh chocolate cake get stale. Should we just cut the cake ourselves?"

"Now you're talking." It was good to be home.

As he examined the cake saver, he recalled the surprise party and delicious cake Emily had made for him. A sharp ache radiated through his whole body. Chris missed Emily so much. Did she miss him too?

CHAPTER 23

EMILY TIPTOED DOWN THE STEPS TO THE KITCHEN. SHE
held a lantern up to guide her way through the dark house. After
lying awake in bed for hours, she had decided to make herself
some Sleepy Time herbal tea as a last-ditch effort to find sleep.
Warm milk did not appeal to her tonight.

As her toes touched the bottom step, she heard her father's
snores rumbling from her parents' bedroom on the other side of
the family room. Smiling, she shook her head. *How does* Mamm
sleep with that racket beside her?

Emily set the lantern on the counter. Then she filled the kettle with water and placed it on the burner. When she turned, she
gasped as a figure came through the doorway.

"*Mamm.*" Emily took deep breaths in an attempt to slow her
racing pulse. "You scared me."

"I'm sorry." *Mamm* walked over to her. "Having trouble
sleeping?"

"*Ya.*" Emily held up the box of tea bags. "I was going to try
some herbal tea."

"May I join you?"

"*Ya.*" Guilt pricked at Emily's nerves. "Did I wake you? I tried
to be quiet."

244

"No." *Mamm* pointed toward the doorway. "Don't you hear that bear growling in my bedroom?"

A laugh burst from deep in Emily's chest, and she clamped her hand over her mouth. Oh, it was so good to laugh again!

"Your *dat* has kept me awake for the past hour. Even though I've poked him and asked him to roll over, the snoring hasn't stopped. I was staring at the ceiling and begging God to give me patience when I saw the light from your lantern. You most certainly didn't wake me up, but I'm thankful for the company." She placed a hand on her hip. "Now, why are you awake?"

"I just can't sleep." Emily shrugged and then retrieved two mugs from the cabinet.

"Emily, you can be honest with me."

Emily set the mugs on the table. "All right. I can't stop thinking about Chris. I imagine he has arrived at his parents' *haus* by now, and I keep wondering how things are going for him." She ran her fingers over the cool ceramic mug. "I hope he and his *dat* can work things out. And I hope he can be *froh*."

She faced her mother as her eyes stung with tears. "I have a hole in my heart, and I don't know what to do about it. Do you think he has thought about me since he left here?"

"*Ach, mei liewe.*" *Mamm* hugged her, and Emily held her breath to prevent herself from crying. "I've suffered with a broken heart before, and I promise you it will get easier. It won't sting like this forever. Just give yourself time to heal."

Emily sniffed and wiped her eyes. "How do I manage the pain until it eases?"

Mamm suddenly snapped her fingers. "I know just the thing." She motioned for Emily to follow her.

Emily pointed to the stove. "The kettle."

"It will be fine. We'll get something from my room and be right back." *Mamm* lifted the lantern. "I'll need both hands, so you'll have to hold this up so I can see."

Emily walked behind her mother as they made their way through the family room to her mother's bedroom. Emily stood in the doorway as *Mamm* set the lantern on the floor in front of her hope chest, and the soft yellow light illuminated part of the large room. The warm glow of the light seemed a stark contrast to the harsh, thundering snores reverberating from the bed at the far end of the room.

Mamm moved to her dresser and opened a small box. She picked up something and then put the top back on the box before returning to the hope chest. The glow of the lantern glinted off a small key in *Mamm's* hand before she slipped it into the lock and turned it.

Mamm lifted the top of the chest, handed the lantern to Emily, and began searching in the glow of the light. Emily peeked over *Mamm's* shoulder. She breathed in the sweet scent of cedar. *Mamm* sifted past linens and a few small boxes before she lifted a small book.

"I found it," she whispered.

Dat gave three short snorts and breathed in deeply before turning over.

Emily clapped a hand to her mouth to prevent a laugh from bursting through her lips.

Mamm rolled her eyes and pointed toward the door. Emily moved to the doorway. *Mamm* closed the lid, locked the hope chest, and slipped the key into the pocket of her robe. She carried the book out of the room, gently closed the door, and walked through the family room with Emily.

The kettle started to whistle as soon as they entered the kitchen. Emily poured two mugs of tea before sitting down at the table beside *Mamm*.

"What is that?" Emily pointed to the small book.

"It belonged to your *mammi*." *Mamm* pushed the book toward her. "It was her favorite devotional, and she marked her favorite verses. This book helped me through some really difficult times, and I thought maybe it would help you too."

Emily admired the frayed cover. It featured an illustration of a rose and the title *God's Love for You*. She flipped through pages decorated with beautiful drawings of nature scenes and flowers, accompanied by Scripture verses. Many of the pages had verses that had been underlined in light pencil. She looked up at *Mamm*.

"Did you mark any of these verses?"

"No, only *Mammi* did. I could have erased them, but I left them that way so I could feel as if I were reading the Scriptures with her."

Emily's chest squeezed. As usual, *Mamm* knew just what Emily needed before she did. "This is perfect. Thank you so much."

"You're welcome." *Mamm* looped her arm around Emily's shoulders and gave her a squeeze.

AFTER THEY FINISHED THEIR CUPS OF TEA, EMILY CARRIED the devotional up to her room. She propped up her pillows and leaned against them while she perused the book by the light of her lantern and her favorite pumpkin spice–scented candle. She read through several verses, but when she came to one, she stopped and stared.

Mammi had underlined it three times and then drawn a heart beside it. The Scripture verse was Psalm 59, verse 16: "But I will sing of your strength, in the morning I will sing of your love; for you are my fortress, my refuge in times of trouble."

Tears sprang to Emily's eyes and then flowed down her cheeks. Oh, that verse spoke right to her soul. She whispered it to herself, repeating it until she had committed it to memory. It was as if *Mammi* had picked that verse out just for her. It was as if *Mammi* could feel Emily's heartbeat and had sent the book to offer her solace.

Hugging the book to her chest, Emily blew out the candle and switched off the lantern before she leaned back against the pillows. She closed her eyes, prayed for Chris, and then cried until she fell asleep.

CHRIS'S ARMS AND BACK ACHED AS HE FOLLOWED PAUL TO the backyard of Paul's house. Chris and a crew of three other men had spent the morning reframing the two exterior walls damaged by the fire. One wall included the stove, sink, and counter space, and the other housed cabinets. It was a miracle the fire damage was contained to only two walls, but the smoke damage had quickly spread throughout the house.

A group of women had spent the morning cleaning. The aroma of smoke, charred wood, and burnt fabric hung in the house like a dense fog, and all the volunteers donned respirators to protect their lungs.

Chris and Paul had picked up sandwiches, brownies, chips, and bottles of water donated by a community member and now sat across from each other at a picnic table. After a silent prayer, Chris unwrapped a ham and cheese sandwich and took a bite.

His legs were grateful for the opportunity to sit after working all morning.

"I can't believe it's Friday already." Paul opened his bottle of water. "The week has flown by."

"It has." Chris pointed toward the large house. "There's plenty to do, but I think we're making *gut* progress. The community has really stepped up to help you. I think you're right that you'll be back in your *haus* by Christmas. Maybe sooner."

"I hope so." Paul took a long draw from the bottle, angled his head to the side, and scrunched his brow. "Why do you seem so surprised the community is helping? You've seen it before. You've grown up here. Remember when the Bender family's barn burned down? I think you were maybe ten."

"*Ya,* I remember that well," Chris said before biting into the sandwich again.

"The whole community came out and rebuilt that barn in a few days. That's what we do."

"*Ya,* that's true." Chris took in the sight of the house. His brother was benefiting from the Amish community's generosity, but what would it take for Chris to actually feel as if he deserved all the community had to offer? The question burned deep in his soul.

"What's going on in your head? You look as though you're contemplating the meaning of life or something."

Chris met his brother's gaze, and Paul cocked an eyebrow.

"Nothing," Chris mumbled. "I'm just grateful for all the help you're getting."

Paul took another long gulp of water. "*Dat* said he had some business to take care of this morning, but he'd come by this afternoon to help us with the walls. I think it will go quicker with another set of hands."

Chris swallowed a groan. Except for meals, he'd managed to steer clear of his father that week, but it would be difficult when they were working side by side. He bit back the bitter taste of shame. Avoiding *Dat* was immature. He had to stop behaving like a boy and face his father like a man.

"Have you talked to him yet?" Paul seemed to sense Chris's evasion.

"No." Chris moved his fingers over the condensation on his bottle of water to avoid his brother's curious stare.

"I didn't think so. How long are you going to wait?"

"I don't know." Chris shrugged. "I guess until the perfect opportunity presents itself."

Paul remained silent. Chris could feel his disapproval, and it sent a familiar resentment bubbling through him. He didn't need Paul to be disappointed in him too.

"Look, Paul." Chris leaned forward and lowered his voice in an effort to keep their conversation private. "*Dat* hasn't tried to talk to me either. He didn't exactly give me a warm welcome when I got here, and he hasn't said much to me since then, except to ask me to pass the mashed potatoes at supper."

Paul sighed. "You're right. I have noticed that, but one of you has to make the first move."

"I just don't know what to say to him." Chris squeezed the bottle of water, and the plastic crackled loudly in protest. "I don't know how to open the conversation, and I know I'm going to lose it when he mentions Gabriel."

"He just might surprise you when that subject comes up."

Chris's gaze snapped to Paul's. "What do you mean?"

It was Paul's turn to lean in close and lower his voice. "I think if you two talked, you'd see you are both feeling guilty."

"What do you mean?"

Paul nodded slowly. "I told you, he shouldn't have bought that horse. And a few weeks ago he finally admitted it to me."

Chris blinked as the words soaked through him.

"So tell me about Bird-in-Hand," Paul said, thankfully changing the subject. "You haven't shared what it was like working in the harness shop with *Onkel* Hank. I want to hear all about it."

"I really enjoyed it, and I learned a lot. Apparently I have a talent for leatherworking." Chris took another bite of his sandwich.

"No kidding." Paul grinned.

"I actually designed a wallet and coin purse that quickly became bestsellers."

As he detailed the story of how customers were looking for souvenirs with a horse and buggy design, and how he drew the new design, Paul periodically nodded. He longed to tell Paul about his friendship with Emily, but he didn't want to run the risk of becoming emotional in public. Instead, he stuck to the subject of leatherworking and soon their lunches were gone.

"I guess we'd better get back to work," Chris said.

"*Ya*, you're right." Paul popped the last piece of brownie into his mouth, then grinned at Chris.

"What?" Chris asked, feeling self-conscious. "Why are you grinning at me like that?"

"I was just thinking about something you said Tuesday night." Paul shoved his trash into the empty chip bag. "You said *Dat* has compared you to me, said you weren't as *gut* at horse training as I am."

"Really, Paul?" Chris deadpanned. "You're laughing about that?"

"No, no, no." Paul shook his head and frowned. "Just give me a chance to finish. What I'm getting at is I've never seen you as excited about horse training as you are about leatherworking. I think you've found your calling."

"Do you think so?" Chris immediately wanted to hide his face with his hands. He loathed sounding like such a needy moron. But he had to admit he craved his brother's approval.

"*Ya*, I do." Paul stood and tossed his trash into a nearby can. "Let's get back to work."

Chris deposited his trash in the can and followed Paul back to the house. As he pulled on his respirator, Paul's words about leatherworking being Chris's true calling echoed through his mind. But if Chris was meant to work in leatherworking, how could he pursue that dream while living under his father's roof?

Chris lifted the receiver and dialed *Onkel* Hank's phone shanty later that evening. After quite a few rings, *Aenti* Tillie's words sounded through the phone line.

"*You've reached Hank and Tillie Ebersol. Please leave us a message, and we will call you back. Thank you.*"

After the beep, Chris took a deep breath. "Hi, *Aenti* Tillie and *Onkel* Hank. This is Chris. I want to let you know I'm fine. I arrived late Tuesday night. The trip was long, but it was *gut*. Everyone is doing well." He paused and leaned back in the chair, stretching his legs out in front of him. "I've been helping with the work on Paul's *haus*. The structural damage was mostly confined to two walls, but there's still a lot of work to be done."

Emily's gorgeous face filled his mind, and he took a deep breath before speaking again. "*Aenti* Tillie, I have a favor to ask of you. Would you please give a message to Emily? Please tell her

I'm sorry I didn't say good-bye to her. Tell her I really miss her, and, well . . ." Regret, longing, and affection tangled inside of him. There was much more he wanted to say to Emily, and so many things he should have said to her. Leaving them on a voice mail message for his aunt and uncle, however, was not the proper way to relay all those things to her.

"I just want to thank you both for everything," he continued. "I really enjoyed staying with you, and I'm so grateful for everything *Onkel* Hank and Leroy taught me. I will talk to you soon. Good-bye."

Chris hung up the phone and sagged in the chair. Regret held him hostage, filling his stomach with painful knots. He pushed himself up from the chair and started toward the back door.

When he entered the house, he found everyone sitting in the family room. He slipped into the room unnoticed and sat in his favorite faded blue wingchair in the corner. Across the room, *Dat* and Paul discussed horse prices as *Mamm* and Rosanna spoke softly, talking about their sewing projects.

Chris settled back into the chair, breathing in the familiar scent of the old, worn fabric. Ever since Chris was a little boy, he had enjoyed sitting in this chair. Turning to his left, he spotted Gabriel's favorite—an old, rickety rocker that had belonged to their grandmother. His lungs squeezed as memories of quiet Sunday afternoons reading in this room rained down on him.

Memories of Gabriel flashed through his mind like a movie. He suddenly recalled Emily's sweet laugh and her gorgeous sky-blue eyes. Would she ever forgive him for leaving without explaining why or saying good-bye?

A tug on his sleeve drew his attention to a small person standing beside him.

"*Onkel* Chris?"

He glanced down at Mamie. She was clad in pink pajamas and had a doll secured under her right arm.

"Hi, Mamie." He smiled and his spirit warmed as she returned the gesture. "How are you?"

"Will you hold me?" She pointed to his lap.

"Of course." He opened his arms to her, and she crawled up on his lap, resting her head against his chest.

Mamie hugged her doll to her shoulder as her thumb found her mouth. Chris absently massaged her soft hair, and she closed her eyes. Soon her breathing slowed and she was fast asleep in his arms. He thought his heart might explode with love for his sweet niece.

Chris suddenly remembered his first conversation with John when he talked about becoming an uncle after Mike and Rachel had a child. Did John miss their softball games?

His thoughts turned to wondering what his life would have been like if he'd stayed in Bird-in-Hand and joined the church. Could he have married Emily someday and started a family? Air whooshed from his lungs, leaving him breathless for a moment. He held Mamie a little tighter as he tried to slow his spinning emotions.

Chris felt someone looking at him, and he glanced across the room to where *Mamm* and Rosanna beamed at him. The love in his mother's eyes overwhelmed him as he smiled back at her. He was grateful to be back with his family, but something was missing.

Leaving Emily behind felt like someone had punched a hole in his chest.

CHAPTER 24

"WOULD YOU GO FOR A WALK WITH ME?" TILLIE ASKED Emily as they stood in Tillie's kitchen Sunday afternoon.

It was an off-Sunday without a church service, and Emily's parents had decided they would visit with Hank and Tillie instead of traveling to visit relatives or other friends.

"What about the dishes?" Emily pointed to the stack on the counter.

Tillie gestured toward where *Mamm* and Rachel were washing and drying utensils. "I think they can handle them. Come on. We'll only be gone for a few minutes."

Emily and Tillie grabbed their sweaters from the mudroom, stepped out into the cool afternoon breeze, and descended the porch steps. Emily had always been close to Tillie, but her request to speak to her alone had piqued her curiosity.

"How are you doing?" Tillie asked as they slowly walked together toward her garden.

"I'm fine." Emily hugged her sweater to her middle. "Rachel's wedding is coming fast, but I think we're ready. The dresses are finally done, and we're working on the table decorations now. Everything is coming together nicely. We have the menu all set, and—"

"That's not what I mean." Tillie put her hand on Emily's arm, and they stopped walking. "You're not one to talk about yourself, are you?"

Emily shrugged, and her cheeks burned with hot embarrassment. "I'm not sure what you mean."

"*Ya*, you do know what I mean because you've been this way your whole life, Emily." Tillie sighed. "I asked you how *you* are. If I wanted to hear about the wedding plans, I would've asked Rachel how her wedding was coming together."

Emily gaped. Tillie always had a way of getting right to the point.

"How are you, Emily?"

Emily swallowed. "I'm okay." It was a sin to lie, but she didn't want to talk about how her heart was shattered. She kept herself busy by helping with Rachel's wedding plans during the day and reading her grandmother's devotional late into the night. Praying helped to comfort her during the most difficult times, which was when she was stuck between staring at the ceiling in her bedroom and sleeping. If she needed to keep her hands busy, she'd work on the quilt she'd started for Chris, even though she doubted she would ever give it to him.

If Emily allowed her thoughts to roam, she drowned in her favorite memories of Chris—his handsome face, the strong line of his jaw, the warmth of his gaze, the sound of his laugh, and those gorgeous blue-green eyes. Her memories had a way of sneaking up on her when she least expected it, taking her by surprise and sending waves of grief radiating through her.

While she was working on *Mamm's* new dress for the wedding last week, she recalled the night she'd joined Chris working in the harness shop. That was the night when he'd poured out his soul to her for the first time, and they'd cried together as he shared the story of Gabriel's accident. Emily had believed she and Chris had bonded that night and formed a lifelong friendship. But if their friendship was really so meaningful, why had Chris left without saying good-bye?

Emily crossed her arms over her chest as if to shield her broken heart. "Really, I'm fine." She hoped she sounded convincing.

Tillie's brown eyes glimmered with tears. "Chris called and left me a message, and he asked me to pass one along to you."

Emily's breath caught. "Chris asked you to give me a message?" She mentally kicked herself for sounding so desperate.

"*Ya*, he called Friday night to let us know he is doing well. He also asked me to tell you he's sorry for leaving without saying good-bye, and he misses you." She frowned. "He started to say something else, but he stopped himself. I suppose it was too personal for him to share with me."

Emily scowled as anger shoved her grief out of its way. If Chris had something personal to say to Emily, why didn't he call her?

Leaving a message through his aunt was impersonal, but as her anger quickly subsided, a glimmer of hope percolated inside of Emily. At least Chris had sent her a message, and it was almost satisfying to know he felt guilty for not saying good-bye to her. Maybe he did still have a conscience after all.

But if Chris cared, why had he hurt her?

"*Danki* for telling me." Emily squeezed her arms closer to her chest.

Tillie touched Emily's cheek. "I believe he cares about you, Emily."

Emily nodded, but doubt had once again ripped through her.

And when would the pain ease as her parents had promised it would?

CHRIS CLIMBED THE STAIRS TO THE SECOND FLOOR IN HIS parents' house and headed down the hallway to the sewing room. He unbuttoned his white shirt as he walked, eager to change out of his Sunday clothes. He'd spent all afternoon in the clothes while relaxing in the family room after the church service, but now he looked forward to going out to the barn to help Paul care for the animals.

He'd ridden to and from the service in Paul's buggy with his family. Mamie had asked Chris to ride with her, which was the perfect excuse to avoid speaking to his father for another day. *Dat* hadn't made any attempts to speak to Chris beyond muttering or nodding a greeting when moving past him in the hallway or asking for a tool or a nail as they worked on Paul's house.

Chris stepped into the sewing room and pulled off his shirt and black trousers, then changed into work clothes. It had been strange to attend church in his former community. Although he'd been gone for only a short time, people welcomed him back as if he'd been gone much longer. Everyone seemed genuinely happy to see Chris again.

His stomach soured as he remembered seeing Salina Chupp. She'd smiled at him from across the barn during the service, and in a split second the memories from the day of Gabriel's accident came crashing over him. He spent the rest of the service staring down at the toes of his shoes as he fought back the threat of volatile emotions. Salina had approached him after the service, and Chris was grateful one of his parents' friends interrupted their brief conversation.

He tucked in his shirt and raked a comb through his hair. As he set the comb on the dresser, he noticed the tool set Emily had given him on the floor next to his duffel bag. He picked it up and ran his fingers over the plastic case. His gaze moved to the bag and the stack of pink envelopes peeking out of the side pocket.

He lifted them and pulled out the encouraging notes Emily had left for him at the harness shop. It felt as though his heart turned over in his chest as he reread her kind and thoughtful words. He wondered if *Aenti* Tillie had given Emily his message. If so, would Emily reach out to him?

Chris squeezed his eyes shut and swallowed a groan. How could Emily contact him if he hadn't asked *Aenti* Tillie to give her his address or phone number? Emily might feel awkward asking for it.

Stupid, stupid, stupid!

Chris set the toolbox on the dresser and then stepped out into the hallway. As he pulled the door shut behind him, he looked over his shoulder to the door at the end of the hallway.

Gabriel's room.

Chris's hands shook and he gnawed his lower lip as he stared at the door. He hadn't walked into Gabriel's room since the accident, but now an invisible force pulled him toward it.

Inhaling a deep breath through his nose, Chris walked down the hall and stepped inside. He flipped on a lantern by the bed and scanned the room. It was exactly as Chris remembered it. Gabriel's favorite green shirt, which *Mamm* had made to match his eyes, hung on a peg on the wall next to his black church hat. The quilt their *mammi* had made Gabriel when he was twelve was smoothed over his double bed. A shelf in the corner was jammed with Gabriel's favorite novels, along with books detailing horse training and farming.

Chris crossed to the dresser and touched the items covering the top of it—a pocketknife, a wallet, a metal tray clogged with coins, a pack of Gabriel's favorite flavor of bubble gum, and a tube of ChapStick. He picked up the pocketknife and pulled out the blade as memories assaulted his mind. He almost expected Gabriel to stomp into the room and tell Chris to stop touching his personal things. He recalled the sound of Gabriel's voice and his contagious laugh.

A burning pit of emotion lodged in his gut. Gabriel would still be alive today if only Chris hadn't told him to take that horrible horse to the pasture.

"Christopher?"

Chris glanced over his shoulder to see *Mamm* observing him from the doorway.

Her face contorted with a frown. "I thought you were going to have a piece of pie. Are you all right?"

"I'm not hungry." His words were strained. "I changed my clothes so I could help Paul with the animals before bed."

"Oh." She eased through the doorway. "May I join you?"

"Ya. I was just, well . . ." Chris shrugged. *What am I doing in here?*

"I come in here sometimes too." *Mamm* lowered herself down onto the edge of Gabriel's bed and glanced around the room. "I can't bring myself to pack up his things or even give away his clothes." She moved her hand over the quilt. "I guess it seems strange to leave the room as it is since it's not used, but sometimes it feels *gut* to be here while I'm thinking about him." She met Chris's gaze. "Does that make sense?"

"Ya." Chris touched the spine of the cold metal blade.

"I miss him." Her sapphire-blue eyes misted. "Sometimes I think he's going to run into the kitchen and ask me to make him a hot dog." Her lower lip trembled.

"I know what you mean," Chris's words were soft, and he

hoped she wouldn't cry. He recalled the calamitous sound of her sobs at the graveside service.

To his surprise, *Mamm* suddenly beamed. "I remember the last conversation I had with him. He asked me if I would trim his hair because he was finally going to ask Sallie Zook to ride home with him after the youth gathering."

"Really?" He clearly remembered his younger brother's interest in Sallie. Gabriel talked about her nonstop some days while they mucked the stalls. He'd had a crush on her since they were in school together, but he was only brave enough to say hello to her, not the equivalent of asking her out on a date.

Mamm's grin brightened, lighting up her entire face. "*Ya*, he had finally worked up the courage."

Chris blinked with a mixture of surprise and awe. "He hadn't told me that."

"I think she would've said yes too. I think she had a crush on him. I remember seeing her watch him during church, and she would blush whenever he walked past her." *Mamm* sighed, touching the quilt once again. "Gabriel was such a *gut bu*. He was so kind and thoughtful. He thought the world of you too."

Unease spread through Chris like wildfire as he recalled the grief in Sallie's eyes when he'd seen her at the graveside service. He was surprised she hadn't blamed him for Gabriel's death once she'd witnessed his father's accusations.

He took a ragged breath and turned his focus to the knife, taking in the inlaid design of a horse.

"Have you spoken to your father?"

The question caught Chris off guard. He shook his head. "No, I haven't. It never seems like the right time, and I also haven't gotten the feeling *Dat* wants to talk to me."

"You should start the conversation."

"Paul has given me the same advice, but I don't even know what to say to *Dat*." Chris leaned a hip against the dresser. "He wasn't exactly welcoming when I arrived last week."

"What do you mean?" *Mamm's* brow wrinkled.

"He barely spoke to me. He's made it clear he doesn't want me here."

Mamm blew out a puff of air. "Would you do me a favor? I've lost one son, and then you left, pushing the knife deeper into my soul. Now you're back, and my family is intact. I can't bear the thought of losing you again. Please don't let your *dat* push you away. Would you talk to him for me? Just do it for my sake to make me *froh*."

Guilt had Chris in its grip. He couldn't possibly say no to her request and risk deepening his mother's bereavement. "*Ya*. I'll try to talk to him . . . when the time is right."

"*Danki*. Now, tell me about your *freind* Emily."

Chris groaned and flipped the blade closed on the pocket-knife. "There's nothing to tell you."

"What do you mean?"

Chris hesitated but then decided to share everything about Emily with her, including their last conversation and how he'd returned to Ohio without saying good-bye to her.

"I'm sure she's given up on me, and I don't blame her. I'm a lost cause."

"You're not a lost cause. Do you love her?"

"*Ya*." Chris rubbed his chin. "I do. She's my best *freind*."

Mamm's blue eyes sparkled, and he recognized that look. She'd had the same excitement when Paul told her he was going to marry Rosanna and again when Paul announced he and Rosanna were expecting.

"Don't get any ideas, *Mamm*. Not only am I not baptized, but she's in Pennsylvania, and I'm here. It could never work between us."

"Christopher, you've always been so cautious and hesitant about decisions. You never rushed into anything, and you've never had any faith in yourself." She frowned. "I've always wondered if it was because your father criticized you, especially for not being as skilled at horse training as Paul is."

"You knew about that?" Chris asked.

"*Ya*, I did." *Mamm* frowned. "I heard your *dat* say something about it, and I asked him to be patient with you. You know how he is. He's very stubborn."

Chris fidgeted with the knife once again.

"It's your decision whether to join the church," she began, "but I hope you're not holding back just to spite your *dat*."

Chris blinked. "I never said that."

"No, you didn't. But you didn't leave the community and go out in the *English* world as some of your *freinden* did, and I've always had the feeling your troubled relationship with your father was holding you back. I know what he said to you at Gabriel's service wounded you too, and I hope if you and your father talk this out, he'll apologize and you'll forgive him."

She looked at him for a moment. "If not because of your father, then why haven't you joined the church? You could have done it well before Gabriel's accident, so it can't be all about that."

He shrugged as anxiety washed over him. "I never felt I was worthy."

"Christopher, none of us is worthy of God's love, but he loves us anyway." She stood and walked over to him, then reached up to place her warm hand against his cheek. "After Gabriel died and you left, I realized how rarely I made a point of telling you *buwe* how proud I am of all of you. Maybe if I had, you would feel better about yourself. But I am proud of you, Christopher. Very proud. You are a *wunderbaar* young man, and if Emily is half as special as you say she is, she will wait for you to figure things out. Just don't make her wait too long."

Dumbfounded, Chris stared at *Mamm* as she turned and walked to the doorway.

She stepped into the hallway and then glanced back over her shoulder at him. "Are you going to join us for dessert? I made apple pie."

"*Ya*, I'll be down in a minute."

"*Gut*." Her focus moved to the knife in his hand. "Keep that pocketknife. Gabriel would want you to have it."

Chris looked down at the knife and then back up at her. "*Danki*." He slipped the knife into his pocket. "I think I'm going to sleep in here tonight."

"Okay." *Mamm* smiled and then disappeared down the hall.

CHRIS SNUGGLED DOWN UNDER GABRIEL'S QUILT LATER THAT evening. He rolled to his side and stared at the shadows on the wall. He was struck by *Mamm's* words from earlier. "*Christopher, none of us is worthy of God's love, but he loves us anyway.*"

Of course she was right. Was she also correct when she accused Chris of refusing to be baptized just to spite *Dat*, the bishop? Had Chris been that immature and vindictive because he was jealous of the close relationship *Dat* shared only with Paul through horse training and the hurt he felt from his father's criticism?

Chris frowned as humiliation coiled in his chest. Ya, Mamm

may have hit the nail on the head. Why haven't I realized the truth on my own?

He closed his eyes and Emily's angelic face filled his mind. *Do I belong with Emily? If she waits for me, does that mean I should go back to Bird-in-Hand to be with her?*

The sudden and urgent need to pray clamped around his rib cage. For the first time since he lost Gabriel, he longed to fully open his heart to God and ask for guidance.

"God," he whispered, his voice soft and unsure in the darkness of Gabriel's room. "My life has been a mess since Gabriel died. Please help me figure out who I am and where I belong. And please help me mend my broken relationship with *Dat*. I know I don't deserve your love or guidance. I'm sorry for all my mistakes and for all the hurt I've caused both to my family members and to Emily. Help me make things right and be a better man. In Jesus' holy name, amen."

Chris closed his eyes and felt himself drifting into a peaceful sleep.

CHAPTER 25

EMILY RAN HER FINGER ALONG THE FENCE AND SHIVERED as she walked toward the back of the pasture. In the distance she could still hear the voices pouring from her parents' house and the surrounding area. Laughter and conversations echoed through the air, transforming into a murmur of happy noise, a stark contrast to her mood.

She looked up at the clear evening sky as guilt and shame sliced through her soul. She had no right to frown or even to run off to be by herself on Rachel's special day. After all, the wedding had been perfect, and Rachel had been happy, absolutely giddy, after the ceremony.

Rachel was radiant in her purple dress as Emily and Veronica stood by as attendants and more than two hundred members of their community packed into her father's largest barn to witness the ceremony. Mike had glowed with equal excitement, and he looked handsome, just as John, Jason, and Mike's cousin Samuel had.

Emily stopped walking and leaned on the fence to watch the horses grazing in the pasture. She was a horrible person for hiding out by the pasture alone. She should be mingling with the guests and celebrating with her family.

She shivered again in the chilly November air. She wasn't

envious of Rachel. In fact, she was thrilled for her sister. Rachel had found happiness after her ex-boyfriend had broken her heart. At the same time, however, Emily had spent most of the wedding thinking about Chris. Her soul ached as memories of their short friendship flashed through her mind.

Not that long ago, Emily had envisioned Chris attending the wedding and celebrating alongside Emily and her family. Yet, in the blink of an eye, Chris told her he wasn't baptized and couldn't be with her. Then she hadn't heard from him since he'd asked Tillie to give Emily that short message. She still pined for him.

Though they had all suggested Emily give Chris time, *Mamm* and her sisters had also encouraged her to attend youth gatherings. She was sure they hoped she'd find someone else and forget both Chris and the hurt he'd caused. She told them she didn't want to go, but they continued to nag her, insisting it would be good for her. Emily vehemently disagreed. She wasn't ready to forget Chris, and she also wasn't ready to have her heart broken by someone else.

"Em?"

Emily turned as Veronica walked toward her, hugging a black sweater to her middle. "Veronica. How did you find me?"

Veronica shrugged. "It was a *gut* hunch. I remember you used to run out here when you were little. You said you liked how the pasture smelled out here."

Emily laughed. "*Ya*, that's true." She breathed in the aroma of wood-burning fireplaces and the moist pasture. Somehow the air was always clearer out here. "You didn't need to come looking for me."

"I wanted to check on you. You've seemed preoccupied today." Veronica leaned against the fence, and her hand moved over her abdomen. Although she still wasn't showing, it seemed to be instinctive for her to prepare for the changes that would soon take place in her body.

"I have?" Emily frowned. "Oh no. Is Rachel upset with me? Did I do something wrong?"

Veronica sighed. "Oh, Emily. You're always so worried about everyone else. You haven't done anything wrong. I just noticed you look unhappy. That's all." She touched Emily's arm. "How are you?"

Emily shrugged. "I'm fine."

Veronica raised an eyebrow. "You're still hurting, aren't you?"

Emily touched the cold wooden fence post. "*Ya*, I am. Every night I beg God to heal my heart, but it still hurts. It hurts a lot."

"I'm sorry." Veronica gave her shoulder a squeeze.

"I miss him." Emily's voice was thick. "I thought he'd be here today. I imagined him sitting with you, Jason, and me while we ate. I thought maybe he'd stay after everyone else left, and we'd sit on the porch together and talk. We used to discuss everything. He was my best—" Her voice broke and she swallowed back a sob.

"*Ach*, Emily." Veronica rubbed her shoulder. "I know how much it hurts to lose someone you love. I know this is different from when I lost Seth, but I still remember the hurt. It gets better. I promise you it does."

"When?" Her voice was louder than she'd expected.

Veronica sighed. "I don't know."

Emily sniffed and wiped away an errant tear. She hated crying in front of Veronica, but she couldn't stop the grief bubbling up inside of her.

"When I lost Seth, he was gone forever. Chris is still alive."

"I know that." Emily looked at her sister.

"Have you thought about reaching out to him?"

"No." Emily shook her head. "If he cared about me, he would reach out to me. I don't want to chase after someone who doesn't love me."

"But he did reach out to you. He sent a message through Tillie. Maybe he's waiting for you to reach back."

Emily paused.

"Didn't you say you were working on a quilt for him for Christmas?"

"*Ya*, I've been working on it when I get a moment, but I haven't had a chance to finish it because I had so much to do for the wedding."

"Have you considered finishing it and mailing it to him as a gesture of friendship?" Veronica smiled. "You could send him the quilt and include a short note just to tell him you're thinking of him. He might think you hate him and that's why he hasn't called you. Maybe if you reach out to him, you'll open the door. He might be inspired to call you, and you can talk things through."

Emily smoothed her hands over the fence post as she contemplated Veronica's idea. Hope flourished deep in her soul, but a thread of doubt taunted her. "What if he doesn't contact me after I send the quilt?"

"Em, I have a feeling he will contact you." She touched Emily's arm. "I can't bear seeing you so sad. You've always been a pillar of strength for Rach and me. You've always told us to be positive and have faith. Now I need you to follow your own advice. I believe Chris loves you and he's just afraid to call you. You need to have faith that I'm right."

Emily smirked. "So I need to take my own advice."

"Right." Veronica grinned. "Do you need help with the quilt?"

"No, *danki*. But I think I'll get back to it right away."

"Good."

Emily hugged Veronica and hoped her sister was right when she said Chris still cared for her.

THE AROMA OF ANIMALS AND HAY PERMEATED CHRIS'S SENSES as he entered the barn, holding a lantern to light his way past the stalls. Today was Rachel's wedding, and as he'd spent the day helping install new cabinets in Paul's kitchen, he couldn't redirect his thoughts away from Emily. Chris smiled. She'd talked endlessly about everything she had to do for the wedding. Had she finished all the preparations on time? He nodded. Certainly she had.

He imagined she looked beautiful in the purple dress she made for the ceremony. Had she sat with a man as they ate the special dinner? The idea of Emily dating someone else nearly caused his stomach to churn with repulsion.

Why should she wait for you? You left her.

He needed to stop thinking about Emily and concentrate on the purpose of his visit to the barn. His nerves were frayed as his back tensed.

He reached the office at the back of the building. *Dat* sat at his desk. A lantern illuminated the small room where he wrote in an accounting book. His face was twisted in an intense frown as if he were contemplating a complicated problem.

Chris leaned a shoulder on the doorframe. He'd promised his mother more than a week ago that he would talk to *Dat*, and it had taken him this long to work up the courage to do it.

Several moments passed, and *Dat* didn't turn or acknowledge

Chris's presence. Chris silently debated turning on his heel and heading back into the house, but he was tired of taking the coward's way out. He not only wanted *Dat* to talk to him; he wanted him to listen. This estrangement had gone on long enough. It was time to hash it out and try to come to some sort of peaceful solution.

It's now or never.

Chris took a deep breath and mustered all the emotional strength he could find deep in his soul.

"*Dat.*" His tone was thin and unsure. Disgusted with himself, Chris nearly rolled his eyes. He needed to be a confident man, not a nervous child.

"*Dat.*" Chris said the word again, with more determination.

Dat turned, faced Chris, and raised his eyebrows. "Yes?"

Chris took a hesitant step into the small office. "I was wondering if I could talk to you."

Dat leaned back against his chair and folded his arms over his wide chest. "Of course." He leveled his gaze. "What would you like to discuss, Christopher? You took off for Pennsylvania without saying good-bye to me. Then when you finally called home, you only left a message for your *mamm.*" His eyes hardened. "Now you finally want to talk to me, so go ahead. Talk."

Chris bristled at his father's sardonic words, but he wasn't going to allow *Dat* to intimidate him. He'd done that to Chris for too long. Chris was a man now, and he was going to stand his ground, no matter how much his father upset him.

"I finally want to talk to you? Is that how you see it?" Chris snapped, his hands shaking. "You didn't go out of your way to talk to me when I got home. In fact, you acted as if you didn't want me back."

"You're the one who ran off." *Dat* sat up straight and pointed at him. "Do you have any idea how much you hurt your *mamm* when you left?"

Tension and fury crawled up Chris's back and settled on his shoulders, coiling the muscles into tight knots. "I had to go." His words trembled.

"Why? I don't remember throwing you out."

"No, but you made it clear you didn't want me here." Chris took another step into the office.

"What do you mean?"

"You took every opportunity you could to remind me it was my fault Gabriel died. You threw it in my face day after day, even when you didn't actually say the words. I didn't want Gabriel to get hurt." Chris's voice cracked. "I never wanted him to die." Tears stung his eyes and choked back his words.

In one swift motion, *Dat* stood and pulled Chris into a tight hug. Chris was so stunned he stiffened. He couldn't remember a time when his father had hugged him. The feeling was so new, so foreign, that he was knocked off balance for a moment.

"I know, son," *Dat* whispered, his voice shaky.

Chris patted his father's back and sniffed back tears.

"I never meant to blame you," *Dat* murmured, his voice now strained. "I'm sorry. I'm so, so very sorry."

Chris blinked. Had he heard his father correctly?

Dat took a step back and wiped his eyes. "You're the bigger man than I am for coming to me. I was too stubborn and prideful to talk to you and apologize when you first arrived home."

Confusion crept through Chris, pushing away his fury. This was not how he imagined this conversation would go.

"I never meant to drive you away. I took out my guilt about

buying that horse on you, and I'm sorry. I'm the bishop, and I'm supposed to be an example for the rest of our community to follow. Instead, I've been nothing but sinful and prideful, blaming you for Gabriel's death, and I'm ashamed. It wasn't your fault."

Chris shook his head while trying to gather his thoughts. "But I was the one who told Gabriel to lead the horse out to the pasture." His voice quavered. "I wanted to try to train it so I could prove myself to you."

Dat's face contorted. "Why did you feel you had to prove yourself to me?"

Chris snorted. *Is he serious?* "I was tired of you comparing me to Paul. You kept saying Paul was much more skilled as a horse trainer by the time he was my age, and I needed to catch up to him. So I felt I had to do something to change your mind." Chris was grateful his words were steady and strong as he shared his most painful feelings. "But I'm not Paul. I'm not good with horses and I don't like working with them."

Dat opened his mouth, but no words passed his lips. For the first time in Chris's life, his father was speechless.

"I left because I was tired of disappointing you. After Gabriel died, things were worse than ever between you and me, and I couldn't take it anymore. That's why I called *Onkel* Hank and asked him if I could stay with him until I figured out what I was going to do with my life. I only came back to help Paul after *Mamm* told me about the fire."

Dat looked stunned for a moment. Then he pointed to a stool across from the desk. "Let's talk this out. Please, sit."

Chris sat down on the stool as *Dat* lowered himself into his desk chair. Chris studied his father, surprised by the anguish in his hazel eyes.

"Christopher," *Dat* began, his tone still thin and wobbly, "I never wanted to push you away. You're my son."

Chris's chest squeezed at the tenderness in the statement.

"I thought you left because you hated me for making you feel guilty," *Dat* admitted.

Chris shook his head with emphasis. "I never hated you, *Dat*. I just wanted you to forgive me for my mistake. I wanted you to be proud of me. I wanted you to look at me the way you always looked at Paul." He folded his shaky arms over his middle.

"I am proud of you. I'm proud of all three of my *buwe*." He gasped and his eyes misted over.

Dat's stricken face left Chris feeling as empty as an echo.

"I'm sorry for comparing you to Paul." *Dat* took a long, deep breath. "I didn't realize those comments had hurt you, and it wasn't fair. You and Paul are unique in your own ways." He fiddled with his beard, a mannerism Chris had always seen him do when he was deep in thought while delivering a sermon in front of their congregation. "I've always seen a lot of myself in you. You have my personality. You're stubborn and tenacious, and I thought you would take to the horse training like I did."

His face contorted into a deep scowl. "I was so disappointed when you never seemed to put any effort into learning how to properly train the horses, when you showed so little interest. Paul was eager to learn even without much encouragement. When he started his own business, I hoped maybe you would finally show some interest so I could leave the farm to you.

"I had worked so hard for so many years to get this farm going, and if none of my sons wanted it, it would have to be sold off. I thought maybe Gabriel might take it over, but then . . ."

Cold knots tightened like a rope around Chris's chest.

"*Dat*, I'm sorry, but I just—"

"Stop apologizing," *Dat* said, interrupting Chris. "You've done nothing wrong. You're welcome here. This is your home." He pointed to the ground. "You're part of this family, and Gabriel's death was not your fault."

Stunned, Chris nodded. For months he'd yearned to hear his father tell him he wasn't to blame for Gabriel's death. Now that *Dat* had said the words, he suddenly felt as though grief would knock him off the stool.

"I'm so sorry about Gabriel," Chris whispered, his voice quavering again. "If I could go back in time and tell him to stay away from that horse, I would. I'm so sorry, *Dat*. Please forgive me." Tears stung his eyes, and his lower lip trembled.

"It's my fault, Christopher, not yours. It was my stubborn pride that made me buy that horse even though Paul told me not to." He leaned forward and touched Chris's arm. "You can't let this eat you up inside."

Chris sniffed, but confusion lingered inside of him. "I don't know how to let it go. I have nightmares about the accident."

Dat winced. "You have nightmares?"

Chris described the dreams, how they always ended with Gabriel dying in front of him. "The nightmares aren't as frequent, but I still have them. I wake up sobbing, and I don't know how to move past the guilt. *Mei freind* Emily said I have to forgive myself, but I don't know how."

"Ask God to help you," *Dat* said. "Only he can heal us."

Chris suddenly recalled what Emily had said about how God could make him whole again. She was right.

"You're not a failure and you're not a disappointment," *Dat* said. "You're my son and I love you, Christopher." He paused, his eyes wet with anguish. "I was too stubborn and prideful to reach out to you when you left, but I hope we can start over and make things right between us."

All the anger and resentment he'd harbored against his father drained from his heart. And what *Mamm* had suggested suddenly rang true. Chris was just as stubborn as *Dat*, and he had held off from being baptized in part to spite him.

"Are you all right?" *Dat* asked. "You have a strange look on your face."

"*Ya*, I'm okay." Chris nodded. "I just realized I'm partly to blame for all the issues we've had between us. I'm so sorry."

Dat's facial features softened. "You and I are very much alike. We're both stubborn and quick-tempered."

"*Ya*, we sure are." He pursed his lips. "Are you disappointed I haven't been baptized?"

Dat gave him a half-shrug. "I always believed you'd come to the faith in your own time."

"How do you know when you're ready to be baptized?"

Dat tapped his chest over his heart. "You know in here."

Chris leaned back against the wall behind him. "I always believed I wasn't *gut* enough for the church. That was one of the reasons I never joined."

Dat blew out a trembling breath as renewed regret glimmered in his eyes. "I'm so sorry, Christopher. Why didn't you tell me how you felt sooner?" He huffed out a sigh. "I know the answer to that question. I'm not very easy to talk to. I hope you can forgive me."

"Of course I can. You're still *mei dat*."

An easy silence fell over them. Chris marveled at how wonderful it was to sit with his father and feel comfortable.

"Who is Emily? How did you meet her?"

Chris hesitated for a moment, unused to sharing with his father. "She lives next door to *Onkel* Hank. Her *dat* is part owner of the harness shop."

"Oh *ya*? She's one of Leroy Fisher's *dochdern*?"

Chris blew out a breath. "*Ya.*"

"Is she *schee*?"

Chris grinned. He and *Dat* had reached a new beginning in their relationship. They were actually talking and listening to each other. His shoulders relaxed, and for the first time in his adult life, he began to speak to his father without hesitation, trusting him with personal details. "*Ya*, she's really *schee*. I actually think I've fallen in love with her."

When Chris finished telling his story, *Dat* pressed his lips together and nodded.

"Emily sounds like a special *maedel*," *Dat* said with a faraway look in his eyes. "Your *mamm* changed my life when I met her nearly thirty years ago."

"Really?" Chris rested his elbows on his thighs.

Dat dropped his arm onto his desk. "Do you know the story of how your *mamm* and your *aenti* Ida came to Ohio to visit a cousin, and they both wound up staying here?"

"*Ya*, I've heard that story. And *Onkel* Hank was the only sibling from their family left in Pennsylvania. Well, except for *Onkel* Naaman, who didn't join the Amish church."

"That's right. I met your *mamm* at a youth gathering. I was sort of a loner, and I thought I would wind up a bachelor for the rest of my life. I didn't think any *maedel* in her right mind would take a chance on me. I was so headstrong and set in my ways, even as a young man."

Chris's eyes widened. Before this day, he'd never heard his father use such self-deprecating words to describe himself.

"But your *mamm* took a chance on me, and here we are so many years later." *Dat* leaned forward in his chair. "Emily sounds just as special as your *mamm*. If you feel she's the one, you should consider your relationship with God and where you stand with the church." He touched his chest again above his heart.

Chris swallowed a gasp. Why hadn't *Dat* ever shared this tender side of himself? "*Danki* for the advice, *Dat*."

"*Danki* for giving me another chance, son."

Chris nodded as affection for his family bubbled up in his soul. He said a silent prayer, asking God for the opportunity for him and Emily to somehow make their relationship work.

CHAPTER 26

EMILY YAWNED AS SHE STARED DOWN AT THE FINISHED
quilt. After the guests had left the wedding reception and the mess
had been cleaned up, she worked on the quilt until late into the
night. She grabbed a few hours of sleep and then started on the
quilt again early that morning, only stopping to quickly eat.

She glanced at the clock on the sewing table. It was almost
four o'clock in the afternoon. Urgency shot through her. She had
to write a letter and find a box, and then she could ask *Dat* to take
her to the post office before it closed.

If she got the box in the mail today, maybe, just maybe, she'd
hear from Chris early next week. Her insides fluttered. She couldn't
wait to hear his voice over the phone. Would the quilt mean so
much to him that he'd long to call her? She hoped it would.

Emily popped up from the chair, grabbed a notepad and pen,
and began to write.

Dear Chris,

I hope you and your family are doing well. I started this lap
quilt the day I made you breakfast and you told me you missed
the quilt your *mammi* made for you. I had hoped to give this to
you in person, but I didn't have a chance to finish it before you
left. I was so wrapped up in Rachel's wedding that I ran out of

time. And then I didn't know you were going to leave. Anyway, I want you to have it.

I thought I should explain the significance of the log cabin quilt pattern. This block pattern is very old and is symbolic of life itself. The center square used to be red to represent the heart or hearth of the home. The strips around the center are said to represent the logs of the cabin. The light side of the block represents the sun in front of the cabin, such as babies, weddings, family, and friends. The dark side represents the shadow behind the cabin, such as death or disaster. The dark moments are supposed to remind us how wonderful the light moments really are. I hope you remember your time in Bird-in-Hand as a light time in your life.

The quilt is made with special material that belonged to *mei mammi*. I hope you like the colors. The blues and greens remind me of your eyes and how they change color depending upon the light reflected off them.

Rachel's wedding was lovely. It's a shame you weren't here to see it. I had hoped you'd be here to celebrate with us.

I'm sorry for arguing with you before you left. You said you didn't know where you belonged, and that upset me because in my heart I thought you belonged in my community. I never meant to push you away.

I keep replaying our last conversation in my mind and I think of things I should have said. I'm sorry if I hurt you. I pray you understand how much your friendship means to me. I miss our talks. I felt as if you and I shared a special bond and connection. I hope you felt that too.

Mamm gave me a devotional book that belonged to *mei mammi*, and the verses *Mammi* underlined really speak to my heart. I want to share one with you that has really helped me lately. Psalm 59, verse 16: "But I will sing of your strength, in the morning I will sing of your love; for you are my fortress, my refuge in times of trouble."

May this quilt keep you warm when you ride in your buggy on cold Ohio nights.

I miss you, Chris.

All my best,

Emily

She reread the letter and then rushed downstairs to find a box. She was thankful she got Chris's address from Tillie yesterday.

"*Mamm!*" Emily called as she headed toward the kitchen.

"Emily?" *Mamm* met her at the doorway. "Is everything all right?" She spotted the quilt in Emily's hand and gasped. "Oh, that is lovely." She ran her fingers over the stitching. "I think this is your best quilt yet."

"You think so?" Emily gnawed her lower lip. "I hope he likes it."

"*Ach, mei liewe.*" *Mamm* touched her cheek. "He will love it. I'm certain he will." She pointed toward the mudroom. "I have the perfect box."

"*Danki.* I want to get it to the post office before it closes." Emily placed the quilt and the letter on the table.

"You tape it up, and I'll call our driver. We'll get you there in time." *Mamm* winked at her. "I'm certain you will hear from Chris next week."

Emily blew out a shaky breath and hoped her mother was right.

CHRIS EXITED THE BARN AND WALKED WITH PAUL AND DAT toward the house at suppertime Tuesday evening. Although his whole body ached after another long day of working on Paul's house, he smiled as he thought about the past few days.

For the first time in years, he felt like a true part of his family and of the community as he worked alongside his brother and father, as well as some other men, installing cabinets and painting the rebuilt kitchen in Paul's house. It was beginning to resemble a home again.

They entered the mudroom, and when the aroma of stew filled his nostrils, his stomach growled. He'd worked up a good appetite. He shucked his coat, hung up his hat, and pulled off his boots.

Chris tapped his right front trouser pocket, confirming that Gabriel's knife was still secure. He started carrying the knife after *Mamm* told him he could keep it. Although it was only an inexpensive pocketknife, it was as if he were carrying a piece of Gabriel with him.

He had awoken this morning with a sense of peace settling over his soul instead of the usual bitter, raging guilt that had plagued him since the accident. He had finally forgiven himself and accepted that the accident wasn't his fault, though certainly he and his father had both made mistakes. His nightly prayers had warmed his soul, just as Emily promised they would.

Rosanna was still setting the table as *Mamm* carried a bowl of green beans over. Betsy sat in a high chair and Mamie was perched on a booster seat.

"Hi." Rosanna beamed at Paul. "How was your day?"

"It was *gut*." Paul kissed her cheek before turning his attention to his daughters.

"How was your day?" *Mamm* looked up at *Dat*.

"It was *gut*, Agnes." *Dat* hugged her, whispering something in her ear that made her giggle.

Chris grinned. He'd never seen his parents show any affection in public, but *Dat* seemed to have changed in the past few days. It was as if his heart had softened after he and Chris had their emotional conversation. Chris felt different inside too.

"Let's eat. Everything is ready." *Mamm* waved a hand toward the table.

Chris sat across from Rosanna and Paul and bowed his head. After a silent prayer, they filled their plates, and the scraping of utensils and murmur of conversation filled the large kitchen.

"How's the work coming along at the *haus*?" Rosanna asked Paul as she handed a bowl of mashed potatoes to Chris.

"It's going well," Paul said. "We're almost done installing the cabinets, and the upstairs is repainted. I think we're right on schedule."

"*Ya*, I think so too," Chris agreed. "I went upstairs and I was impressed by the painting. The *haus* looks brand new, and the smoke odor is almost gone."

"Oh good." Rosanna blew out a sigh. "What a relief."

"Christopher," *Mamm* said. "A package arrived for you today."

"A package for me?" he asked.

"*Ya*. It's over there." *Mamm* nodded toward the counter across the room.

Chris spotted the large cardboard box. Who would send him a package?

"Go on." *Mamm* grinned. "Open it."

He took in his mother's smile with suspicion. She looked as if she had a secret.

"Just go open it, Chris," Rosanna said. "If you don't open it, I will."

Were the women conspiring? He stood and crossed the room. His name was written in familiar penmanship on the box. When he read the return address, hope sparked through him—*E. Fisher.* The package was from Emily! What would she send him?

He fetched a steak knife and cut through the copious amount of packing tape. He pulled the box flaps apart and searched through the pool of tissue paper until his fingers found an envelope and a quilt.

Chris pulled out the quilt. It featured blue and green material shaped like boxes. He held the quilt to his chest and inhaled, finding a faint scent of strawberries. He closed his eyes, imagining Emily's beautiful face as she looked at him.

Mamm and Rosanna gasped in unison as they rushed over to him.

"Look at that quilt." Rosanna smoothed her hand over the material. "Look at that stitching, *Mamm*! I can't imagine how long that took to make. She did it by hand."

"Oh, that is fantastic. That is the most *schee* log cabin design I have ever seen." *Mamm* clicked her tongue. "I could never stitch like that."

Chris handed the quilt to his mother, and she and Rosanna continued to cluck over it as he opened and read the letter.

His eyes stung as he took in Emily's sweet words. She'd started creating the quilt the day he mentioned the quilt his grandmother had made. That was the first day he was nice to her. They weren't even close yet, but she had started to make him a quilt out of precious material from her own grandmother.

She missed him, and she seemed to blame herself for their argument, apologizing for pushing him away. Why would she think she pushed him away when he had left her without even saying good-bye?

Chris absorbed the Scripture verse. Yes, God was his refuge in times of trouble. He'd begun praying every night, and his soul was refreshed. He was whole once again.

Chris remembered a conversation he had with Mike the night John invited Chris to come over to Emily's for supper. Mike explained he didn't think he'd met Rachel at the right time since his father was so gravely ill. But then Mike said he met Rachel at the perfect time because it was when he'd needed her most. *"It's funny how God works. As Rachel once told me, we think we know God's plan for us, but we don't know what his plan is until he reveals it to us."*

Chris *belonged* with Emily. Excitement and exhilaration exploded through him, and he could feel it all the way to his bones. He needed to go to Emily. He had to join the church and marry Emily.

God had sent him to Bird-in-Hand to find his future, and Emily was that future.

"Christopher?" *Mamm's* hand was gentle on his bicep. "Are you all right?"

"*Ya.*" Chris grinned down at his mother. "I've never been better."

Mamm's eyebrows knitted together.

"How would you feel about me moving to Bird-in-Hand permanently?" Chris looked from his mother to his father, who sat at the table looking at him with his eyebrows careening toward his hairline. "I'd miss you all terribly, but I want to join the church there and be a part of that community. I want to work at *Onkel* Hank's harness shop. I've realized leatherworking is my future. I never loved horse training the way you and Paul do, *Dat*. I'm better at working with my hands."

Dat nodded slowly. "If you feel in your heart that you belong in Bird-in-Hand, then I will support you. Leatherworking is a fine profession."

Chris looked down at his mother again. "*Mamm*? I won't go without your blessing."

Mamm sniffed and touched Chris's chest. "Are you going for Emily?"

"*Ya*, I am, but I don't want to hurt you again. I want you to be honest with me." He held his breath as a tear sprinkled down his mother's pink cheek.

"I will give you my blessing if you make me one promise," *Mamm* began.

"All right."

"You have to promise you and Emily will come and visit us at least once a year."

"That is a promise!" Chris laughed and then picked up his mom and spun her around.

His mother laughed and *Dat*, Paul, and Rosanna joined in. Betsy and Mamie clapped and giggled too.

Chris began ticking off a list on his fingers. "I need to call *Onkel* Hank. And I need to pack, and I need to call the bus station." He looked at his brother. "I should wait until your *haus* is done. I'll go after Christmas."

Paul waved off the comment. "Go, Chris. The *haus* is almost done. You've helped so much already. Go start your new life."

"Absolutely," Rosanna agreed as she sat down next to Paul.

"*Danki* for all you've done for us. We'll come visit you next year, right, Mamie?"

"*Ya,*" Mamie agreed with another clap. "I want to see your *haus.*"

"I'd like that." Chris rubbed his chin. "I have so much to do. I have to figure out when I can leave. I should call *Onkel* Hank now."

"Slow down," *Mamm* said. "Take your time."

Chris grinned down at his mother. "*Ya,* you're right. Emily and I have the rest of our lives."

He turned and bolted for the door, rushing out to the phone shanty. He couldn't wait to begin the rest of his life with Emily Fisher.

EMILY HANDED A CUSTOMER HIS CHANGE AND PUT THE WALlet and coin purse in a brown paper bag. They were the last wallet and coin purse Chris had made. She bit back the urge to tell the man he couldn't buy them for his daughter because she wanted to cherish them forever.

"Thank you for coming to see us." She forced a smile. "Come back again soon."

Once the customer was gone, Emily slumped on the stool and blew out a deep sigh. If the postal clerk was correct in her calculations, Chris had received the package on Tuesday. It was now Friday afternoon, and Emily still hadn't heard from him. She'd checked with Tillie every morning and afternoon since Tuesday to see if Chris had left a message on her phone. Every time Emily asked, Tillie frowned and shook her head, and sadness radiated through every pore of Emily's body.

Emily couldn't understand why she hadn't heard from Chris.

Had her letter come on too strong? Had she been too honest? Maybe he didn't like the quilt or considered the gift too extravagant for their friendship.

And her worst fear of all—had Emily become just a memory from his past, an old friend who no longer held any significance for him?

She leaned forward on the counter and stared down at the accounting books she'd tried to complete all week. She couldn't concentrate long enough to make sense of the numbers. She had tried to work on the receipts, but her mind kept wandering back to all the time she and Chris had spent together. He was at the forefront of her mind, and nothing else seemed to matter except hearing from him.

The hum of an engine drew her attention to the three parking spaces in front of the store. A yellow taxi parked in the middle space, and Emily turned and looked toward the work area.

"*Dat*? Hank? Are you expecting someone to come in a taxi today?"

"Nope." *Dat* looked up from the table. "Are you, Hank?"

"I'm not sure." Hank shrugged and then smiled. "Would you please go see who it is, Emily?"

She paused. "All right. Please answer the phone if it rings. I'll be right back."

Hank muttered something in response, but she couldn't comprehend the words from the front of the store. She hopped down from the stool, pulled her sweater tighter, and opened the door, then stepped out onto the sidewalk.

An Amish man leaned in the driver side window paying for the ride. The man stood. When she took in his handsome profile, her heart fluttered like a hummingbird and then her pulse soared.

Chris!

Was Chris truly standing in front of her, or was she dreaming?

Chris looked over at her and his lips quirked up in a smile. "Hi, Em."

Emily couldn't speak as a tear sprinkled down her cheek.

Chris set his duffel bag on the sidewalk. The taxi backed out of the parking space and disappeared down the street.

Chris took a step toward her and she breathed in his familiar scent. He'd come back!

"You're really here. I can't believe it." She croaked the words with thick emotion, and for a moment she stared into his chest. "When I didn't hear from you, I-I was afraid you didn't like the quilt or were offended by my letter."

His grin faded. "You could never offend me. I came to thank you in person for the beautiful quilt and letter. And to say you were right about everything."

She looked up into his blue-green eyes.

"What do you mean?"

"You were right when you said I had to open my heart to God and let him make me whole." He touched her arm. "I prayed and gave my burdens to him, and he put me back together. I worked things out with *mei dat*, and I made things right with *mei bruder* and *mamm*. I also came to terms with Gabriel's death. It wasn't my fault, despite the mistakes I made, and I learned I had to stop blaming myself. That burden was tearing me apart."

"I'm so *froh* for you." Emily pressed her hands together as if in prayer. "That's *wunderbaar* news."

"Now I need to make things right with you, Em." He took a deep breath, and emotion shimmered in his eyes. "I'm so sorry for leaving without saying good-bye. I was a coward. In fact, I've been a coward most of my life, running away from my problems instead of facing them and fixing them. I never wanted to hurt you, and I hope you can forgive me."

"Of course I can." Her voice shook with tenderness. "You're forgiven."

"In your letter, you said you hoped I remember my time in Bird-in-Hand as a light time in my life. But my time here hasn't been just light; it's been the most brilliant, most wonderful time of my life. I guess you could say it's the lightest."

Emily sniffed as tears of joy filled her eyes. She tried to speak, but a rush of emotion blocked her words.

"I have a gift for you, but I couldn't figure out how to wrap it." He smiled as he brushed his finger down her cheek, sending shivers of electricity dancing down her spine. "I couldn't figure out how to wrap my heart."

Emily closed her eyes and leaned into his touch. Oh, how she'd missed him.

Wait. What did he say?

She opened her eyes. "Your heart?"

"You've had my heart since the day you made breakfast for me at your parents' *haus*. You're my best *freind*. You're my first thought in the morning and my last thought before I go to sleep at night. You've helped me work through all my messy family issues, and you made me realize I am worthy of the church and the community. I believe God sent me to Bird-in-Hand to find you. I'm certain to the depth of my soul that you and I belong together."

He rested both of his hands on her cheeks, and she drew in a deep breath as her body trembled with excitement.

"What I'm trying to say is I love you, Emily Fisher." His eyes searched hers. "I want to join the church and then I want to be with you. I don't have much, but I'll find a way to build you a *haus*. I want to spend the rest of my life with you. I want to have a family with you."

Emily sniffed as tears rolled down her cheeks. She had to be dreaming. This seemed too good to be true! But it was real.

"What do you think?"

"I love you too," she whispered. "I've been dreaming of this moment, and I can't believe it's actually coming true."

Chris's eyes softened. He leaned down, and Emily's breath hitched in her lungs. He brushed his lips across hers, sending her stomach into a wild swirl. She closed her eyes and savored the feeling of his mouth against hers. Her most fervent prayers had been answered.

After their lips parted, Chris rested his forehead against hers and he smiled. Emily beamed and silently thanked God for sending Chris back to her.

EPILOGUE

"MAMM!" EMILY CALLED AS SHE RACED DOWN THE STAIRS. *"Mamm!"*

She went into the kitchen, and when she didn't see her mother there, she stepped out onto the porch and shivered against the bitter December wind. Her mother had said she was going over to the harness shop, but she should have been back by now.

Hugging her arms to her chest, Emily moved back into the mudroom and then headed through the family room toward her parents' bedroom.

She'd been working feverishly on quilts that would be Christmas gifts for Mike and John, and she still had to make one for Jason. But with Christmas only two weeks away, she was quickly running out of time, and now she'd run out of material. She wanted to ask her mother's permission to look for more material in her hope chest, and if she couldn't find what she needed there, then in her closet.

When Chris showed his quilt to them at a recent family dinner, Mike and Jason raved about it. Emily would make lap quilts for them as a simple but personal gift from both her and Chris.

Chris and I are now a couple! Her cheeks heated. Although they couldn't officially date, they were enjoying each other's company and taking their time getting to know each other better. She looked forward to his baptism next fall so they could make their relationship official.

Chris continued to live with Hank and Tillie and work in the harness shop full-time. His wallets and coin purses had quickly become two of the most popular items they had to sell, and both Chris and Emily were saving money to build a house at the back of his uncle's property. Chris's parents had also offered to help, contributing a generous sum of money to Chris's savings account. Emily's chest fluttered as she imagined what it would be like to live together as husband and wife. She couldn't wait for their future together to begin.

Emily stood in the doorway to her parents' bedroom and stared at the hope chest. Would *Mamm* mind if she looked in it without asking? *Mamm* kept it locked, and she probably locked it for a reason.

She worried her bottom lip and looked at her mother's dresser, recalling where *Mamm* had found the key the last time she'd unlocked it. Would *Mamm* be upset if she opened the chest herself?

Emily approached the dresser and lifted the top to the small box. She spotted the key and swallowed a groan. What was she doing? *Mamm* might be very upset with her if she opened the chest without checking with her first. But she wanted to take full advantage of the time she had to work on the quilts this afternoon.

Emily swallowed her guilt, took the key, and knelt in front of the hope chest. She slipped the key into the lock and turned it, then lifted the lid and breathed in the sweet scent of cedar as she rummaged through the linens and small boxes. She sifted through to the bottom and found a large envelope.

She lifted the envelope and turned it over in her hands. On the front, she read "Leroy and Martha Fisher" written in neat handwriting. Martha was her mother's given name. She opened it, and an official government document fell out. It said "Certificate of Death," and the name on it was Jacob Petersheim Fisher. She also found a lock of blond hair in a small zippered storage bag, parchment paper with tiny footprints and handprints, and a birth certificate.

Questions swirled through Emily's mind. Who was Jacob Petersheim Fisher? Was he a cousin or a friend?

She looked closer at the death certificate. Her parents' names were listed as the infant's parents. A gasp escaped her with a whoosh. Jacob had been born more than a year before Veronica!

I had an older bruder? *Was he stillborn? And why was his middle name Petersheim?*

"What are you looking at?"

Emily's eyes were wide as she turned toward *Mamm* watching her from the doorway. She held up the birth and death certificates. "I had a *bruder?*"

Mamm's face contorted with pain and shock.

"Why didn't you tell us?" Emily stood. "I don't understand."

Mamm sank onto the corner of the bed and rubbed her temple. "I never felt the need to tell you or your *schweschdere.*"

"Please tell me. I need to know."

Mamm heaved a heavy sigh and reached for the documents in Emily's hand. Emily released them and *Mamm* examined them for a long moment.

"I will tell this story only once," *Mamm* whispered. "Call Veronica and Rachel and ask them to come over tomorrow for a sisters' day. I'll share the story then."

"Okay." Emily started for the door and then stopped, guilt pricking at the back of her neck. "*Mamm,* I'm sorry. I didn't mean to snoop. I was looking for material so I could make Jason's quilt."

Mamm nodded with a bleak smile. "It's all right. It's time for you and your *schweschdere* to learn the truth."

Emily blinked. She couldn't imagine what tomorrow would bring.

ACKNOWLEDGMENTS

As always, I'm thankful for my loving family, including my mother, Lola Goebelbecker; my husband, Joe; and my sons, Zac and Matt. I'm blessed to have such an awesome and amazing family that puts up with me when I'm stressed out about a book deadline. Thank you to my sons, who don't mind having cookies for lunch on Saturdays when I'm too focused on my book to stop and make a sandwich. Special thanks to Matt, a.k.a. Mr. Thesaurus, for helping me find synonyms. I couldn't ask for a more adorable wordsmith!

I'm more grateful than words can express to Janet Pecorella and my mother for proofreading for me. I truly appreciate the time you take out of your busy lives to help me polish my books. I'm also grateful to my special Amish friends, who patiently answer my endless stream of questions. Thank you also to Karla Hanns for her quilting expertise and to Jason Clipston for his firefighting information. Thank you also to Jessica Miller, RN, for her medical research for this book.

Thank you to my wonderful church family at Morning Star Lutheran in Matthews, North Carolina, for your encouragement, prayers, love, and friendship. You all mean so much to my family and me. Special thanks to Pastor John Mouritsen, who inspired the faith message in this book. You are a blessing to our congregation!

ACKNOWLEDGMENTS

Thank you to Jamie Mendoza and the fabulous members of my Bakery Bunch! I'm so thankful for your friendship and your excitement about my books. You all are amazing!

To my agent, Natasha Kern—I can't thank you enough for your guidance, advice, and friendship. You are a tremendous blessing in my life.

Thank you to my amazing editor, Becky Philpott, for your friendship and guidance. Love you, girl!

Thank you also to Julee Schwarzburg for her guidance with the story. I always learn quite a bit about writing and polishing when we work together. Thank you for pushing me to become a better writer. I hope we can work together again in the future!

I'm grateful to Jean Bloom, who helped me polish and refine the story. Jean, you are a master at connecting the dots and filling in the gaps. I'm so thankful that we can continue to work together!

I also would like to thank Samantha Buck and Kristen Golden for tirelessly working to promote my books. I'm grateful to each and every person at HarperCollins Christian Publishing who helped make this book a reality.

To my readers—thank you for choosing my novels. My books are a blessing in my life for many reasons, including the special friendships I've formed with my readers. Thank you for your e-mail messages, Facebook notes, and letters.

Thank you most of all to God—for giving me the inspiration and the words to glorify you. I'm grateful and humbled you've chosen this path for me.

Special thanks to Cathy and Dennis Zimmermann for their hospitality and research assistance in Lancaster County, Pennsylvania.

ACKNOWLEDGMENTS

The author and publisher gratefully acknowledge the following resource used to research information for this book:

C. Richard Beam, *Revised Pennsylvania German Dictionary* (Lancaster, PA: Brookshire Publications, Inc., 1991).

DISCUSSION QUESTIONS

1. Chris is devastated after his younger brother is killed in an accident. Have you faced a difficult loss? What Bible verses helped you? Share these with the group.

2. What role did the quilt play in Emily and Chris's relationship? Can you relate the quilt to an object that was pivotal in a relationship you've experienced in your life?

3. Emily feels guilty for being jealous of her sisters' happiness and the events going on in their lives. Have you ever been in a similar situation? If so, how did it turn out? Share your experience with the group.

4. Emily pours herself into Rachel's wedding plans as a way to deal with her grief after Chris returns to Ohio. She also finds solace in her grandmother's devotion book. Think of a time when you felt hurt or betrayed. Where did you find your strength? What Bible verses would help with this?

5. Near the end of the novel, Chris finally finds the courage to confront his father about his feelings, and he's surprised by the outcome of the conversation. What do you think Chris learned about his father during the course of their discussion? What do you think Chris learned about himself? How did this conversation change

Chris's feelings regarding his family and his place in the community?

6. Chris feels lost at the beginning of the book. He is convinced he isn't worthy enough to join the Amish church through baptism, and he is also afraid of opening his heart to Emily. By the end of the story, he realizes he's ready to be baptized and pursue a relationship with Emily. What do you think caused him to change his point of view throughout the story?

7. Wilmer (Chris's father) is cold and distant when Chris first arrives home in Ohio. His demeanor toward Chris changes after Chris finally confronts him. What do you think caused Wilmer to change near the end of the book?

8. Which character can you identify with the most? Which character seemed to carry the most emotional stake in the story? Was it Chris, Emily, Wilmer (Chris's father), or someone else?

9. What role did John play in Chris's introduction to the Bird-in-Hand community and also the Fisher family? How did John affect Chris's feelings about his own self-worth?

10. What did you know about the Amish before reading this book? What did you learn?

DON'T MISS THE REST OF THE
AMISH HEIRLOOM SERIES!

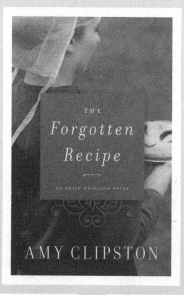
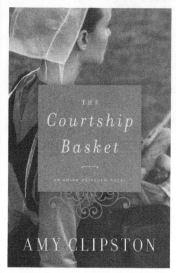
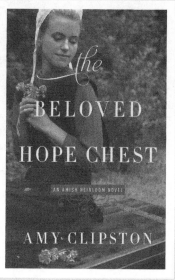

Four women working at the
Lancaster Grand Hotel find their
way through life and love.

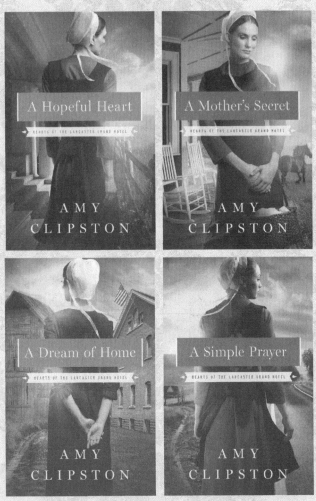

Available in print and e-book

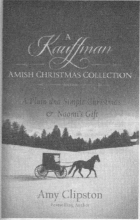

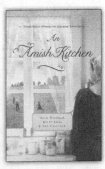

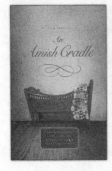

ABOUT THE AUTHOR

AMY CLIPSTON IS THE AWARD-WINNING and bestselling author of the Kauffman Amish Bakery, Hearts of Lancaster Grand Hotel, Amish Heirloom, and Amish Homestead series. Her novels have hit multiple bestseller lists including CBD, CBA, and ECPA. Amy holds a degree in communication from Virginia Wesleyan University and works full-time for the City of Charlotte, NC. Amy lives in North Carolina with her husband, two sons, and three spoiled rotten cats. Visit her online at AmyClipston.com, Facebook: AmyClipstonBooks, Twitter: @AmyClipston.

Visit her online at amyclipston.com
Facebook: AmyClipstonBooks
Twitter: @AmyClipston
Instagram: @amy_clipston